Crash and Fred
An Adventure of Epic Absurdity

Chase Fiore

ISBN-13 Digital: 979-8-9994370-0-6

ISBN-13 Paperback: 979-8-9994370-3-7

ISBN-13 Hardcover: 979-8-9994370-4-4

ISBN-13 Paperback (First Edition): 979-8-9994370-1-3

ISBN-13 Hardcover (First Edition): 979-8-9994370-2-0

Library of Congress Control Number: 2025914220

Printed in the United States of America

10 9 8 7 6 5 4 3 2

Cover illustration by:

Katarzyna Surman

www.CrashandFred.com

To my wife.

I found my heart, in San Francisco.

Chapter 1
The Daily Grind

A bell tolls in the crisp morning fog. Strips of wood smolder on cold steel. Crash, surfing the running board of the Hyde line, is neither awake nor asleep; for now, the only place he's going is down one hill, and up another.

He feels the city waking up around him, the hum of distant traffic, the murmur of early risers, and the rhythmic rattle of the cable car beneath his feet. The fog clings to the streets like a heavy blanket, muffling the sounds, softening the edges of the world. Yet, through it all, the clang of the bell cuts sharp, ringing in a new day.

Crash rides the rails with practiced ease, his hand gripping the cold metal bar as the car sways and jolts down the incline. The familiar route is like muscle memory—down one hill, up another, the city rolling by in a blur of pastel-painted houses and weathered storefronts. He's made this journey a thousand times, but today, it feels different. The city, with all its beauty and decay, seems to whisper something just out of reach.

As the car crests the next hill, the fog lifts slightly, revealing a glimpse of the bay in the distance, its waters as grey and restless as the thoughts swirling in his mind. Crash closes his eyes for a moment, letting the cool air brush against his face, the scent of saltwater mingling with the faint aroma of fresh-brewed coffee wafting from a nearby café. The sensation is grounding, a small comfort in the monotony of his daily routine.

But comfort isn't what he's after—not anymore. He opens his eyes as the car begins its descent, the city sprawling out before him, a patchwork of dreams and disappointments. He knows the path too well, but today, a restlessness tugs at him, a need for something more. The clang of the bell echoes in his ears as if urging him to wake up, to see the world with new eyes.

By the time he hops off the car at his usual stop, Hyde and Union, the sun has started to burn through the fog, casting long shadows over the cracked pavement. He pulls his hoodie tighter against the morning chill and starts the short walk to the Anuman Family Store, where his mother and grandmother are already bustling around inside, preparing for another day. The smell of burnt toast greets him before he even reaches the door—a scent as familiar as the streets he's just traveled.

Inside, everything is as it always is: shelves stocked with an eclectic mix of groceries, old family photos hanging slightly askew on the walls, and the hum of a small radio playing a scratchy tune from another time. It's a place of warmth and routine, but to Crash, it feels more like a cage with invisible bars. He knows every inch of this store, every creak in the floorboards, every chip in the paint. And while there's comfort in the familiarity, there's also a growing itch—a need to break free, to find something beyond these walls.

But for now, he pushes those thoughts aside, slipping into the back to wash up before starting his shift. The day stretches out ahead of him, just like all the days before it, a series of tasks and routines that have become as automatic as breathing. Yet beneath the surface, something stirs, a quiet longing that he can't quite name.

Crash heads into the tiny restroom in the back to wash his hands before serving customers. As he dries his hands on a worn towel, he catches his reflection in the cracked mirror above the sink. The face staring back at him is the same one he's seen every day for years, but today, there's a flicker of something new in his eyes— something that wasn't there before.

It's faint, but it's there.

The bell tolled this morning, and for the first time in a long while, Crash felt like it was calling for him.

Crash steps into the front of the store, greeted by the soft hum of the refrigerator units and the warm, familiar scent of spices that have soaked into the wood over the years. His grandmother, a small woman with iron-grey hair pulled into a tight bun, is already bustling around behind the counter, sorting through the morning's delivery of fresh produce. She moves with a practiced efficiency, her hands deft and sure, but there's a slight tremor to them that Crash can't help but notice.

"Morning, Grandma," he says, trying to inject some brightness into his voice.

She glances up, her lined face breaking into a smile that doesn't quite reach her eyes. "Good morning, Crash. The apples came in a bit bruised, but they'll do. Can you check the stock in the back? We might need to reorder the rice."

Crash nods, slipping into the rhythm of the store. It's a dance he's known all his life, one step after another, each movement as familiar as the last. But today, his steps feel heavier, as if something is pulling him back, holding him down.

He passes by his mother, who's arranging the flowers by the front window. She's humming softly to herself, a tune he can't quite place, her hands moving with the same careful precision she's always had. There's a peace to her movements, a contentment that Crash has never been able to find in himself.

"Morning, Ma," he says, pausing to kiss her on the cheek.

"Morning, sweetheart," she replies, her voice as warm as the sun that's just starting to filter through the window. "I made your favorite—burnt toast and overcooked eggs."

Crash chuckles, the sound more genuine than he expected. "Just how I like it."

They exchange a smile, a brief moment of connection that lingers in the air before slipping away like smoke. Crash wants to hold onto it, to let it fill the emptiness that's been growing inside him, but it slips through his fingers, intangible and fleeting.

As he moves to the back of the store, checking the stock as his grandmother asked, Crash can't shake the feeling that something is missing. It's a feeling that's been with him for a while now, a quiet dissatisfaction that he's tried to ignore, but it's growing harder to push aside.

The store is their life, their legacy, but to Crash, it feels like a chain, binding him to a future he never chose. He knows the sacrifices his family made to keep it going, the long hours, the sleepless nights, the endless worries about bills and suppliers. He knows they depend on him, that the store is more than just a business—it's a lifeline, a connection to the community that has supported them through thick and thin.

But knowing that doesn't make the weight any easier to bear.

He finishes his tasks in the back and returns to the front, where his grandmother is now chatting with Mrs. Lee, one of their regular customers. The old woman is holding a bunch of wilted carrots, her expression one of mild concern as she inspects them.

"They're a bit soft, aren't they, Jan?" she says, looking over at Crash's grandmother.

Jan Anuman gives a slight nod. "They are, Mrs. Lee. I'll knock a bit off the price for you."

Crash watches the exchange, noting the ease with which his grandmother handles the situation, her words smooth and comforting. She's always had a way with people, a natural gift for making them feel at ease, for making them feel heard.

It's a gift that Crash wishes he had.

Mrs. Lee catches sight of him and gives a warm smile. "Ah, Crash! How are you this morning?"

He forces a smile in return. "I'm good, Mrs. Lee. How are you?"

"Better now that I've seen you," she replies with a wink. "You know, my granddaughter was asking about you the other day. I told her you're a good boy, always helping out at the store. She said she might come by later this week."

Crash feels a flush of embarrassment rise in his cheeks. Mrs. Lee has been trying to set him up with her granddaughter for months now, and while he's always polite about it, the thought of yet another awkward encounter makes his stomach churn.

"That's nice of her," he says, trying to deflect. "I'll keep an eye out."

Mrs. Lee beams, clearly pleased with herself. "You do that, dear."

Crash's grandmother gives him a knowing look as Mrs. Lee shuffles out of the store with her carrots. "She means well, you know."

"I know," Crash replies, rubbing the back of his neck. "But I'm not really..."

"Interested?" Jan finishes for him, her tone gentle.

Crash nods, grateful that she understands. "Yeah."

Jan sighs, her eyes softening as she looks at him. "You're a good boy, Crash. I know you feel like you're stuck sometimes, but you're doing the right thing by being here. This store... it's our home. It's your father's legacy."

The mention of his father sends a pang through Crash's chest, and he swallows hard, pushing the emotion down. "I know, Gran. I know."

She reaches out, placing a hand on his arm, her touch light but reassuring. "He would be proud of you. We all are."

Crash nods, unable to find the words to express the conflicting emotions churning inside him. Instead, he gives her a small smile, one that doesn't quite reach his eyes, and excuses himself to the back of the store once more.

As he leans against the cool wall, out of sight from his family, he lets out a breath he didn't realize he was holding. The store is more than just a building to them—it's a symbol of everything they've worked for, everything they've lost. But to Crash, it's starting to feel like a cage, one that's closing in on him a little more each day.

And as much as he loves his family, as much as he wants to make them proud, he can't shake the feeling that there's something out there, beyond these walls, that's waiting for him. Something that could fill the void he's been carrying for so long.

He just doesn't know what it is yet.

But today, as he stands in the quiet of the stockroom, listening to the muted sounds of the city outside, he feels a spark of determination flicker to life within him. Maybe today will be different. Maybe today he'll find what he's been searching for.

Or maybe, he thinks as the bell over the door jingles, signaling another customer, it's just another day like all the rest.

Crash looked up from the register, where he'd been absently straightening a stack of bills, and saw Mr. Ruiz hobbling in, his cane tapping rhythmically on the worn hardwood floor.

"Morning, Mr. Ruiz," Crash called out, forcing a brightness into his voice. The elderly man had been a fixture in the neighborhood for as long as Crash could remember—a retired dockworker with a penchant for cigars and stories of the good old days.

"Morning, Crash," Mr. Ruiz replied, his voice gravelly from years of smoking. "Just here for my paper and a pack of Camels."

Crash grabbed the items from behind the counter, ringing them up with practiced speed. "How's the leg treating you today?"

Mr. Ruiz shrugged, the movement making his leather jacket creak. "Same as always. This weather doesn't help, though. Makes the joints ache something fierce."

Crash nodded sympathetically as he handed over the paper and cigarettes. "If you need anything else, just let me know."

The old man gave a nod of thanks and turned to leave, but then paused, glancing back at Crash with a frown. "You look tired, kid. You alright?"

Crash hesitated, caught off guard by the question. "Yeah, just didn't sleep well last night, I guess."

"Hmm," Mr. Ruiz grunted, clearly unconvinced. "You're too young to be walking around like you've got the weight of the world on your shoulders. Don't let this place grind you down, eh?"

Crash managed a small smile. "I'll try not to."

With a final nod, Mr. Ruiz shuffled out the door, leaving Crash standing behind the counter, the old man's words echoing in his mind.

He returned to his task, his hands moving automatically as he restocked the gum and candy near the register, but his thoughts were elsewhere. The customers who came through their doors every day were as much a part of the store as the products on the shelves— each one with their own stories, their own struggles. Some, like Mr. Ruiz, had known better days, while others were just trying to make it through the week.

Crash had grown up listening to their stories, their laughter, and their complaints, all woven into the fabric of his daily life. But as he watched them go about their routines, he couldn't help but wonder if this was all there was—if he, too, would one day become another regular with nothing more to look forward to than a newspaper and a pack of cigarettes.

The bell jingled again, breaking through his reverie, and Crash looked up to see a young mother wrestling with a toddler who was determined to escape her grasp. The little boy, no more than three or four, was a bundle of energy, wriggling free and darting down the aisle toward the candy display.

"No, no, no!" the mother called, exasperation clear in her voice as she chased after him. "We're not buying any candy today!"

Crash watched with a mixture of amusement and sympathy as she finally caught up to the boy and scooped him into her arms, his chubby hands still reaching for the brightly colored wrappers.

"Sorry about that," the woman said breathlessly as she approached the counter, juggling the squirming child and a basket filled with groceries. "He's a handful."

"No problem," Crash replied with a grin. "I've seen worse."

As he rang up her items, the woman tried to calm her son, who was now pouting and kicking his legs in frustration. "I swear, he's like a little tornado. Keeps me on my toes."

Crash handed her the receipt with a smile. "Looks like you've got your hands full, but you're doing great."

The woman gave him a tired but grateful smile. "Thanks. Some days, it doesn't feel that way."

Crash watched as she struggled to gather her bags and keep hold of the still-wriggling toddler. Without thinking, he stepped out from behind the counter to help her with the bags, a small gesture, but one that seemed to ease her burden just a little.

"Thank you," she said, genuine appreciation in her voice as she balanced the bags on one arm and shifted the boy to her hip. "It's nice to know there are still some helpful young men out there."

Crash shrugged, feeling a slight blush creep into his cheeks.

She gave him one last smile before heading out the door, her son already wriggling again in her arms. Crash returned to his spot behind the counter, his mind lingering on the brief exchange.

He'd always taken pride in being someone people could rely on, someone who could make their day a little easier, even if it was just by carrying a bag or offering a kind word. But lately, that pride had been overshadowed by a gnawing sense of dissatisfaction, a feeling that these small gestures weren't enough—weren't what he was meant to be doing with his life.

The day wore on, and more customers came and went, each one greeted with a smile and a bit of small talk. There was Mr. Patel, who ran the corner newsstand and always stopped by for a coffee and a chat before starting his shift; Mrs. Delgado, who bought fresh bread every morning and never left without reminding Crash to "eat something, you're too skinny!"; and old Mrs. Walters, who always took an extra minute to rummage through her purse for exact change.

They were all part of the rhythm of the store, part of the life that Crash had known since he was a boy. The Anuman Family Store had been a fixture in the neighborhood for over four decades, a small, unassuming building nestled between a laundromat and a barbershop. Its once-bright blue awning had faded to a dull grey, and the wooden sign that bore their family name was chipped and weathered, its letters barely legible.

Inside, the store was a patchwork of memories and practicality. The narrow aisles were lined with shelves that groaned under the weight of cans, jars, and boxes, a mix of familiar brands and specialty items that spoke to the diverse tastes of their customers. The floor was a mosaic of cracked hardwood, worn smooth in places by years of foot traffic. It creaked underfoot, a sound that had become as familiar to Crash as the ticking of a clock. The ceiling clad in stamped tin and crown moulding from decades before his grandfather purchased the building.

Behind the counter, the walls were adorned with old photographs, faded by time but still full of life. There was his grandfather, standing proudly in front of the store on its opening day, a wide grin on his face and a sparkle in his eyes. In another photo, his grandmother, much younger but still with that same determined set to her jaw, stood behind the register, a baby Crash perched on her hip.

The store had been their life's work, passed down from father to daughter, a legacy of hard work and dedication. It had weathered the storms of time, the economic downturns, and the rise of big-box stores, surviving on the strength of the community that had grown up around it. For years, it had been a place where people could find not just groceries, but a sense of belonging—a place where they were known by name, where their stories were remembered, where they were more than just customers.

But the store had also seen its share of losses. Crash's mother and father had taken over the business when his grandfather passed away, pouring his heart and soul into keeping it afloat. It was a responsibility he carried with quiet pride, never letting on how much it weighed on him—until the day it all became too much. The heart attack had come suddenly, taking him away before Crash could even say goodbye. He was just a boy then, too young to understand the weight of the legacy that had just been handed to him.

Since then, the store had become a place of both comfort and burden for Crash. It was where he had grown up, where he had learned the value of hard work and community. But it was also where he had seen the toll it had taken on his father, the long hours, the sleepless nights, the constant worry. And now, with his father and grandfather gone, it was up to Crash to carry that burden, to keep the store—and their family's legacy—alive.

Every corner of the store held a memory, every item on the shelf a reminder of the people who had passed through its doors over the years. The old candy jars by the register, the same ones his grandfather had filled when Crash was a boy, now stood half-empty, a testament to changing tastes and tighter budgets. The deli counter, once bustling with activity, now served only a few loyal customers, its glass display case a little emptier each day.

And yet, despite its age and wear, the store still had a warmth to it, a sense of history that wrapped around Crash like a comforting blanket. It was a place where the past was always present, where the stories of those who had come before him were written into the very walls. But it was also a place where the future seemed uncertain, where the weight of responsibility sometimes felt too heavy to bear.

As Crash looked around, taking in the familiar sights and sounds, he felt a pang of nostalgia mixed with a deep sense of restlessness. This was his life, his inheritance, but he couldn't shake the feeling that there was something more out there for him— something beyond the shelves and the aisles, beyond the store and the neighborhood he had always known.

But for now, as the bell over the door jingled again, signaling another customer, Crash pushed those thoughts aside and turned his attention back to the task at hand, forcing a smile as he greeted them. The store might feel like a cage, but it was his cage, and until he found a way out, this was where he would stay.

The midday lull had settled over the store, a brief respite from the steady trickle of customers. Crash leaned against the counter, pulling his phone from his pocket. The device was a few models old, its screen slightly cracked at the corner from a drop he didn't want to remember. But it still worked, and for now, it was his lifeline to a world that felt both tantalizingly close and frustratingly out of reach.

With a few swipes, Crash opened the MeTube app, scrolling through the recommended videos until he found the familiar names of his favorite streamers. These were the people who seemed to have it all—freedom, success, the kind of life Crash could only dream about. Their lives were a constant stream of adventures, collaborations, and behind-the-scenes glimpses into a world that felt like the exact opposite of his own.

He tapped on a video from "TechNomad," a popular channel run by a streamer named Jordan who traveled the world reviewing the latest gadgets and tech. The video began with a flashy intro, all neon colors and upbeat music, before cutting to Jordan standing in front of a futuristic skyline that Crash could only guess was somewhere in Tokyo.

"What's up, TechNomads? It's your boy, Jordan, coming to you live from one of the most high-tech cities in the world! Today, we're diving into the latest innovations in wearable tech—stuff that's going to blow your mind!"

Crash watched as Jordan flashed a winning smile at the camera, exuding the kind of confidence that came from knowing millions of people were hanging on his every word. The video cut to sleek shots of cutting-edge gadgets, all displayed in a setting that looked like something out of a science fiction movie. It was a world so far removed from the worn floorboards and flickering fluorescent lights of the Anuman Family Store that it might as well have been on another planet.

As the video played, Crash found himself lost in the fantasy of what it would be like to live a life like Jordan's. To wake up in a different city every week, to be at the forefront of technology and innovation, to have a voice that people actually listened to. It wasn't just the gadgets that fascinated him—it was the freedom, the sense of possibility that came with being a part of something bigger than himself.

His thoughts drifted to another streamer he followed, "NomadAnnie," a travel vlogger who explored remote corners of the world, sharing stories of cultures and places that seemed untouched by time. Annie's videos were always filled with vibrant colors, the sounds of bustling markets, and the laughter of children playing in sun-drenched villages. Her life seemed like a never-ending adventure, each day bringing something new and exciting.

Crash couldn't help but feel a pang of envy as he watched her latest video, filmed in a small coastal town in Greece. The camera panned over whitewashed buildings with blue-domed roofs, the sparkling Mediterranean stretching out to the horizon. Annie's voice-over was calm and soothing, a stark contrast to the chaotic energy of the store around him.

Chapter 2
The Fish That Got Away

"This place," she was saying, "is a reminder that there's still so much beauty in the world, even in the smallest, most unexpected corners. It's about finding those moments of peace, those little pockets of joy, and holding onto them."

Crash paused the video, letting her words linger in the air. It was hard not to compare his own life to the ones he saw on screen, to feel like he was missing out on something vital, something that could give his life the meaning and excitement he craved. The world beyond his tiny sliver of San Francisco felt so vast, so full of possibilities, while his own life seemed to be shrinking, closing in on itself with each passing day.

He scrolled through more videos, each one a glimpse into a life that felt just out of reach. There was "ChefZ," a culinary expert who toured the world's best restaurants, sampling dishes that Crash could barely pronounce. There was "ExtremeSports," a channel dedicated to adrenaline Jankies who pushed the limits of what the human body could endure. And then there was "GamerX," a streamer who played the latest video games in front of millions, his commentary turning even the most mundane moments into something thrilling.

Crash wasn't just watching these videos—he was living vicariously through them, imagining what it would be like to be the one on the other side of the screen, to have people care about what he had to say, to be a part of a world where anything seemed possible.

But it wasn't just the content creators that fascinated him. There was another figure, always looming in the background, a man whose name was synonymous with the platform itself: Leonard Trice, the CEO of TechSpan, the company that owned MeTube. Leonard's influence was everywhere, from the algorithms that decided which videos got recommended, to the monetization policies that allowed streamers to make a living doing what they loved.

Leonard Trice was a name that carried weight, a name that was spoken with equal parts reverence and fear in the online world. He was known for his ruthless business acumen, his ability to turn anything into a profit, and his vision for a future where technology was woven into every aspect of human life. Some saw him as a visionary, a man who was pushing the boundaries of what was possible. Others saw him as a manipulator, someone who was more interested in control than in the freedom he purported to offer.

Crash had seen interviews with Leonard before—always calm, composed, with a hint of something unreadable in his eyes. There was a coldness to him, a sense that everything he did was calculated, every word carefully chosen. And yet, despite the unease Leonard sometimes provoked, Crash couldn't help but admire the man's success, his ability to create something that had changed the world.

In one of the videos he watched, Leonard had been asked about the future of content creation, about where he saw platforms like MeTube going in the next decade. Leonard had leaned back in his chair, his hands steepled in front of him, and replied, "The future is limitless. We're just beginning to scratch the surface of what's possible. The world is becoming smaller, more connected, and those who are able to harness that connectivity will shape the future. It's not just about creating content—it's about creating a new way of living, of interacting with the world around us."

Crash had replayed that line in his head more times than he could count. A new way of living. That's what he wanted—a life that wasn't defined by the confines of the store, by the same routines and faces, day in and day out. He wanted to be part of something bigger, to have a voice, to be seen.

He glanced around the store, at the shelves filled with canned goods and cleaning supplies, at the scuffed floors and the flickering lights. It was a world he knew inside and out, a world that had given him everything he had. But it wasn't enough—not anymore.

Crash looked back at his phone, at the smiling faces of the streamers who seemed to have figured it all out, who had found their place in the world. He wanted that. He wanted the freedom, the excitement, the sense of purpose that came with it.

But more than anything, he wanted to be someone who mattered.

The bell over the door jingled, snapping Crash out of his reverie. He quickly tucked his phone back into his pocket and straightened up, ready to greet the next customer. But as he did, the words of Leonard Trice lingered in his mind, a reminder of the world that was out there, just waiting to be discovered.

A new way of living.

Maybe, just maybe, there was a way for him to find it.

The store had settled into its usual afternoon rhythm—a quiet hum of distant traffic outside, the soft buzz of the fluorescent lights overhead, and the gentle rustle of the newspaper pages as Crash's grandmother flipped through the morning edition at the counter. Crash was in the middle of restocking the shelves, his mind still buzzing with thoughts of the streamers he'd been watching earlier.

Crash looked up and saw old Mr. Thompson shuffling into the store, his gnarled hand gripping the handle of his cane as if it were the only thing keeping him upright. The elderly man moved slowly, his steps hesitant, as though he wasn't entirely sure where he was. His clothes hung loosely on his frail frame, and his eyes, though clouded with age, still held a spark of determination.

Crash felt a pang of sympathy for the old man—he'd been a regular customer for as long as Crash could remember, coming in almost every day for as long as the store had been around. Mr. Thompson was one of those customers who everyone in the neighborhood knew by name, who always had a kind word and a smile for everyone he met. But as sweet as the old man was, Crash also knew that this encounter was going to be anything but quick.

Crash forced a warm smile onto his face as he stepped out from behind the shelves. "Afternoon, Mr. Thompson. What can I help you with today?"

Mr. Thompson peered at Crash as though seeing him for the first time, his brow furrowing in concentration. "Ah, Crash, my boy," he said slowly, his voice shaky with age. "I'm looking for... now, what was it again? Ah yes, that brand of sardines I like. You know the one, right? The ones in the blue tin with the little fish on the front."

Crash resisted the urge to roll his eyes. He'd had this conversation with Mr. Thompson more times than he could count. The brand he was asking for had been discontinued years ago, something Crash had explained to him countless times, but the old man seemed to forget that fact every time he walked through the door.

Crash's smile tightened slightly. "I'm sorry, Mr. Thompson, but we don't carry those sardines anymore. They stopped making them a while back. But we do have some other brands you might like—how about we take a look?"

Mr. Thompson's face fell, a look of confusion crossing his features. "Stopped making them? Well, that doesn't make any sense. They were the best ones! Are you sure you don't have any in the back?"

Crash's patience was wearing thin, but he kept his tone gentle. "I'm sure, Mr. Thompson. We've been out of stock for a long time now. But why don't I show you the other options we have? Maybe there's something else you'll like just as much."

The old man hesitated, his eyes darting around the store as if he was trying to remember something important. "I suppose... well, alright then, let's take a look."

Crash guided Mr. Thompson toward the aisle where the canned fish was stocked, his mind already half on the task, half elsewhere. He knew this was going to take some time—Mr. Thompson would likely want to inspect every single can on the shelf, comparing them to the ones he remembered. It was a small thing, really, but to the old man, it was important. And Crash couldn't bring himself to brush him off, no matter how much he wanted to.

As they reached the aisle, Crash began to pull a few cans off the shelf, holding them up for Mr. Thompson to inspect. "Here's one that's pretty popular," Crash said, "as popular as sardines are anymore," he thought while handing the can to the old man. "It's packed in olive oil, just like the ones you used to get."

Mr. Thompson took the can, turning it over in his hands as he squinted at the label. "Hmm... doesn't look quite right. The fish on the front isn't smiling like the old ones."

Crash bit back a sigh. "No, it's not exactly the same, but the quality is just as good. And the flavor is really nice—I've had a lot of customers tell me they like this brand," he lied.

Mr. Thompson nodded slowly, but his expression remained doubtful. "I don't know, Crash. Maybe... maybe we should check the other aisle? There might be something there."

Crash knew that there wasn't anything else to find, but he also knew that Mr. Thompson wouldn't be satisfied until they'd checked every possible spot. It was frustrating, sure, but he couldn't help but feel a sense of duty to the old man—a need to help him find some semblance of the familiar in a world that was slowly slipping away from him.

As they made their way down the aisle, Crash's attention drifted, his mind wandering back to the videos he'd watched earlier. He couldn't help but imagine what it would be like to just drop everything and go—leave the store, the city, and all its obligations behind, and set out on an adventure of his own. It was a tempting thought, one that lingered in the back of his mind like a persistent itch he couldn't quite scratch.

He was so lost in his thoughts that he didn't notice the subtle rustling sound coming from the front of the store, the soft padding of something moving stealthily across the floor. A sleek, dark figure moved with practiced ease, sticking to the shadows as he made his way toward the fish section, his whiskers twitching with anticipation.

Meanwhile, Crash continued to humor Mr. Thompson, who was now insisting on checking behind the jars of pickles for the elusive sardines. "I'm sure I saw them here last time," the old man muttered, his brow furrowed in concentration.

"Maybe it was a different store," Crash suggested gently, though he knew it wouldn't make a difference. "We haven't had them in a long time."

Mr. Thompson sighed, finally accepting defeat as he handed the can of sardines back to Crash. "Maybe you're right, Crash. I suppose I'm just getting old. Can't keep track of things the way I used to."

Crash gave him a sympathetic smile, placing the can back on the shelf. "You're doing just fine, Mr. Thompson. And hey, if we ever get those sardines back, you'll be the first to know."

The old man managed a weak smile in return. "I appreciate that, son. I really do."

Crash nodded, guiding Mr. Thompson back toward the front of the store, still unaware of the stealthy visitor lurking in the store.

As Crash rang up Mr. Thompson's purchase—just a small loaf of bread and a carton of milk—his mind was still elsewhere, still caught between the reality of his life and the fantasy of something more. He handed the old man his change, bidding him a warm goodbye.

The door closed behind Mr. Thompson with a soft jingle, the sound lingering in the air as Crash let out a slow breath. He watched the old man shuffle away down the sidewalk, his form gradually disappearing into the late afternoon haze. Crash leaned back against the counter, absently running a hand through his hair as he tried to shake off the lingering sense of unease that clung to him like the San Francisco fog.

The store was quiet now, the lull between the lunchtime rush and the after-work crowd. It was the kind of quiet that left room for thoughts to drift, to wander into places Crash usually tried to avoid. He looked around the store, his eyes tracing the familiar lines of the aisles, the shelves stocked with goods, the walls that had seen more than a lifetime's worth of memories.

The interaction with Mr. Thompson had left a strange taste in Crash's mouth—one part sympathy, one part frustration, and a dash of something he couldn't quite name. The old man's confusion, his insistence on searching for something that wasn't there, had hit closer to home than Crash wanted to admit. There was something about the way Mr. Thompson kept looking, kept hoping, that struck a chord deep within him.

Crash had been doing the same thing, hadn't he? Searching for something that he couldn't quite find, hoping for a spark of excitement, a moment of clarity that would show him the way out of the rut he felt trapped in. The store, the neighborhood, the endless parade of familiar faces—it was all too much and not enough at the same time. He couldn't help but feel like he was living someone else's life, following a script that had been written long before he was born.

He closed his eyes for a moment, letting the familiar smells of the store wash over him—fresh bread, ripe fruit, the faint tang of cleaning supplies. It was comforting, in its own way, but it was also stifling. The walls felt like they were closing in, the ceiling pressing down, the air growing thick and hard to breathe.

Crash's thoughts drifted back to the videos he'd been watching earlier, to the streamers who seemed to have it all figured out. They were out there living their lives, chasing their dreams, while he was stuck here, going through the motions, day in and day out. They had the freedom he craved, the excitement he longed for, and they made it look so easy.

But was it really that simple? Or was he just fooling himself, imagining a life that didn't exist, one that was just as unattainable as the sardines Mr. Thompson kept searching for?

Crash sighed, opening his eyes and letting them roam the store once more. He knew he was lucky to have what he did—a family that loved him, a roof over his head, a job that kept them all afloat. But there was a restlessness in him, a gnawing desire for something more, something that he couldn't quite put into words.

He pushed himself off the counter, feeling the need to move, to do something with his hands, if only to distract his mind. He walked toward the back of the store, where the fresh fish were kept on ice, their silvery scales glinting in the dim light. It was one of the last parts of the store that still felt vibrant, still carried a sense of newness amidst the wear and tear of everything else.

Crash reached down, adjusting a few of the fish that had shifted out of place, their cold, slick bodies cool against his fingers. As he did, he caught a movement out of the corner of his eye—just a flicker of something in the shadows, something that shouldn't have been there.

He straightened up, his eyes narrowing as he scanned the area, but there was nothing out of the ordinary. The store was empty, just as it had been a moment before. He shook his head, chalking it up to his overactive imagination, a byproduct of too much time spent lost in his own thoughts.

Still, the feeling of unease didn't leave him. There was something off, something that didn't quite sit right. It was as if the air had shifted, the atmosphere in the store subtly different from what it had been just moments ago.

Crash turned his attention back to the fish, rearranging them neatly on the ice, but his mind was elsewhere, still caught up in the tangle of thoughts and emotions that had been swirling inside him all day. He knew he couldn't go on like this, couldn't keep pretending that everything was fine when it wasn't. But what could he do? Where could he go?

He didn't have the answers, not yet. But maybe—just maybe—the first step was recognizing that he needed to ask the questions.

Maybe it was time to stop searching for the sardines that were never coming back and start looking for something new, something that would actually satisfy the hunger that had been gnawing at him for so long.

As Crash finished arranging the fish, he glanced around the store once more, still feeling that strange sense of being watched, of something lurking just out of sight. But there was nothing there, just the quiet aisles, the humming refrigerators, the faint sound of his grandmother's radio playing a scratchy old tune.

Crash found himself once again behind the register, his attention half on the screen of his phone, where one of his favorite streamers was mid-rant about the latest gaming controversy. The familiar banter was a welcome distraction from the monotony of the day, pulling him into a world that felt both exciting and far removed from the reality of the store.

His grandmother was at her usual spot by the counter, her glasses perched on the end of her nose as she flipped through the pages of her Thai newspaper. Occasionally, she'd glance up at the small bank of security monitors behind her, making sure everything was as it should be. The system more for watching for customers than for security now, the built in VCR long broken. Crash did manage to rig an online feed of the cameras using a Raspberry Pi so they could check in from home, but a bank of harddrives to record to was well out of their budget. His mother was somewhere in the back, restocking the shelves and humming a soft tune that blended with the crackle of the radio playing an old jazz standard.

Crash absently scrolled through the comments section of the stream, his mind half-tuned to the chatter, when something on one of the security monitors caught his grandmother's eye. She peered at the screen for a moment, her brow furrowing slightly before she shook her head and returned to her paper. Crash barely noticed, lost in the rhythm of the stream, but something about her hesitation lingered in the back of his mind.

Meanwhile, a few aisles away, a very different sort of drama was unfolding.

The sleek figure of a sea lion, surprisingly nimble for its size, was doing its best to navigate the narrow aisles of the Anuman Family Store without drawing attention. Its glossy fur shone under the fluorescent lights, but what stood out most was the green bucket hat perched precariously on its head—a relic of another life, stolen during a daring escape from a place that felt like a distant nightmare.

A sea lion—moved with a mix of clumsiness and caution, his large body not quite suited for the tight spaces between shelves stocked with cereal boxes and canned goods. He paused every few steps, his whiskers twitching as he scanned the area, his keen eyes searching for any signs of movement. It wasn't easy being a sea lion in a human world, but the sea lion had learned to adapt—most of the time.

As he crept forward, his belly sliding against the cool floor, he caught sight of Crash's mother moving between the aisles, her back to him as she rearranged a display of pasta. the sea lion froze, holding his breath as she bent down to pick up a box that had fallen. His heart—or whatever the sea lion equivalent was—thudded in his chest, his instincts screaming at him to make a run for it. But the scent of fresh fish was too strong, too tempting to resist.

With a quick glance to make sure she hadn't noticed him, the sea lion ducked into the next aisle, his hat tilting dangerously to one side. He adjusted it with a flick of his head, muttering something that sounded suspiciously like a sea lion's version of a curse word. The hat had been with him since the day he escaped that cursed research ship, and it was as much a part of him now as his flippers. He wasn't about to lose it to a stack of canned beans.

As the sea lion inched closer to the back of the store, where the fish lay enticingly on their bed of ice, he was forced to dodge yet another obstacle—Crash's grandmother, who had just decided to stretch her legs and take a stroll through the store. She moved slowly, her gaze shifting from the shelves to the security monitors, her senses still sharp despite her age.

the sea lion pressed himself flat against the floor, his whiskers brushing the base of a shelf as she passed by, barely a foot away. He could feel his nerves on edge, every muscle in his body coiled tight, ready to bolt if she so much as glanced in his direction. But she didn't, her focus more on finding a snack than on the odd figure creeping through her store.

As soon as she was out of sight, the sea lion bolted—well, as much as a sea lion could bolt—toward the back of the store, his eyes locked on the prize. The fish were laid out in neat rows, their scales glistening under the lights, the scent almost overwhelming. He could practically taste them already, the promise of a good meal making his mouth water.

Crash, still absorbed in his stream, leaned back in his chair, his phone propped up on the counter as the streamer ranted on about the latest drama in the gaming world. The sounds of the store faded into the background as he lost himself in the virtual world, his attention drifting away from the here and now.

But then, something pulled him back—an odd sound, like a soft thud, followed by the faintest rustle. It was enough to make Crash glance up from his phone, his eyes narrowing as he tried to locate the source. For a moment, he didn't see anything out of the ordinary—just the usual rows of shelves, the familiar flicker of the overhead lights, and the quiet hum of the refrigerators.

Then he saw it.

Or rather, he saw a glimpse of it—a flash of movement at the back of the store, something dark and low to the ground. Crash blinked, wondering if he was imagining things, but then it happened again—a quick, darting motion, too fast to be one of the neighborhood cats that sometimes wandered in.

Curiosity piqued, Crash stood up, his eyes fixed on the spot where he'd seen the movement. He took a few steps forward, his gaze scanning the aisles, his heart starting to beat a little faster. What on earth was that?

As he rounded the corner of the aisle, his breath caught in his throat.

There, just a few feet away, was the last thing he ever expected to see in his store: a sea lion, its sleek body partially hidden behind a display of paper towels, its dark eyes wide and alert. And perched on its head, as if it were the most natural thing in the world, was a green bucket hat.

For a moment, neither of them moved. Crash stood frozen, his mind struggling to make sense of what he was seeing, while the sea lion held his ground, his whiskers twitching as he sized up this strange human who had caught him in the act.

Crash blinked, half-expecting the sea lion to disappear like a mirage, but it remained stubbornly in place, as real as the shelves and the tiles underfoot. And then, without warning, the sea lion moved—darting forward with surprising speed for an animal of his size, making a beeline for the fish display.

"Hey!" Crash finally found his voice, the shock giving way to instinct as he took off after the sea lion, his sneakers squeaking on the floor as he rounded the corner.

the sea lion was fast, but not fast enough. Crash reached the fish display just in time to see the sea lion skidding to a halt in front of the ice, his eyes locking onto the fish with a hunger that Crash recognized all too well.

For a split second, Crash hesitated. There was something almost comical about the sight before him—a sea lion in a green bucket hat, eyeing the fish like a kid in a candy store. But there was also something else, something that made Crash pause, something that felt strangely... familiar.

Before he could make sense of it, the sea lion lunged forward, his flippers sending ice scattering as he reached for the nearest fish.

Crash reacted on instinct, diving forward and grabbing the sea lion by the hat, pulling him back just before he could snag his prize.

the sea lion let out a startled bark, twisting around to face Crash, his eyes wide with a mix of surprise and indignation. Crash tightened his grip on the hat, his heart pounding in his chest as he stared down at the creature in front of him, not quite sure what to do next.

For a moment, they simply stared at each other—human and sea lion, caught in a standoff that neither of them had expected.

Then, slowly, the sea lion's eyes narrowed, his expression shifting from surprise to something that looked suspiciously like mischief. With a sudden, jerking motion, the sea lion pulled back, his flippers flailing as he tried to slip out of Crash's grasp. But Crash held on tight, determined not to let the sea lion get away, even as his own grip started to slip.

It was a battle of wills, and Crash wasn't sure who would win—until, with a final, desperate tug, the sea lion wrenched himself free, sending Crash stumbling backward as the hat slipped from the monster's head and on to the wooden floorboards

The sea lion didn't waste a second. With a triumphant bark, he grabbed the nearest fish in his jaws and made a break for it. His beloved green bucket hat a temporary victim of his clumsiest caper to date.

Crash, still reeling from the encounter, could only watch as the sea lion made his escape, the sound of his grandmother's voice calling out from the front of the store, asking what all the commotion was about.

But Crash didn't answer. He was too busy staring at the door, his mind racing, his heart pounding, and one thought echoing in his head.

What the hell just happened?

Crash didn't have time to think. The moment the sea lion bolted out of the store, fish in tow, instinct took over. He leaped over the counter, barely registering his grandmother's startled gasp as she called after him. The bell over the door jangled wildly as Crash burst through, his sneakers skidding on the pavement outside.

The sea lion was already several yards ahead, his sleek form darting down the sidewalk with surprising speed for a creature his size. The great Otariinae bobbed comically as he weaved between pedestrians, dodging the occasional stroller or shopping bag. It would have been almost funny if Crash wasn't so focused on catching up.

The streets were alive with the usual afternoon hustle—cars honking, people chatting, the occasional bus rumbling by—but all of it blurred into the background as Crash zeroed in on the fleeing sea lion. The scent of the stolen fish lingered in the air, mingling with the smell of street food and the faint tang of salt carried on the breeze from the bay.

Crash pushed himself to run faster, his breath coming in sharp bursts as he closed the distance. the sea lion, however, was no easy target. He darted into a narrow alleyway, slipping past a row of stacked crates and knocking over a trash can in his haste. Crash followed, nearly tripping over the spilled garbage as he squeezed between the tight walls.

The alley opened up into a small courtyard, its edges lined with colorful murals and potted plants that overflowed with greenery. the sea lion hesitated for just a second, his gaze darting around as if calculating his next move, before he spotted an open gate leading to the street beyond.

"Stop!" Crash shouted, though he knew it was pointless. His voice echoed off the walls, barely reaching the sea lion's ears as the sea lion made a break for the gate.

Chapter 3
In Which a Sea Lion Evades Arrest

But the sea lion wasn't alone in the courtyard. An elderly woman with a bright red scarf around her neck and a shopping cart full of fresh produce stood frozen in place, her eyes wide as she watched the scene unfold. She was one of the neighborhood regulars—Mrs. Chao, if Crash remembered correctly—always smiling and quick to offer a kind word.

Now, though, she looked more bewildered than anything else.

"Excuse me!" Crash gasped as he darted past her, barely avoiding a collision. "Sorry!"

Mrs. Chao blinked in surprise, her hand fluttering to her scarf as she watched the boy and the sea lion disappear through the gate, her groceries forgotten for the moment.

Out on the street again, the sea lion had picked up speed, his belly sliding smoothly over the sidewalk as he made his way toward the heart of the neighborhood. Crash was right on his tail—literally—his eyes fixed on the green bucket hat that bobbed up and down with every flippered stride.

The neighborhood around them was a vibrant mix of cultures and colors, the streets lined with small businesses that catered to the diverse community. Thai restaurants with colorful awnings, family-owned notions stores, and boutiques selling everything from handmade jewelry to vintage clothing created a lively atmosphere. The air was thick with the scent of spices, the sound of different languages mixing together in a harmonious cacophony.

But there was no time to appreciate any of it. the sea lion was heading toward a busy intersection, the light just about to change. Crash pushed himself harder, his legs burning as he closed the gap, but the sea lion was already halfway across the street, dodging between the cars that had started to move.

"Watch out!" Crash shouted as he reached the curb, narrowly avoiding a Uber that screeched to a halt just in time. The driver honked angrily, but Crash barely noticed, his attention fixed on the fleeing sea lion.

the sea lion's path took them past a row of street vendors, their carts laden with everything from steaming bowls of noodle soup to intricately woven baskets. One of the vendors, a young man with a shock of blue hair and a wide grin, watched in amusement as the sea lion darted past, his eyes widening when he saw Crash in hot pursuit.

"Hey, is that...?" the vendor began, but Crash was already gone, weaving between the carts and barely avoiding a stack of crates that toppled over as the sea lion brushed past them.

The chase took a sharp turn down another alleyway, this one narrower and darker than the last. The walls were covered in graffiti, a kaleidoscope of colors and shapes that seemed to pulse with energy as Crash sprinted past. He could hear the sea lion's breathy grunts ahead, the sound bouncing off the walls, guiding him through the twists and turns.

But the sea lion was clever. Just as Crash thought he was getting closer, the sea lion made a sudden turn, darting through a half-open door that led into the back of a small restaurant. Crash skidded to a stop, his heart pounding in his chest as he stared at the door, half-expecting the sea lion to reappear.

Instead, he heard a startled shout from inside, followed by a clatter of pots and pans. A moment later, the door burst open again, and the sea lion came barreling out, a string of noodles somehow tangled around his neck like a makeshift scarf. The sight was so absurd that Crash couldn't help but laugh, even as he resumed the chase.

They emerged onto a side street that led uphill, the steep incline forcing Crash to push even harder to keep up. the sea lion, for all his bulk, was surprisingly agile, using his flippers to propel himself forward with surprising speed. Crash's lungs burned, his muscles aching as he struggled to maintain the pace.

At the top of the hill, the street opened up into a small park, the trees casting dappled shadows over the grass. the sea lion didn't slow down, his gaze fixed on the other side of the park where another street led downhill. But the park wasn't empty.

A group of kids were playing soccer, their shouts of excitement filling the air as they chased the ball back and forth. One of them—a boy with a shock of curly hair—spotted the sea lion first, his eyes going wide as he pointed and shouted, "Look! A sea lion!"

The other kids stopped in their tracks, their game forgotten as they watched the sea lion barrel through the park, the noodles trailing behind him like a ridiculous cape.

Crash was right behind him, barely managing to shout out, "Watch out!" as he swerved to avoid the kids, who scattered with delighted shrieks. One of them—probably the bravest—gave chase, laughing as he tried to keep up with Crash.

the sea lion, however, had no time for games. He reached the edge of the park and took a flying leap onto the street, sliding down the steep incline with a grace that only a sea lion could manage. Crash skidded to a stop at the top of the hill, his breath coming in gasps as he stared down at the street below.

For a moment, he considered giving up—the sea lion was fast, and the chase had taken them far from the store. But something in him refused to quit, a stubborn determination that drove him forward.

With a deep breath, Crash took off down the hill, his momentum carrying him faster than he expected. The wind whipped through his hair, his feet pounding the pavement as he tried to keep his balance on the steep descent. Ahead of him, the sea lion was still in the lead, but the gap was closing.

The street at the bottom of the hill led directly to the cable car tracks, the familiar clang of the bell ringing out in the distance. the sea lion seemed to know exactly where he was going, his movements purposeful as he headed toward the tracks. Crash could only guess that this wasn't the first time the sea lion had taken this route.

As they neared the intersection, Crash could see the cable car approaching, its bright red and yellow paint standing out against the grey of the street. the sea lion was heading straight for it, his eyes locked on the moving target as he pushed himself to go faster.

Crash's heart pounded in his chest as he realized what the sea lion was about to do. "No way..." he muttered under his breath, his eyes widening in disbelief.

the sea lion reached the tracks just as the cable car approached, and without missing a beat, he launched himself onto the side of the car, his flippers gripping the railing as he pulled himself up. The green bucket hat wobbled but stayed in place, as if by sheer force of will.

The passengers on the cable car let out startled gasps, some laughing in disbelief as they watched the sea lion hitch a ride. One of them—a woman with a camera—snapped a photo, her face lit up with excitement.

Crash, still running, skidded to a stop at the edge of the street, watching in stunned silence as the cable car continued down the tracks, the sea lion safely aboard.

He could only watch as the sea lion, now out of reach, disappeared around the corner, the clang of the cable car's bell fading into the distance.

Breathless and defeated, Crash bent over, his hands on his knees as he tried to catch his breath. The chase was over—for now. But as he stood there, his mind racing, he couldn't shake the feeling that this wasn't the last he'd see of the sea lion with the green bucket hat.

Crash stood at the intersection, hands on his knees, still catching his breath. The clang of the cable car glided into the distance, along with any hope of catching the mysterious sea lion. He straightened up, glancing around as if expecting the sea lion to reappear from some hidden corner, but the streets had returned to their usual rhythm, oblivious to the wild chase that had just taken place.

Pedestrians walked by, some giving him curious looks, but most just carried on with their day. The city moved around him, unaware of the bizarre encounter that had left him standing there, breathless and bewildered.

Crash wiped the sweat from his brow, his mind racing as he replayed the chase in his head. A sea lion... in a bucket hat... stealing fish. It sounded ridiculous even to him, but there was no denying what he had seen. The image of the sea lion—sliding through the streets, bobbing and weaving like some kind of slippery escape artist—was burned into his memory.

But what now? He hadn't caught the sea lion, and he had no idea where the sea lion had disappeared to. The whole thing felt surreal, like something out of one of the ridiculous videos he watched online. But it had been real enough. And it left him with more questions than answers.

Crash took one last look down the street where the sea lion had disappeared, his thoughts already shifting gears. He might not have caught the sea lion today, but that didn't mean he was giving up.

With a final deep breath, Crash turned back toward the grocery store.

The walk back to the grocery store was slower, more deliberate. Crash's legs ached from the chase, and his mind was still spinning from the surreal events that had just unfolded. A sea lion... in a green bucket hat... stealing fish. It sounded like something out of a children's book, not the reality he was supposed to be living in.

As he walked, the city's rhythm gradually returned to normal around him. The honking of cars, the chatter of pedestrians, the occasional roar of a city bus—all of it filled the air, blending into the familiar background noise of San Francisco. But for Crash, everything felt slightly off-kilter, as if the world had tilted on its axis and he was the only one who noticed.

He couldn't stop replaying the chase in his head, the absurdity of it all gnawing at him. What kind of life was this, where he found himself running after a fish-stealing sea lion through the streets? And why did he feel so compelled to catch it, to solve the mystery of the creature that had so brazenly invaded his family's store?

Lost in thought, Crash barely noticed where his feet were taking him until he found himself standing in front of a small coffee shop. The windows were slightly fogged from the warmth inside, the smell of freshly brewed coffee wafting out every time the door swung open. He glanced up, catching sight of his own reflection in the glass.

For a moment, he almost didn't recognize the person staring back at him.

A short, lanky figure, with scruffy black hair that never seemed to stay in place, no matter how much he tried to tame it. The hoodie he wore, a deep charcoal gray, was worn but well-loved, its edges darned carefully by his grandmother's skilled hands. The Vans sneakers on his feet were untied, the laces tucked inside, a habit he'd picked up in middle school and never quite grew out of.

His eyes—dark, tired, yet still searching—bore into his own reflection, and in that moment, Crash felt a wave of something unfamiliar wash over him. It wasn't just fatigue, or confusion, or even the lingering adrenaline from the chase. It was something deeper, something that gnawed at the edges of his consciousness, whispering truths he wasn't sure he was ready to face.

Who was he? A boy in his mid 20's working at his family's grocery store, running after fish thieves and dreaming of a life that felt like it belonged to someone else? The reflection in the window seemed to mock him, a reminder of the life he was leading—one that felt increasingly small, confined to the narrow aisles of the store and the routines that had become as automatic as breathing.

As Crash stared at himself, he realized how little he thought of his own life so far. He was going through the motions, day after day, without ever really considering what he wanted, what he needed. The chase with the sea lion—absurd as it was—had sparked something in him, a realization that he couldn't keep living this way, drifting aimlessly through his days.

He took a step closer to the window, his breath fogging the glass as he peered more closely at his reflection. Was this all he was? A boy in a hoodie and untied sneakers, stuck in a life that didn't fit, running after shadows in the streets?

The thought left him hollow, an emptiness settling in his chest that he couldn't quite shake. There had to be more to life than this, more than the endless routine of stocking shelves and ringing up customers, more than the quiet expectations of his family and the weight of a legacy he hadn't chosen.

Crash felt a flicker of something in his chest—anger, frustration, maybe even hope. It was hard to tell, but it was there, simmering just beneath the surface. He didn't know what it meant, or what he was supposed to do with it, but he knew one thing for certain: he couldn't keep living like this, letting life happen to him without ever taking control.

He needed to figure out who he was, what he wanted, and how to find it. The chase with the sea lion had shown him that there was a world outside the store, a world full of possibilities and absurdities and challenges that he'd never even considered. Maybe it was time to start exploring it, to take a risk and see where it led him.

Crash took a deep breath, stepping back from the window. The reflection faded, replaced by the sight of the bustling coffee shop inside, people laughing and talking over cups of coffee, oblivious to the storm of thoughts raging in his head.

He turned away, heading back toward the store. The questions still buzzed in his mind, but they didn't feel as overwhelming now. There was something liberating about acknowledging the absurdity of his situation, about seeing himself for who he really was—a boy on the brink of something new, something bigger than the life he'd been living.

As he walked, his steps felt a little lighter, the weight of his thoughts lifting just enough to let in a sliver of hope. He didn't have all the answers yet, but he knew one thing: he wasn't going to settle for a life that didn't feel like his own. Not anymore.

And if that meant chasing after sea lions in bucket hats, so be it.

As Crash continued his slow walk back toward the store, a crisp breeze rolled in from the direction of the bay, cutting through the late afternoon air. It carried with it the unmistakable scent of salt and seaweed, a sharp reminder that fall had quietly replaced summer, bringing with it shorter days and colder nights. Crash pulled the hood of his sweatshirt up over his head, tucking his hands into his pockets as the chill settled in.

But it wasn't just the weather that felt different. With each step, Crash felt his fresh perspective on his own life begin to widen, stretching out to encompass the world around him. It was as if the chase with the sea lion had jarred something loose in his mind, making him see things he'd long since stopped noticing.

The neighborhood he had walked through every day now seemed strangely unfamiliar, the details sharper, more pronounced. He saw things now that he hadn't really seen before, or at least hadn't paid much attention to—the slow, creeping decline of the place he called home.

There were more homeless people on the streets than he remembered. They were huddled in doorways, wrapped in blankets that did little to keep out the cold, their eyes distant and hollow. Cardboard signs leaned against crumbling walls, scrawled with pleas for help that seemed to go unanswered. Crash had always known they were there, but now, it was impossible to ignore how many of them there were, how their numbers seemed to have grown, spreading out like shadows across the city.

He walked past a row of shops, their once-vibrant windows now boarded up, the remnants of old signs barely visible through the layers of dust and graffiti. What had once been a bustling stretch of local businesses—a bakery, a small bookstore, a tailor's shop—had been slowly emptied out, one by one, until all that remained were the faded memories of what they used to be.

Crash paused for a moment, his eyes tracing the outlines of the boarded-up windows, the cracked pavement in front of them. He remembered coming to this part of the neighborhood as a kid, holding his grandmother's hand as they picked up fresh bread from the bakery. The smell of warm, yeasty dough had filled the air, mingling with the sweet scent of pastries cooling on the racks.

Now, the bakery was gone, replaced by a cold, empty shell, its windows covered in plywood, its door chained shut. The tailor's shop next door had fared no better—its windows shattered, its interior gutted and left to decay. The bookstore, too, was just a memory now, the rows of shelves that had once been filled with stories now bare and collecting dust.

Crash sighed, the weight of it all pressing down on him. He had been so wrapped up in his own life, in his own dissatisfaction, that he hadn't noticed how the neighborhood around him had withered away. What had once been a community, a place full of life and energy, was now little more than a collection of empty buildings and forgotten faces.

As he walked on, the signs of decline only grew more apparent. At a busy intersection, a group of self-driving taxis sat in a traffic jam of their own making, their sleek, driverless bodies motionless as their sensors tried to make sense of the confusion. They clogged the streets, blocking the flow of traffic, their engines humming quietly as they waited for some unseen command to set them back in motion.

Crash watched as a pedestrian tried to weave through the gridlock, dodging between the stalled cars with a look of frustration on his face. The driverless taxis, once hailed as the future of transportation, now seemed more like a nuisance, their mindless wandering only adding to the chaos of the streets. They were symbols of progress, but progress that had left the neighborhood behind, trapped in a cycle of decline that no amount of technology could fix.

As he turned down another street, Crash noticed a row of parked cars, their back windows smashed in, glass littering the pavement like broken dreams. The work of brazen burglars, no doubt—another sign of the times, of a neighborhood struggling to keep itself afloat. The sight of it all filled him with a deep, gnawing sadness, a realization that the world he had grown up in was changing, slipping away from him one broken window at a time.

He kept walking, his steps slower now, more thoughtful. The city had always been a place of contrasts—old and new, rich and poor, thriving and decaying—but it had never felt as stark, as unavoidable, as it did now. Everywhere he looked, there were reminders of the slow decline that had taken hold of the neighborhood, the signs of a world that was moving on without him.

But there was something else, too—something that hadn't been there before. It was a flicker of determination, a small, stubborn spark that refused to be extinguished by the weight of what he was seeing. Crash wasn't sure where it had come from, or what it meant, but he knew one thing: he couldn't just keep walking through life with his eyes closed, pretending not to see what was right in front of him.

The cold wind whipped through the streets, but Crash hardly noticed. His thoughts were still tangled up in the events of the day, the absurdity of the chase, and the unsettling realization of how much his neighborhood had changed. It felt like the world was shifting beneath his feet, and he wasn't sure where to step next.

In an attempt to distract himself, Crash pulled out his phone, the familiar weight of it in his hand offering a small measure of comfort. The screen lit up, and with a few quick swipes, he was back on MeTube, scrolling through his favorite streamers. Their voices, filled with energy and enthusiasm, poured through his earbuds, drowning out the noise of the city around him.

He let himself get lost in their world for a moment, the bright colors and fast-paced edits of the videos pulling him away from the cold streets and the unsettling thoughts that had been gnawing at him all day. It was a temporary escape, but it was one he desperately needed.

Then, in an instant...

Crash barely had time to register the blur of movement out of the corner of his eye before he felt the sharp tug on his hand. His phone was snatched from his grip so quickly that it took a second for his brain to catch up to what had just happened.

"Hey!" he shouted, his heart leaping into his throat as he saw the figure sprinting away, his phone clutched tightly in their hand.

Instinct took over, and Crash started running after the thief, but his body protested. He was already sore and tired from the chase with the sea lion, his legs heavy and uncooperative. Each step felt like dragging himself through thick mud, his muscles screaming in protest.

He pushed himself to go faster, but it was no use. His untied shoelaces, which had always been more of a fashion statement than anything else, betrayed him. They tangled around his feet, tripping him up at the worst possible moment.

Crash stumbled, his arms flailing as he tried to regain his balance, but it was too late. He went down hard, the impact jarring through his bones as he hit the pavement.

The world spun around him, the breath knocked out of his lungs as he lay there for a moment, stunned and disoriented. The thief was already gone, disappearing into the maze of streets, taking Crash's phone—and his connection to the world beyond—with them.

He groaned, rolling onto his back and staring up at the cloudy sky, his chest heaving as he tried to catch his breath. The pain in his hands and knees was sharp and immediate, but what hurt more was the frustration, the helplessness that welled up inside him.

"Great," he muttered to himself, wincing as he pushed himself up into a sitting position. His palms were scraped, tiny bits of gravel embedded in the skin, and his knees throbbed from the impact. He felt like he'd been run over, not just physically, but emotionally too.

This was the last thing he needed. The phone had been his lifeline, the one thing that connected him to the world he wanted to be a part of. And now, just like that, it was gone, snatched away in the blink of an eye.

Crash glanced around, but there was no sign of the thief. The street was quiet, the only sounds the distant rumble of a bus and the murmur of a few passing pedestrians. No one had noticed the theft, or if they had, they didn't care. It was just another day in the city, another petty crime that would go unnoticed, unreported.

He sighed, pulling his knees up to his chest and resting his forehead on them. The adrenaline from the chase had faded, leaving him feeling hollow and exhausted. It was as if the universe was conspiring against him, throwing one obstacle after another in his path, testing his resolve.

Crash lifted his head, looking down at his untied sneakers, the laces still tangled around his feet. He'd never thought much about it before—how he always wore them this way, never bothering to tie them properly. It was just something he did, a small act of rebellion against the mundane, against the expectations that had been placed on him.

But now, it just felt foolish. Another sign that he was stumbling through life, tripping over himself at every turn, never quite getting it right.

He untangled the laces, his fingers moving slowly, deliberately, as he tied them properly for the first time in who knows how long. It felt strange, but also... right. Like maybe it was time to start taking things a little more seriously, to stop letting life just happen to him.

Crash sighed again, climbing to his feet. His body ached, but he ignored it, brushing himself off and taking a deep breath. There was no point in dwelling on what was lost—he had to keep moving forward, no matter how hard it seemed.

But as he started walking again, the weight of the day settled heavily on his shoulders. He was tired, sore, and now completely disconnected from the world he so desperately wanted to be a part of. The city felt even colder, even more unwelcoming, as he made his way back to the store.

The more he thought about it, the more his chest tightened, a familiar feeling of panic rising up, threatening to choke him. He could almost hear his mother's voice in his head, the worry and disappointment that would edge into her tone when she found out. She always tried to hide it, to be strong for him and his grandmother, but Crash knew how much she depended on him, how much she needed things to go smoothly.

He couldn't bear the thought of letting her down, not again. Not after everything she had done to keep the store—and their family—going after his father passed. She had enough on her plate without worrying about him, about something as stupid as a stolen phone.

Crash felt the panic clawing at him, his breaths coming quicker and shallower as the full weight of what had happened began to sink in. He felt the tears pricking at the corners of his eyes, but he blinked them away, trying to keep it together, trying to stay calm.

But it was no use. The panic swelled inside him, his thoughts spiraling out of control as the realization of what he'd have to do—what he'd have to tell his mom—loomed over him like a dark cloud.

He stopped walking, his hands trembling as he tried to take a deep breath, but the air seemed to get stuck in his throat. The city around him blurred, the noises fading into the background as his own heartbeat pounded in his ears.

Crash ran a hand through his hair, his fingers digging into his scalp as if he could somehow force himself to calm down, to think clearly. But all he could think about was how stupid he'd been, how he should have been more careful, how he should have tied his damn shoes.

He squeezed his eyes shut, feeling the hot sting of tears building up again. He hated this—hated feeling so out of control, so helpless. He was supposed to be strong, supposed to be the one who kept things together. But here he was, standing on a street corner, on the verge of breaking down over something as ridiculous as a stolen phone.

Chapter 4
Conversations with Strangers

It wasn't just the phone, was it? It was everything—the store, the neighborhood, the feeling that his life was slipping away from him, one small failure at a time.

Crash pressed his hands to his face, trying to steady his breathing, trying to pull himself together. But the thought of going back to the store, of facing his mom, was like a weight pressing down on his chest, making it hard to breathe, hard to think.

He couldn't do this. Not right now. Not when everything felt like it was falling apart.

Crash sank down onto a nearby bench, dropping his head into his hands as the panic and frustration and exhaustion finally caught up with him. He sat there for what felt like hours, the tears finally spilling over, silent and hot as they streaked down his cheeks. The cold breeze continued to blow through the streets, but Crash barely felt it, lost in the storm of emotions that raged inside him.

He knew he couldn't stay there forever, that eventually, he'd have to get up, go back to the store, and face whatever was waiting for him. But right now, all he could do was sit there and let it all out, let the tears fall, let himself feel everything he'd been holding back.

It was only after the tears started to dry up, leaving his cheeks sticky and his eyes sore, that he finally forced himself to take a deep breath. He wiped his face with the sleeve of his hoodie, the fabric dampening as it soaked up the last of his tears.

He had to go back. He had to tell his mom. It wouldn't be easy, but it was better to get it over with, to face the music and deal with whatever came next.

Crash pushed himself up from the bench, his legs shaky but holding. He ran a hand through his hair again, smoothing it back as best he could, trying to regain some semblance of composure. He could do this. He had to.

With one final deep breath, Crash turned back toward the store, his steps slow but steady as he prepared himself for the conversation ahead. The weight of the day still hung heavy on his shoulders, but there was a small flicker of determination deep inside him—a reminder that he was stronger than this, that he could handle whatever came his way.

As he walked, he rehearsed what he would say in his head, trying to find the right words, the right way to explain what had happened. But no matter how many times he went over it, the pit of anxiety in his stomach refused to go away.

Still, he kept walking, one step at a time, until the store finally came into view. The familiar sight of the building, with its weathered sign and cracked windows, filled him with a mix of dread and relief.

This was it. He couldn't turn back now.

Crash paused at the door, taking one last deep breath before pushing it open. The bell jingled softly as he stepped inside, and for a moment, everything felt normal again—just another day at the store, just another problem to solve.

But as he spotted his mom at the counter, her face lighting up with a smile when she saw him, Crash felt the anxiety surge back to the surface. He braced himself, ready to face whatever came next.

"Mom," he began, his voice trembling slightly. "We need to talk…"

The glow of the ancient CRT monitor cast a dim, flickering light across the small room, barely illuminating Crash's tired face as he stared at the screen. The family's desktop computer was a relic from another era, its bulky hard drive humming loudly as it struggled to keep up with even the simplest of tasks. It sat precariously on his grandmother's sewing table, surrounded by spools of thread, fabric scraps, and old patterns that hadn't been touched in years.

Crash's fingers moved sluggishly over the keyboard, the keys sticky from years of use. He was trying to log into his social media accounts, to check the latest updates from his favorite streamers, but the browser was slow to load, the images and videos lagging as the old machine struggled to keep up.

The loss of his phone had left him feeling disconnected, adrift in a world that moved too fast for him to catch up. This old computer was his only lifeline now, a poor substitute for the sleek, modern device he had carried with him everywhere. It was a constant reminder of how far behind he was, how much he longed for the life he saw online, the life that now felt even more out of reach.

Crash leaned back in the creaky wooden chair, running a hand through his scruffy black hair. His hoodie, worn and comfortable, was pulled tight around him, but it did little to soothe the frustration gnawing at his insides. It was going to take forever to save up for a new phone, especially with the store barely breaking even. He didn't even want to think about how long it would take to get back to the life he had taken for granted.

"Crash, dinner's ready!" his mother's voice called from the kitchen, her tone warm but with a hint of exasperation. She had been trying to get him to the table for the past fifteen minutes, but Crash couldn't tear himself away from the computer, desperate for even a small taste of the normalcy he had lost.

"I'll be there in a minute, Ma," Crash muttered, not really paying attention as he clicked on another link, only to be met with another slow-loading page. His frustration bubbled over, and he slapped the side of the monitor, as if that would somehow speed things up.

The noise brought his grandmother into the room, her small frame almost lost in the oversized cardigan she wore to ward off the evening chill. Jan Anuman was a quiet woman, her movements deliberate and slow, but her eyes were sharp, always observing, always aware of what was happening around her.

"Crash," she said gently, placing a hand on his shoulder. "You need to eat. The computer will be here later."

Crash sighed, knowing she was right but still unwilling to give up the fight. "I just... I need to check a few things, Gran. I'm almost done."

His grandmother's gaze softened, and she gave his shoulder a reassuring squeeze. "I know it's hard, losing something you rely on. But you need to take care of yourself too. Come eat with us, then you can try again."

Crash looked up at her, seeing the concern in her eyes. It wasn't just about dinner—she was worried about him, about the way he had been spiraling since the theft. His mother, too, had noticed, though she hadn't said much. They knew how much that phone had meant to him, even if they didn't fully understand why.

"Alright," he relented, pushing the chair back with a groan. The computer whirred loudly as if protesting his decision to leave, but Crash ignored it, turning away from the screen and letting his grandmother guide him toward the kitchen.

The smell of warm, home-cooked food filled the air, and Crash realized just how hungry he was. His mother had outdone herself tonight—a spread of rice, stir-fried vegetables, and a steaming bowl of tom yum soup sat on the small table, the aromas comforting and familiar.

"Finally!" his mother said with a teasing smile as Crash took his seat. Somjai Anuman was a petite woman with strong, capable hands and a kind face that belied the hard work she put into running the store and caring for their family. She set down a plate of crispy fried fish, her own addition to the meal, and joined them at the table.

"I was starting to think you'd forgotten where the kitchen was," she joked, ladling soup into bowls with practiced ease.

Crash managed a small smile, though it didn't quite reach his eyes. "Sorry, Ma. The computer... well, it's not exactly the fastest."

His mother sighed, her expression softening as she handed him a bowl. "I know it's hard, Crash. I know how much you relied on that phone. But we'll figure something out. It might take some time, but we'll get you back on your feet."

Crash nodded, grateful for her support but still feeling the weight of the loss. He picked up his spoon, stirring the soup absently as his mind drifted back to the streamers he'd been watching before everything went wrong. They were out there, living their lives, chasing their dreams, while he was stuck here, struggling to keep up.

The envy gnawed at him, a constant reminder of everything he didn't have, everything he wanted but couldn't reach. It was hard not to compare himself to them, to see their success and wonder why he couldn't have the same. The feeling was as bitter as the soup was spicy, and it left him with a knot in his stomach that even the warm meal couldn't soothe.

His grandmother noticed his silence and gave him a gentle nudge. "You know, when I was your age, we didn't have phones or computers. We had to make do with what we had. But that didn't stop us from finding happiness in the small things. You're stronger than you think, Crash. Don't let this setback get the best of you."

Crash looked up at her, her words sinking in slowly. His grandmother had always been the rock of their family, steady and unyielding even in the face of hardship. She had lived through more than he could imagine, and yet she still found joy in the little things—a warm meal, a quiet evening with family.

"I'll try, Gran," he said quietly, the frustration still there but softened by her words. He took a bite of the fish, savoring the crispiness, letting the familiar flavors ground him in the moment.

His mother smiled, reaching across the table to ruffle his hair. "We're here for you, Crash. No matter what happens, we'll get through it together."

Crash nodded, feeling a little of the weight lift off his shoulders. The world outside might be spinning out of control, but here, at this table, with his mother and grandmother beside him, he found a small measure of peace.

The dinner plates had been cleared away, and the remnants of the meal sat on the countertop, a testament to the quiet, steady routine that defined their evenings. Crash, his mood somewhat lifted by the warmth of the food and the presence of his family, leaned back in his chair, feeling the familiar comfort of home settle around him.

His grandmother, Jan, was carefully folding a cloth napkin in her lap, her movements soft and deliberate. Across from her, Crash's mother, Somjai, sipped on a cup of tea, her eyes distant as if she were lost in thought. The usual post-dinner chatter had lulled, giving way to a comfortable silence that seemed to invite reflection.

Crash glanced between the two women, sensing there was something unspoken in the air. He wasn't sure what it was, but he could feel the weight of it, like a shared memory hovering just out of reach.

Finally, it was his grandmother who broke the silence, her voice soft but steady. "You know, Crash, your father was always so proud of you. He used to say that you had his spirit—that you were a dreamer, just like him."

Crash looked up, surprised by the sudden mention of his father. It wasn't something they talked about often, the loss still raw even after all these years. But there was a gentleness in his grandmother's tone, a warmth that made him want to listen, to hear more.

"Your father," Jan continued, her gaze turning inward as she spoke, "was the kind of man who never let anything stop him. He always had big dreams, always looking for the next adventure. It was what made him... so special."

Crash felt a pang in his chest, the familiar ache that came whenever he thought of his father. The man who had taught him how to ride a bike, who had taken him to baseball games and cheered louder than anyone in the stands. The man who had always seemed larger than life, until the day he was gone, leaving behind a void that Crash had never quite known how to fill.

"He was so excited when your grandparents asked him and your mother to take over the store," Jan said, her eyes misting slightly as she remembered. "He felt like he was carrying on something important, something that mattered. It wasn't just a job to him—it was a legacy."

Somjai nodded, her hands wrapped around her cup as if seeking comfort from its warmth. "Your father and I were so honored," she added, her voice quiet. "We knew how much the store meant to your grandparents, how hard they had worked to build it from the ground up."

Jan's gaze softened as she looked at Crash, a faint smile playing on her lips. "Your grandfather and I... we didn't have much when we started. Just a few dollars and a lot of hope. But we were determined to make something of ourselves, to build a life for our family. The store was our dream, our way of giving back to the community that had welcomed us when we had nothing."

Crash listened intently, picturing the stories he'd heard before but never fully appreciated. His grandparents, immigrants from Thailand, had arrived in America with little more than the clothes on their backs and a fierce determination to succeed. They had worked tirelessly, saving every penny they could until they were able to open the small grocery store that would become the heart of their family.

"The early days were hard," Jan continued, her voice tinged with both pride and nostalgia. "We had to do everything ourselves—stocking the shelves, ringing up customers, even delivering groceries on foot. But we didn't mind. We were building something, something we could be proud of."

Crash could see the pride in her eyes, the deep sense of accomplishment that came from knowing she and his grandfather had created something lasting, something that had supported their family for generations.

"And when we asked your father and mother to take over," Jan said, her voice growing softer, "it was because we trusted them. We knew they would take care of the store, that they would continue the work we had started."

Somjai smiled, though it was a bittersweet expression. "Your father threw himself into it," she said, her gaze distant as she remembered. "He wanted to make the store the best it could be, to honor your grandparents' hard work. He was always looking for ways to improve things, always coming up with new ideas. He was... so proud to be part of it. But that doesn't mean it needs to be your dream too, Crash. Your grandmother and I know this isn't the life a young man dreams about anymore."

Crash felt his throat tighten as he listened to his mother's words. He could picture his father, standing behind the counter with that big, infectious grin, talking to customers as if they were old friends. He had always seemed so at home in the store, so sure of his place in the world.

But then, one day, he was gone. No warning, no time to prepare. Just gone, leaving behind a hole that nothing seemed to fill.

"He loved you so much, Crash," Somjai said, her voice trembling slightly. "You were everything to him. And he would be so proud of the young man you've become."

Crash blinked back the tears that threatened to spill over, nodding wordlessly. He missed his father every day, but hearing these stories, feeling the love and pride his father had for him, made the loss just a little easier to bear.

The room fell silent again, the weight of the memories hanging in the air like a heavy blanket. But it wasn't an oppressive silence—it was one filled with love, with shared history, with the knowledge that no matter what happened, they would always have each other.

Crash looked around the small, cluttered kitchen, the place where so many of his family's stories had been told, where so much laughter and joy had been shared. The store might be their legacy, but this—this was their home, the heart of everything they had built together.

He took a deep breath, feeling the warmth of his family's love wrap around him like a comforting embrace. No matter how hard things got, no matter how much the world outside seemed to change, he knew he could always find strength in the stories of those who had come before him.

And maybe, just maybe, he could find a way to honor them, to carry on the legacy they had worked so hard to create.

"Thank you," he whispered, his voice barely audible, but the words carrying the weight of his gratitude, his love for the two women who had given him so much.

His grandmother reached across the table, placing her hand over his, her touch warm and reassuring. "We're a family, Crash. We'll get through this together."

His mother smiled, the sadness in her eyes giving way to something brighter, something filled with hope. "Your father would want us to keep going, to keep fighting. And we will. For him, and for us. We will be fine if you decide this isn't the life for you."

As the evening light faded outside, casting long shadows across the room, Crash felt a sense of peace settle over him. The road ahead might be difficult, but he knew he wasn't alone. And with that knowledge, he found the strength to keep moving forward, to face whatever challenges lay ahead.

For his father, for his family, and for himself.

The house was quiet, the soft hum of the old refrigerator in the kitchen the only sound breaking the stillness. Crash sat on the edge of his bed, the worn fabric of his hoodie bunched up in his hands as he stared at the floor. The conversation with his mother and grandmother still echoed in his mind, the weight of their words pressing down on him like a heavy blanket.

It had been a long day—longer than most. The chase, the stolen phone, the reflection on his life and the state of the neighborhood, and now, the conversation that had stirred up so many emotions he usually kept buried deep inside.

Crash leaned back against the wall, closing his eyes as he let out a slow breath. His mind was a tangled mess of thoughts and feelings, all swirling together in a chaotic jumble that made it hard to think straight.

He had always known that his life was different from the lives of the streamers he admired, the ones who traveled the world, chased their dreams, and lived life on their own terms. But today, that difference felt sharper, more pronounced, like a gulf that he would never be able to cross.

On one hand, there was his family—the people who had given him everything, who had worked so hard to build a life for him, who depended on him to help keep the store running. His grandmother and mother had sacrificed so much, and the thought of letting them down, of walking away from the life they had built, filled him with guilt and a deep sense of responsibility.

The store was more than just a business; it was their legacy, a testament to the hard work and determination of his grandparents, and later, his parents. It was a symbol of everything they had accomplished, everything they had overcome. And now, with his father gone, it was up to Crash to help carry that legacy forward, to honor the sacrifices his family had made.

But on the other hand, there were his dreams—the dreams that had been growing inside him for as long as he could remember, the dreams that had been ignited by the streamers he watched every day. He wanted more than the life he had, more than the routine of stocking shelves and ringing up customers. He wanted adventure, excitement, a chance to see the world and make a name for himself.

Crash opened his eyes, staring up at the ceiling as he wrestled with the conflict inside him. How could he balance these two parts of himself? How could he honor his family's legacy while still pursuing the life he wanted? Was it even possible to do both?

The questions gnawed at him, filling him with doubt and uncertainty. He wanted to make his family proud, to live up to the expectations they had for him, but he couldn't ignore the growing restlessness inside him, the feeling that he was meant for something more.

His mind drifted back to the chase with the sea lion, the absurdity of it all, and how it had made him feel—alive, in a way he hadn't felt in a long time. There was something about that moment, about the thrill of the unknown, that had sparked something in him, something that refused to be extinguished.

But then there was the store, the sense of duty he felt to his mother and grandmother, the knowledge that they depended on him to keep things going. How could he walk away from that? How could he leave them behind?

Crash sighed, running a hand through his hair as the weight of it all pressed down on him. He didn't have the answers, didn't know what the right thing to do was. All he knew was that he couldn't keep living like this, caught between two worlds, never fully committing to either one.

Something had to change. He couldn't keep going through the motions, day after day, pretending that everything was fine when it wasn't. He had to find a way to reconcile these two parts of himself, to find a path that would allow him to honor his family while still pursuing his dreams.

It wouldn't be easy. It would mean making tough choices, taking risks, stepping out of the comfort zone he had built for himself. But if there was one thing Crash knew for sure, it was that he couldn't keep living with this internal conflict, this constant push and pull between duty and desire.

He had to make a decision, to choose a direction, to take control of his life in a way he never had before.

Crash sat up, the resolve building inside him. He wasn't sure how he was going to do it, wasn't sure what the future held, but he knew one thing: he was going to find a way to make his dreams a reality, to create a life that was true to who he was.

With that thought, Crash felt a sense of peace settle over him, a clarity that he hadn't felt in a long time. The road ahead was uncertain, but for the first time, he felt ready to face it, to take the first steps toward the life he wanted.

He didn't have all the answers, but he had a direction, a purpose. And that was enough to get started.

Crash stood up, feeling lighter than he had in weeks. He walked over to the window, looking out at the city below, the lights twinkling in the distance like stars.

"I'll figure it out," he whispered to himself, a small smile tugging at the corners of his lips. "One step at a time."

And with that, Crash made a promise to himself—a promise to keep moving forward, no matter how hard it got, no matter what obstacles lay in his path.

He was going to change his life, to find a way to honor his family and pursue his dreams. And nothing was going to stop him.

The soft glow of the kitchen light spilled into the hallway, casting long shadows that danced across the floor as Crash quietly made his way down the stairs. The house was still, the silence of the night wrapping around him like a blanket, but the weight of his thoughts kept him restless, unable to sleep.

As he reached the bottom of the stairs, Crash noticed the faint sound of the television playing in the living room. The volume was low, the familiar hum of late-night news providing a comforting background noise. He hesitated for a moment, then moved toward the kitchen, where he could see a familiar figure sitting at the table.

His grandmother, Jan, was there, her small frame hunched over a cup of tea, steam rising in delicate tendrils from the surface. She looked up as Crash entered the room, her eyes softening with a smile when she saw him.

"Couldn't sleep?" she asked gently, her voice a soothing balm in the quiet of the night.

Chapter 5
The Lair Beneath the Powerhouse

Crash shook his head, pulling out a chair and sitting down across from her. "Just... too much on my mind, I guess."

Jan nodded, her gaze thoughtful as she took a sip of her tea. "I understand. It's been a long day."

Crash looked down at the table, tracing the grain of the wood with his finger. The kitchen, with its familiar smells and warm light, had always been a place of comfort for him, a sanctuary from the worries of the outside world. But tonight, it felt different—heavier, somehow, as if the walls themselves could sense the turmoil inside him.

They sat in companionable silence for a few moments, the only sound the soft ticking of the clock on the wall. Crash could feel the words building up inside him, the thoughts he had been trying to suppress all day, but he didn't know where to start. How could he explain the conflict that was tearing him apart? How could he put into words the pressure he felt to live up to his family's expectations, while also chasing his own dreams?

His grandmother seemed to sense his struggle. She reached across the table, placing her hand over his, the warmth of her touch grounding him in the moment.

"Crash," she said softly, her eyes full of understanding. "You don't have to carry this burden alone. Whatever is on your mind, you can share it with me."

Crash looked up at her, the kindness in her gaze making it easier to open up, to let the words spill out. "It's just... I don't know what to do, Gran. I feel like I'm stuck between two worlds. I want to make you and Mom proud, to take care of the store and honor Dad's memory, but... I also have my own dreams. I want more than this life, but I don't want to let you down."

Jan listened quietly, her expression thoughtful as Crash spoke. When he finished, she gave his hand a reassuring squeeze before leaning back in her chair, her gaze drifting to the window as she considered her response.

"Your father was the same way, you know," she said after a moment, her voice tinged with nostalgia. "He had big dreams, too—always looking for something more, always pushing himself to do better. It was one of the things I loved most about him, but it also made life difficult for him at times."

Crash blinked, surprised by the revelation. He had always seen his father as someone who had everything figured out, who had embraced the family business without hesitation. But hearing his grandmother's words made him realize that maybe his father had struggled with the same feelings of doubt and conflict that he was experiencing now.

"He was so proud when we asked him to take over the store," Jan continued, her eyes shining with the memories. "But that pride didn't come without its own challenges. He felt the weight of the responsibility, just as you do now. But he found a way to balance it, to honor the past while still making room for his own dreams."

Crash leaned forward, his eyes locked on his grandmother's as he absorbed her words. "How did he do it? How did he find that balance?"

Jan smiled, a soft, knowing smile that spoke of years of wisdom. "He didn't do it alone, Crash. He had your mother, and he had us, his family, to support him. And he learned that sometimes, it's not about choosing one path over the other—it's about finding a way to weave them together, to create something new from the threads of the old and the new."

Crash's mind whirred as he processed what she was saying. It was a perspective he hadn't considered before, the idea that maybe his dreams didn't have to be separate from his family's legacy. Maybe there was a way to honor both, to find a path that allowed him to be true to himself while still carrying on the work his father had started.

"Gran, do you ever feel like... like the world has changed too much?" Crash asked, his voice hesitant. "Like the things that mattered so much before aren't as important now?"

Jan's smile faded slightly, replaced by a more serious expression. "I do, sometimes. The world is always changing, Crash. What was important to one generation might not seem as important to the next. But that doesn't mean we should forget where we come from. Our roots are what keep us grounded, even when everything around us is shifting."

Crash nodded slowly, understanding the truth in her words. The store, the family's legacy, it was his roots—his connection to his past, to the generations that had come before him. But it didn't have to be a chain that held him back. It could be a foundation, something solid to build on as he pursued his own dreams.

"I don't want to lose myself," Crash admitted, his voice barely above a whisper. "I don't want to get so caught up in the store, in the expectations, that I forget who I am."

"You won't," Jan said firmly, her gaze intense as she met his eyes. "You are your father's son, Crash. You have his spirit, his drive, but you also have something more—your own dreams, your own path to follow. Don't be afraid to chase those dreams, but don't forget the people who love you, who believe in you. We will always be here, supporting you, no matter what path you choose."

Crash felt a lump form in his throat, the emotions he had been holding back all day threatening to overwhelm him. He squeezed his grandmother's hand, the gesture a silent acknowledgment of the love and support she had always given him.

"Thank you, Gran," he whispered, his voice thick with emotion. "I needed to hear that."

Jan smiled, her eyes warm with affection. "I'm always here for you, Crash. Remember that."

They sat together in the quiet kitchen for a while longer, the connection between them strengthened by the words they had shared. Crash knew that the road ahead wouldn't be easy, that he would still face challenges and tough decisions. But for the first time, he felt like he wasn't alone in his struggle, like he had the support he needed to find his way.

As the first light of dawn began to peek through the window, Crash felt a sense of peace settle over him, a resolution forming in his heart. He would find a way to honor his family's legacy while still pursuing his dreams. He would find that balance, just as his father had, and he would make both his family and himself proud.

He wasn't sure how he would do it yet, but he knew he would. And with his grandmother's words guiding him, he felt ready to take the first steps toward that new path.

The first rays of dawn crept through the curtains, casting a soft, golden light across the kitchen. The night had been long, filled with heavy conversations and unspoken emotions, but as the world outside began to wake, a sense of calm settled over the small room.

Crash and his grandmother, Jan, remained seated at the kitchen table, the remnants of their tea now cold in the cups before them. The air between them was thick with the shared understanding that had blossomed during their heart-to-heart, a quiet acknowledgment of the burdens each of them carried.

For a while, neither of them spoke. The silence was comforting, a reprieve from the weight of the words they had exchanged, but it was also filled with something more—an unspoken bond that had always been there, but had deepened in the past few hours.

Crash looked at Jan, taking in the familiar lines of her face, the way her eyes, though softened with age, still held a spark of determination. She had always been the pillar of their family, the one who kept everything together, even when the world seemed to fall apart. And now, sitting here with her, Crash felt that strength radiating from her, wrapping around him like a protective embrace.

Jan met his gaze, a small smile tugging at the corners of her lips. She didn't need to say anything; the understanding between them was clear. She knew how much he was struggling, how hard it was for him to balance the expectations of the past with the dreams of the future. And in that moment, she wanted him to know that she saw him, truly saw him, and that she was proud of the man he was becoming.

Crash felt a lump form in his throat, the emotions he had been holding back threatening to overwhelm him once again. But this time, there was no panic, no fear—only a deep, abiding love for the woman sitting across from him, the woman who had given him so much, who had always been there, quietly supporting him, even when he didn't realize he needed it.

Jan reached across the table, her hand finding his in a gentle, reassuring touch. Her skin was soft, warm, and as she squeezed his hand, Crash felt a wave of gratitude wash over him—gratitude for her, for the sacrifices she had made, for the love she had always shown him.

"You're stronger than you know, Crash," Jan said softly, her voice filled with quiet conviction. "And no matter what path you choose, I will always be here for you."

Crash swallowed hard, nodding as he blinked back the tears that threatened to spill over. "Thank you, Gran," he whispered, his voice thick with emotion. "I... I don't know what I'd do without you."

Jan's smile widened, and she gave his hand another squeeze before letting go. "You'll find your way, Crash. You've got the heart for it. And remember, it's okay to lean on your family when you need to. That's what we're here for."

The warmth in her words filled the room, dispelling the last remnants of the night's tension. Crash felt a sense of peace settle over him, a quiet resolution that had been born from their conversation, from the understanding that they shared.

For a moment, they simply sat there, the early morning light filtering through the windows, casting everything in a soft, golden hue. The world outside was beginning to stir, but inside the kitchen, time seemed to slow, the bond between grandmother and grandson taking center stage.

Crash knew that the road ahead would still be challenging, that there were difficult decisions to be made and obstacles to overcome. But in this moment, he felt ready to face them, buoyed by the love and support of his family, by the quiet strength of the woman who had always been his guiding star.

He glanced at Jan again, his heart swelling with affection and admiration. She had been through so much in her life, had weathered so many storms, but she had never lost her kindness, her ability to see the good in people, to believe in the strength of family.

"Gran," he said softly, his voice steady now, "I promise, I'll find a way to make you and Mom proud. I'll find a way to balance everything."

Jan's eyes sparkled with pride as she looked at him, her smile warm and full of love. "You already make us proud, Crash. Just by being yourself."

Crash felt a warmth spread through his chest, the words sinking deep into his heart. He didn't have to have all the answers right now—what mattered was that he was trying, that he was willing to face the challenges ahead with courage and determination.

As the sun continued to rise, casting a brighter light over the kitchen, Crash felt a renewed sense of purpose. He wasn't alone in this journey—he had his family by his side, and with their support, he knew he could face whatever came his way.

"Let's make some breakfast," Jan said suddenly, breaking the silence with a soft chuckle. "I think we could both use something warm and comforting after the night we've had."

Crash smiled, feeling lighter than he had in days. "Yeah, that sounds good, Gran."

Together, they stood and moved toward the stove, the familiar routine of preparing a meal bringing a sense of normalcy back into their world. As they worked side by side, the bond between them felt stronger than ever, a testament to the power of family, of love, and of the quiet moments of understanding that could bridge even the widest generational divides.

The morning light streamed through the kitchen windows, bathing the small room in a warm glow as Crash finished his porridge with this grandmother. The conversation from the night before still lingered in his mind, giving him a sense of calm he hadn't felt in a long time. But as he cleared his plate and washed his hands.

Crash wandered into the small living room, where the old desktop computer sat on its precarious perch atop Jan's sewing table. The CRT monitor, bulky and outdated, flickered to life as he switched it on, the familiar hum of the hard drive filling the quiet room.

He sat down, the chair creaking under his weight as he clicked through the slow-loading pages of the browser, navigating to MeTube. The homepage loaded, and Crash was immediately greeted by the vibrant thumbnails and enticing titles of the latest videos from his favorite streamers.

For a moment, he let himself get lost in it, his imagination taking over as he pictured himself in their shoes. He could see it so clearly—the bright lights of a well-designed studio, the high-end camera capturing every moment, the audience hanging on his every word as he shared his thoughts, his adventures, his life with the world.

Crash could almost feel the thrill of it, the excitement of living a life where every day was an adventure, where he wasn't just another kid working in a family store but a personality, a creator, someone with a voice that mattered. He imagined the sponsors lining up to work with him, the fan messages flooding in, the opportunities to travel the world, to meet new people, to do things he had only ever dreamed of.

He leaned back in his chair, a small smile tugging at the corners of his lips as he allowed himself to dream. In his mind's eye, he was already there—on the screen, sharing his life with millions, making a name for himself, living the kind of life that the streamers he admired had made look so effortless.

But then, just as quickly as the dream had taken hold, it was shattered by the voice of his mother calling to him from the other room.

Crash's eyes snapped open, the fantasy evaporating like smoke as reality crashed back in. He blinked, momentarily disoriented as the weight of the world he had been trying to escape settled back onto his shoulders.

"Crash?" Somjai called from the doorway, filled with warmth but tinged with the usual note of concern. "I just wanted to check in before I head out to the store. How are you doing this morning?"

Crash hesitated, the remnants of his dream still clinging to him, making the reality of the conversation feel even more distant. "I'm... I'm okay, Ma," he said, forcing himself to sound normal, even as the frustration of his current situation gnawed at him. "Just, you know, getting ready for the day."

His mother gave him one of those looks when she knew he wasn't telling the whole truth, but she didn't want to push him.

"Alright," Somjai said finally, her voice softening. "Just remember, if you need anything, or if you want to talk about anything, I'm here for you, okay? Don't bottle it up."

Crash nodded, even though she couldn't see him. "I know, Ma. Thanks."

After a few more words of encouragement and a promise to help out at the store later, the silence that followed feeling heavier than before. He stood there for a moment, the dream of being a MeTuber still fresh in his mind, but now it felt more like a distant fantasy—something that was out of reach, something he might never have.

He walked back into the living room, his gaze drifting to the old desktop computer, the MeTube homepage still glowing faintly on the screen. The thumbnails of the successful streamers stared back at him, mocking him with their success, their seemingly perfect lives.

Crash sighed, feeling the weight of reality pressing down on him once again. He couldn't just abandon everything to chase a dream that might never come true. He had responsibilities—his family, the store, the legacy they had built. It wasn't as simple as just deciding to become a MeTuber. There were bills to pay, shelves to stock, a life that demanded his attention.

But even as he reminded himself of all the reasons he couldn't just drop everything, the dream refused to die. It was there, a stubborn ember that refused to be extinguished, no matter how much reality tried to smother it.

Crash sat back down at the computer, staring at the screen as if it held the answers he was searching for. He wanted so badly to be more than what he was, to break free from the life that felt like it was closing in on him. But he didn't know how to make that happen without disappointing the people who mattered most to him.

His eyes drifted to the corner of the screen, where a small window showed the feed from the store's security cameras. The grainy black-and-white image of the store's interior flickered on the monitor, the empty aisles and stocked shelves a stark contrast to the vibrant, exciting world of MeTube.

Crash watched the feed for a moment, the store that had been his life for so long feeling like a prison and a sanctuary all at once. He couldn't just walk away from it, from the people who depended on him. But he also couldn't ignore the call of something more, something bigger.

The tension between his dreams and reality tightened its grip on him, leaving Crash feeling trapped, torn between two worlds that seemed impossible to reconcile.

He reached for the mouse, his fingers hovering over the button that would close the browser, shut down the computer, and bring him fully back to the world he had always known. But he hesitated, the pull of the dream still strong, the desire for something more still burning inside him.

As he scrolled, a thumbnail caught his eye—bright, bold text announcing an opportunity that made his heart skip a beat. He clicked on the video, leaning in closer as the familiar face of a moderately well-known MeTuber filled the screen.

"Hey, everyone! Big news!" the MeTuber announced, his enthusiasm practically jumping off the screen. "We're looking to add a new member to our creator's house! That's right—you could be the next big thing in the world of MeTube, living with us, creating content, and building your brand! All you have to do is submit the most unbelievable video you can think of to prove you belong in our incubator of success. Show us what makes you unique, and you could be the one we choose!"

Crash's heart pounded in his chest as he watched the video, the words echoing in his mind. This was it—this was the opportunity he had been waiting for, the chance to break free from the life he was living and step into the world he had always dreamed of.

But as the video ended and the screen faded to black, the reality of his situation crashed down on him. He didn't have a phone. He didn't have a way to create the video that could change his life. The frustration surged up inside him, a wave of anger and helplessness that left him feeling like he was suffocating.

He pushed away from the computer, pacing the room again as his thoughts spiraled. How could he make this work? How could he seize this opportunity when everything seemed to be stacked against him?

And then it hit him—in the security camera feed he could just make out a green bucket hat half pushed under a shelf. The sea lion in the green bucket hat, the one who had somehow managed to outsmart him, the one who had slipped through the streets of San Francisco with the agility of a seasoned thief. It was the most unbelievable thing Crash had ever seen!

The sea lion could be his ticket out. A video of the sea lion—smart, sneaky, and undeniably unique—would be the perfect entry for the competition. It was just the kind of content that could catch the attention of the MeTuber and his team, something that no one else could possibly match.

But as quickly as the idea came, the reality set in. He didn't have a phone. He didn't have a way to record the video that could change everything.

The frustration bubbled up again, a knot of anger and disappointment tightening in his chest. It felt like the universe was playing some cruel joke on him, dangling the possibility of escape just out of reach, only to yank it away at the last second.

Crash clenched his fists, his nails digging into his palms as he struggled to keep his emotions in check. He had finally found a way out, a way to change his life, but it was slipping through his fingers because of something as simple as not having a phone.

He couldn't do it. He couldn't make this dream a reality, no matter how badly he wanted it.

"Crash?" His mother's voice broke through the storm of thoughts swirling in his mind, gentle and concerned.

Crash turned to see Somjai standing in the doorway, her brow furrowed as she took in the tension in his posture, the frustration written all over his face. She stepped into the room, closing the door behind her as she approached him.

"What's wrong?" she asked softly, placing a hand on his arm. "You seem so upset."

Crash wanted to brush her off, to say it was nothing, but the words caught in his throat. He felt the tears prick at the corners of his eyes, the emotions he had been trying to hold back threatening to spill over.

"I... I had a chance, Ma," he finally managed to say, his voice thick with emotion. "A chance to change everything. But I can't do it. I don't even have a phone."

Somjai's eyes softened with understanding, and she pulled him into a gentle hug, her arms wrapping around him as she held him close. "Oh, Crash," she murmured, her voice full of sympathy. "I'm so sorry. I know how much that thing meant to you."

Crash buried his face in her shoulder, his tears finally escaping as he let out a shaky breath. "It's not fair, Ma. I just want something different. I want to do more, to be more, but I haven't even get started."

Somjai held him tighter, her hand smoothing his hair as she whispered soothing words of comfort. "I know it feels unfair, Crash. And I know how frustrating it is to feel like your dreams are just out of reach. But don't give up, okay? You're smart, you're resourceful. We'll figure something out. There's always a way."

Crash pulled back slightly, looking up at her through tear-filled eyes. "But how, Ma? How can I do this without a phone? How can I make this happen?"

Somjai smiled gently, brushing a tear from his cheek. "Maybe the answer isn't as far away as you think. Sometimes, the solutions to our problems come from the most unexpected places. Don't lose hope, Crash. We'll find a way."

Crash nodded, sniffling as he wiped his eyes with the back of his hand. "Thanks, Ma," he said quietly. "I just... I don't know what to do."

"We'll figure it out together," Somjai assured him, her voice firm with the kind of certainty that only a mother could have. "You're not alone in this, Crash. We're a team, remember?"

Crash managed a small smile, the knot of frustration in his chest loosening just a bit. "Yeah, I remember."

Somjai gave him one last comforting squeeze before stepping back. "Why don't you take a break, get some fresh air? Clear your head. Sometimes a little distance helps us see things more clearly."

Crash nodded, taking a deep breath as he tried to steady himself. "Okay. I think I'll do that."

As he headed toward the door, his mother's words echoed in his mind. There was always a way. He just had to find it.

Chapter 6
Tea, Tuna, and Trust Issues

The sun was well into the sky by the time Crash arrived at the store, the familiar sight of its weathered facade greeting him like an old friend. But today, that familiarity felt tinged with frustration, a reminder of the obstacles he was facing.

Without his phone, everything seemed more complicated. Tasks that had once been second nature now required extra effort, extra time. The digital world that had once made his life easier now felt like a distant memory, replaced by the analog reality of working without the tools he had come to rely on.

As Crash stepped inside, the bell above the door chimed softly, and he was immediately greeted by the comforting smells of the store—fresh produce, spices, and the faint scent of cleaning supplies. But instead of the usual sense of calm that these familiar smells brought, today they only served to remind him of how much he was struggling. He noticed the green bucket hat in the lost and found box behind the register, his mother no doubt noticed it first thing when she walked in.

He headed to the back room, where his mother had left him a list of tasks for the day. Normally, he would have snapped a picture of the list with his phone, using it as a reference as he moved through the store. But today, that wasn't an option. Instead, he found himself carefully folding the piece of paper and tucking it into his pocket, hoping he wouldn't misplace it or forget something important.

The first task on the list was to restock the shelves with the new shipment of canned goods that had arrived earlier that morning. Simple enough—except that without his phone, Crash couldn't quickly pull up the inventory app to check what had been delivered or cross-reference it with the stock in the back room. He had to do it the old-fashioned way, manually counting the cans and checking them off against the paper invoice.

As he worked, Crash found himself growing increasingly frustrated. It wasn't that he couldn't do the tasks without his phone— it was that everything took so much longer. The efficiency he had prided himself on was gone, replaced by a slow, tedious process that left him feeling like he was constantly behind.

Halfway through restocking, Crash realized he needed to check something in the front of the store. Normally, he would have shot a quick text to his mom or pulled up the security feed on his phone to see if she was available. But now, he had to walk to the front, weaving through the aisles and customers, just to ask her a simple question.

"Mom, do we still have the extra cans of coconut milk in the back?" Crash asked as he reached the counter where Somjai was helping a customer.

Somjai looked up, momentarily puzzled, before nodding. "Yes, they should be on the second shelf from the top. Why? Can't you check?"

Crash hesitated, feeling the familiar sting of frustration. "I would... but without my phone, it's taking me forever to find anything."

Somjai's expression softened with sympathy, but before she could respond, the customer she was helping chimed in.

"Lost your phone, huh? I can't imagine trying to get through the day without mine," the customer said with a shake of their head. "But hey, you're making it work. That's something."

Crash forced a smile, appreciating the attempt at encouragement but still feeling the weight of his struggles. "Yeah, just doing what I can."

Back in the stockroom, Crash resumed his work, doing his best to stay focused. But the lack of his usual tools made every task feel like a slog. From checking the inventory to answering customer questions, everything required more time, more effort.

At one point, a customer asked about a specific brand of rice, and Crash found himself fumbling for an answer. Normally, he would have quickly looked it up on his phone, but now he had to excuse himself and go check the back room, leaving the customer waiting longer than he would have liked.

It wasn't just the practical challenges that were getting to him—it was the constant reminder of how much he relied on his phone for everything. Without it, he felt disconnected, out of sync with the world around him. And as the day wore on, that feeling only grew stronger, feeding the frustration that simmered just beneath the surface.

But despite the challenges, Crash refused to let himself give up. He knew he couldn't rely on his phone forever—this was just a temporary setback, something he had to push through. And as much as he hated it, he knew that this experience was teaching him something important: how to adapt, how to be resourceful, how to find solutions even when the tools he was used to weren't available.

As he finished restocking the shelves and moved on to the next task, Crash tried to focus on the positives. He was still getting the work done, still keeping the store running smoothly, even if it took a little longer. And maybe, just maybe, this experience would make him stronger in the long run, more capable of handling whatever challenges life threw his way.

But that didn't mean it wasn't frustrating. Every time he reached for his pocket, expecting to find his phone only to remember it wasn't there, he felt a fresh wave of irritation. Every time a task that should have taken minutes stretched into half an hour, he had to bite back the urge to curse under his breath.

By the time the afternoon rolled around, Crash was exhausted—not just physically, but mentally. The constant effort of trying to compensate for the lack of his phone had taken its toll, leaving him feeling drained and more than a little defeated.

But as he stood at the front of the store, taking a brief moment to catch his breath, Crash reminded himself why he was doing this. He wasn't just working to keep the store running—he was working toward something bigger, something that would take him beyond these walls and into the life he wanted.

It wasn't going to be easy, and he knew he still had a long way to go. But if there was one thing Crash was sure of, it was that he wasn't going to let anything stop him—not even the loss of his phone.

With renewed determination, Crash headed back to the stockroom, ready to tackle the next task on the list. He might be struggling now, but he knew that every challenge he faced, every obstacle he overcame, was bringing him one step closer to the future he was fighting for.

The bell above the door chimed softly as another customer entered the store. Crash, standing behind the counter, glanced up with a tired but friendly smile. The day had been a long one, filled with challenges and frustrations, but he was determined to keep pushing through.

The customer, a middle-aged woman with a kind face, approached the counter with a hesitant expression. She held a shopping list in one hand and a small jar of an unfamiliar spice in the other.

"Excuse me," she began, her voice tinged with uncertainty. "I'm trying to make a dish my grandmother used to cook, but I can't remember exactly what spice she used. I found this one, but I'm not sure if it's the right one. Could you help me figure out if this is what I need?"

Crash took the jar from her, turning it over in his hands as he read the label. The name of the spice wasn't one he recognized immediately, and he felt a familiar pang of frustration—normally, he would have pulled out his phone, done a quick online search, and given the customer an answer in seconds. But today, that wasn't an option.

Instead, he had to rely on his memory and resourcefulness.

"Well," Crash said slowly, thinking through what he knew about spices, "I can't be certain without checking, but this spice is commonly used in a lot of traditional dishes. If your grandmother used something similar, there's a good chance this might be what you're looking for."

The woman frowned slightly, still unsure. "Is there any way to check? I'd hate to buy the wrong thing and mess up the recipe."

Crash hesitated, his mind racing as he tried to think of a solution. Without his phone, he couldn't look up recipes or cross-reference the spice with others. But then an idea came to him.

"You know," Crash said, "we keep a couple of old cookbooks in the back that belonged to my grandmother. They might have a recipe or two that could help us figure this out. Would you mind waiting a moment while I go check?"

The woman's face brightened, clearly relieved by the offer. "That would be wonderful, thank you."

Crash nodded and quickly made his way to the back room, where he knew Jan kept a small collection of well-worn cookbooks on a shelf near the pantry. The books were old, their pages yellowed with age and marked with handwritten notes in the margins. They had been passed down through the family, containing recipes that had been staples in their household for generations.

He carefully pulled one of the books off the shelf and flipped through the pages, scanning the recipes until he found one that matched the customer's description. There, in faded ink, was a recipe that listed the spice in question as an ingredient.

Crash felt a small surge of satisfaction—he had found the answer without relying on his phone. It wasn't the fastest method, but it had worked, and that was what mattered.

He returned to the front of the store with the open cookbook, showing the customer the recipe he had found. "I think this might be what you're looking for," he said, pointing to the name of the spice in the list of ingredients. "It seems to match what you're describing."

The woman's eyes lit up as she read the recipe, a smile spreading across her face. "Yes, this is it! Thank you so much for finding this. I can't tell you how much it means to me."

Crash smiled back, feeling a sense of pride in having been able to help, even without the convenience of his phone. "I'm glad I could help. Let me know if there's anything else you need."

After the customer paid for her items and left the store, Crash returned to the counter, the cookbook still in his hands. He glanced down at the pages, at the handwritten notes and the well-loved recipes, and felt a pang of nostalgia. These books had been a lifeline for his family, a way of preserving their traditions and sharing them with others.

But as he stood there, the satisfaction of helping the customer slowly gave way to a deeper sense of reflection. He realized just how much he had come to rely on his phone—not just as a tool for work, but as an escape from the monotony of his daily life.

Every spare moment, every lull in the day, he would pull out his phone, scrolling through MeTube or social media, immersing himself in the lives of others, in a world that seemed far more exciting and fulfilling than his own. It had become a crutch, a way to avoid facing the dissatisfaction he felt with his current situation.

Crash set the cookbook down on the counter, his mind drifting back to the idea of becoming a MeTuber. The thought had been simmering in the back of his mind for a while now, but today, it felt more urgent, more necessary. He had always seen it as a dream, something to strive for, but now he was beginning to see it as a potential escape—a way out of the life that was slowly suffocating him.

He knew it wouldn't be easy. The challenges he had faced today had shown him just how dependent he had become on technology, how much he relied on it to get through the day. But they had also shown him that he could adapt, that he could find solutions even when the tools he was used to weren't available.

Crash knew that if he was going to pursue this dream, he would need to be resourceful, to find ways to make it work even when things didn't go according to plan. He would need to rely on more than just his phone—he would need to rely on his creativity, his determination, and the support of the people who cared about him.

He looked around the store, at the shelves stocked with items that his family had carefully selected, at the register where his mother worked tirelessly every day, and felt a deep sense of responsibility. This store was his family's legacy, their livelihood, and it was a part of him, too. But it wasn't all he wanted.

Crash took a deep breath, feeling the weight of his decision settling over him. He couldn't ignore the pull of his dreams any longer. He couldn't keep using his phone as a way to escape from the reality he was living. It was time to start working toward something more, something that would allow him to live the life he wanted while still honoring the legacy his family had built.

As the day wore on and more customers came and went, Crash found himself feeling more focused, more determined. He didn't have all the answers yet, and he knew there would be challenges ahead. But for the first time in a long time, he felt like he was moving in the right direction.

And that was enough to keep him going.

It was late in the afternoon, and the store was winding down for the day. The sun hung low in the sky, casting long shadows across the pavement outside. Crash stood by the front window, absently watching the few remaining customers as they made their way in and out of the store. The familiar routine of restocking shelves and ringing up purchases had given him a moment of quiet, a rare break in the steady rhythm of the day.

His thoughts drifted, circling back to the events of the past week—the chase with the sea lion, the loss of his phone, the growing frustration that seemed to hang over him like a cloud. He felt torn between the life he was living and the life he wanted, between his duties at the store and his desire for something more.

As he gazed out the window, something caught his eye. A flash of movement at the edge of the parking lot, near the line of dumpsters. Crash squinted, trying to make out what it was. And then, there he was—the sea lion, the sea lion in the green bucket hat, skulking around the back of the store as if he owned the place.

Crash's heart skipped a beat. It was back.

For a moment, the familiar thrill of the chase surged up inside him, the adrenaline kicking in as he watched the sea lion move with surprising agility for a sea lion. It was almost comical, the way the sea lion darted between the dumpsters. Crash could almost hear the playful tone of his streamers' voices narrating the absurdity of the scene.

But just as quickly as the thrill came, it was tempered by a heavy sense of responsibility. Crash's gaze flickered back to the interior of the store, to the customers browsing the aisles, to his mother and grandmother working tirelessly to keep everything running smoothly. He felt the weight of their expectations, the duty he had to help them, to keep the store going, to be the dependable son and grandson they needed.

He hesitated, torn between the urge to chase after the sea lion and the need to stay and finish his work. The thought of pursuing the sea lion, of capturing a video of the elusive sea lion, tugged at him like a siren's call. It was exactly the kind of content that could help him stand out, that could kickstart his dream of becoming a MeTuber.

But he didn't have a phone. And even if he did, could he really abandon his responsibilities to chase after a sea lion… again? Could he justify leaving his family to fend for themselves while he pursued a dream that felt more and more out of reach?

Crash clenched his fists, frustration bubbling up inside him. He wanted so badly to follow the sea lion, to see where the thing would go, to capture the moment and make it his own. But at the same time, he knew that his family needed him here. The store needed him here.

The thrill of the chase warred with the sense of duty that had been instilled in him from a young age. He had been raised to take care of his family, to put their needs above his own. But lately, that duty had begun to feel like a chain, binding him to a life he wasn't sure he wanted.

Crash took a deep breath, forcing himself to look away from the sea lion. The sea lion was still there, rummaging around the dumpsters, but Crash couldn't bring himself to move. He couldn't abandon his post, couldn't leave his family to chase after something as fleeting as a dream.

With a heavy heart, Crash turned away from the window, the thrill of the chase fading into the background as he refocused on his duties. The customers in the store, the shelves that needed restocking, the responsibilities that weighed on him—they were all still there, waiting for him to step up and do what needed to be done.

But even as he forced himself to stay, a small part of him couldn't help but wonder what might have happened if he had followed the sea lion. What if he had taken the risk, chased after the sea lion, and found something more?

The thought lingered in the back of his mind, a nagging reminder of the life he longed for, even as he pushed it aside to focus on the task at hand. There would be other chances, he told himself. Other opportunities to chase after his dreams.

But as he went back to work, the image of the sea lion in his green bucket hat stayed with him, a symbol of the life that was just out of reach, waiting for him to make the leap.

But as he gripped the edge of the counter, his knuckles white with the effort, Crash felt a different impulse rising within him— one that was quieter but no less powerful. It was the voice of responsibility, the one that had been instilled in him by his family, the one that reminded him of his duties and the people who depended on him.

His eyes flickered to the store, taking in the scene before him. His mother was chatting with a regular customer near the produce section, her face lit up with a warm smile. His grandmother was in the back, no doubt going over inventory or preparing something for the next day. The customers milling about were familiar, part of the rhythm of the store that had been his life for as long as he could remember.

This was where he was needed. Not out in the streets chasing after a sea lion, but here, helping to keep the store running, supporting his family, ensuring that the business his grandparents had built from the ground up continued to thrive.

Crash let out a slow breath, the tension in his chest easing as he made his decision. He wasn't going to pursue the sea lion. Not today. The thrill of the chase, as tempting as it was, couldn't outweigh the importance of his responsibilities.

It wasn't an easy choice. The excitement of the unknown, the possibility of adventure, tugged at him, urging him to give in, to follow his curiosity wherever it might lead. But this time, Crash chose differently. He chose to stay, to do what was expected of him, to honor the commitments he had made to his family.

It was a moment of growth, a recognition that sometimes the right choice wasn't the most exciting one, but the one that reflected the person he was becoming—the person he wanted to be.

As he turned away from the window, Crash felt a mix of emotions. There was a sense of loss, a twinge of regret at the adventure he was leaving behind, but there was also a quiet pride in the decision he had made. He was growing up, learning to balance his desires with his responsibilities, understanding that maturity wasn't just about making the easy choices, but the right ones.

He glanced back one last time, catching a glimpse of the sea lion disappearing around the corner of the building.

As the day wore on, the memory of the sea lion's fleeting appearance faded into the background, replaced by the steady rhythm of the store and the satisfaction of a job well done. Crash knew that he had made the right choice, and that knowledge gave him a sense of peace.

He wasn't abandoning his dreams—far from it. But he was learning to prioritize, to balance his aspirations with the reality of his life. It was a lesson in maturity, one that he knew would serve him well in the days to come.

The store was quiet as the last few customers filtered out, the hum of the fluorescent lights overhead filling the silence. Crash moved methodically through the aisles, straightening the shelves and tidying up as he prepared to close for the night. The routine was familiar, almost comforting, but his mind was elsewhere.

No matter how hard he tried, Crash couldn't shake the image of that sea lion from his thoughts. The absurdity of a it in the green bucket hat, still sitting in his lost and found box, wandering the streets of San Francisco was something that would have amused anyone, but for Crash, it was more than just a funny story. It was a mystery, a puzzle that begged to be solved.

As he wiped down the counter and swept the floor, his mind kept drifting back to that moment earlier in the day when he had seen Fred by the dumpsters. The decision not to pursue him had been the right one—Crash was sure of that. But the choice had left something unresolved, a lingering curiosity that gnawed at him even now.

Who was this sea creature, really? Where had he come from? How had he managed to escape notice for so long? And why did he keep appearing around the store, as if he had some unspoken connection to this place?

Crash picked up the hat out of the box behind the register. It was old, warn, and smelled strongly of the sea. The fabric was thick and the hat well made. On the inside was an industrial label with what looked like a random part number stamped in faded ink letters. On the back side in indelible ink was the name "Fred" written deliberately and dark. "Nice to meet you Fred," thought Crash.

Crash's thoughts whirled with questions, each one more insistent than the last. He found himself replaying the scene over and over in his mind, trying to piece together the fragments of what he knew, searching for a pattern, a clue, something that might make sense of the bizarre situation.

He knew there was more to Fred than met the eye. The sea lion's behavior, the way he seemed to know exactly where to go and how to avoid being caught, hinted at a level of intelligence that was far beyond what Crash would have expected. It was almost as if Fred was playing a game, testing the limits of his own abilities and Crash's curiosity at the same time.

As Crash locked the front door and turned off the lights, he couldn't help but feel a sense of unfinished business. Fred was still out there, somewhere in the city, and the more Crash thought about it, the more he felt a pull to find out the truth. It wasn't just about the thrill of the chase anymore—there was something deeper, something more personal, that was driving him to understand who or what Fred really was.

He stepped out into the cool evening air, locking the door behind him, and paused for a moment on the sidewalk. The city was alive with its usual nighttime energy—cars honking, people chatting, the distant sound of music drifting from a nearby bar. But for Crash, the world felt strangely quiet, as if it were holding its breath, waiting for something to happen.

Crash glanced down the street, in the direction where he had last seen Fred. The urge to follow, to find out where Fred had gone, tugged at him again, but he resisted. It wasn't the right time—not yet. He had responsibilities, and he couldn't afford to get distracted.

But that didn't mean the curiosity was gone. If anything, it had only grown stronger, fed by the mystery and the unanswered questions that swirled around Fred like a cloud of fog.

Crash knew that he couldn't ignore this curiosity forever. Sooner or later, he would have to confront Fred, to find out the truth, to solve the puzzle that had been laid out before him. But until then, he would have to be patient, to bide his time, to wait for the right moment.

As he turned and began walking home, Crash felt the tension between his duties and his curiosity pulling at him from opposite directions. It was a familiar feeling, one that he had been grappling with for weeks now, but tonight it felt more pronounced, more urgent.

Fred was out there, somewhere in the city, and Crash knew that their paths would cross again. When that happened, he would be ready. He would find out who Fred really was, and what he was doing in San Francisco.

But for now, all he could do was wait and wonder, the curiosity simmering just below the surface, ready to boil over at a moment's notice.

As Crash walked through the darkened streets, his thoughts still swirling with questions, he made a silent promise to himself: the next time he saw Fred, he wouldn't hesitate. He would follow, he would find out the truth, and he would finally satisfy the curiosity that had taken root deep inside him.

Chapter 7
The Unseen Network

The afternoon sun filtered through the windows of the store, casting long, golden shadows across the floor. Crash had just finished helping a customer find a rare ingredient when he caught sight of his grandmother, Jan, watching him from the back of the store. Her expression was thoughtful, her eyes tracking his movements with the keen awareness that only a grandmother could have.

Crash had been trying his best to keep his frustration in check throughout the day, but he knew he hadn't been entirely successful. The struggle of navigating his tasks without the convenience of his phone had worn on him, leaving him feeling irritable and short-tempered. He had hoped to hide it from his family, but as he met Jan's gaze, he realized that she had noticed everything.

Jan moved slowly toward him, her hands clasped gently in front of her. She had always been a quiet presence in the store, offering support and guidance without drawing attention to herself. But now, as she approached Crash, there was a deliberate intent in her steps, as if she had made up her mind about something.

"Crash," she said softly, her voice carrying the warmth and calm that had always been a source of comfort for him. "You've been working hard today. Why don't you take a break?"

Crash managed a small smile, though it didn't quite reach his eyes. "I'm fine, Gran. Just trying to get everything done."

Jan nodded, her gaze never leaving his face. "I know you are. But I can see that something's bothering you."

Crash hesitated, unsure of how to respond. He didn't want to burden his grandmother with his frustrations, but at the same time, he knew he couldn't hide from her. Jan had a way of seeing through him, of understanding his feelings even when he didn't fully understand them himself.

"It's just been a tough day," Crash admitted, his voice low. "I'm not used to doing everything without my phone. It's... frustrating."

Jan's eyes softened with sympathy, and she reached out to place a gentle hand on his arm. "I can see that. But you've done well, Crash. You've handled it with grace, even if it hasn't been easy."

Crash felt a lump form in his throat at her words, the tension he had been carrying all day threatening to spill over. He looked away, not wanting her to see how much he was struggling.

But Jan wasn't fooled. She gave his arm a reassuring squeeze, her touch grounding him in the moment. "You know, when I was your age, we didn't have phones or computers to help us with our work. We had to rely on our instincts, our hands, and our wits. And sometimes, when things got tough, we had to find other ways to make things work."

Crash glanced back at her, curious. "What do you mean?"

Jan smiled, a twinkle of mischief in her eyes. "I mean that sometimes, when life takes something away from us, it's an opportunity to find new strengths we didn't know we had. You've been doing that today, even if you didn't realize it."

Crash thought about her words, letting them sink in. She was right—despite the frustration, he had managed to get through the day, finding solutions to problems he would have normally solved with a quick online search. It hadn't been easy, but he had done it.

"Thanks, Gran," Crash said quietly, feeling a swell of gratitude for her understanding. "I guess I just... wish things were easier sometimes."

Jan's smile softened, and she nodded in agreement. "We all do, Crash. But it's the challenges that make us stronger, that teach us what we're really capable of. And you, my dear, are capable of so much."

Crash looked at her, his heart full of affection for this woman who had always been there for him, always known just what to say to make him feel better. He felt a wave of emotion wash over him, a mix of love, gratitude, and something deeper—something that reminded him of why he was so determined to change his life, to make something of himself.

"Gran," Crash began, his voice hesitant, "I've been thinking a lot about what you said the other night. About finding a way to balance everything, to chase my dreams while still honoring the family. I want to do that, but... I don't know how yet."

Jan's eyes shone with understanding, and she reached up to cup his cheek, her touch gentle and full of love. "You'll find a way, Crash. I believe in you. And when you do, I'll be right here, cheering you on every step of the way."

Crash swallowed hard, blinking back the tears that threatened to spill over. "Thank you, Gran. That means everything to me."

Jan nodded, her smile warm and full of pride. "Now, why don't you take a break? Go outside, get some fresh air. You've earned it."

Crash hesitated for a moment, then nodded. "Alright. I think I will."

As he stood there, gazing out at the familiar streets of his neighborhood, Crash knew one thing for certain: whatever path he chose, whatever decisions he made, he wouldn't be alone. His grandmother would be there, supporting him, guiding him, just as she always had.

Jan sat quietly on her usual seat at the front of the store, sipped her tea, newspaper folded to one side. The events of the day played over in her mind, particularly the moments she had shared with Crash. His frustration had been palpable, his struggles evident in every line of his face, and it pained her to see him so burdened.

She had always known that Crash was a dreamer, much like his father. He had that same restless spirit, that same drive to reach for something beyond the ordinary. But unlike his father, Crash was navigating a world that was changing rapidly, a world where technology and connection were intertwined with every aspect of life.

As she sat there, Jan thought about the way Crash had been forced to adapt without his phone. He had handled it well, but she could see how much it had weighed on him. The phone wasn't just a tool for him—it was his lifeline, his connection to the world he longed to be a part of, a world that offered him a glimpse of the life he wanted.

Jan's thoughts drifted back to the conversation they had shared earlier, the way Crash had opened up to her about his dreams and his struggles. She had seen the determination in his eyes, the desire to make something more of himself, and it had filled her with a deep sense of pride. But she also knew that he couldn't do it alone. He needed support, guidance, and sometimes, a little push in the right direction.

Her gaze fell on the small, worn purse that sat on the counter nearby. Inside, tucked away in a hidden compartment, was a modest sum of money she had been saving for a rainy day. It wasn't much, but it was enough to make a difference. Enough to buy Crash a new phone, something that could help him get back on his feet and chase the dreams that meant so much to him.

Jan set her teacup down and reached for the purse, her fingers brushing against the soft fabric as she thought about what she was about to do. It was a small gesture, but one that she knew would have a profound impact on Crash's life.

She had always believed in the power of family, in the importance of supporting one another through thick and thin. And now, as she prepared to make this decision, she felt a deep sense of certainty. This was what Crash needed—a way to reconnect with the world, to find his path, to pursue the life he had always dreamed of.

Jan knew that a new phone wouldn't solve all of Crash's problems. It wouldn't magically make his dreams come true or take away the challenges he faced. But it would give him the tools he needed to take the next step, to keep moving forward, to find his way.

And that was worth everything to her.

With a quiet resolve, Jan stood up and slipped the purse over her shoulder. She stood out front of the store and hopped on the next cable car heading toward downtown. She hopped off at Union Square, walked into the Apple store, and purchased a brand new phone for Crash. It wasn't top of the line, and had the least amount of storage; but it still put a significant dent in the small amount of savings she had amassed.

She knew Crash might protest, might insist that she didn't need to spend the money on him, but she also knew that deep down, he would understand why she had done it.

The morning light filtered through the curtains of the Anuman house, casting a warm glow across the kitchen as Jan carefully placed a small, neatly wrapped box on the table. Her hands lingered on the paper, smoothing out the creases with a tender touch. She had woken up early to prepare this surprise, her heart filled with a mixture of excitement and a hint of nervousness.

Crash would be awake soon, and she knew that the moment he saw what was inside the box, his world would shift—just a little, but enough to make a difference.

As she stood there, waiting, Jan's thoughts drifted back to her own childhood. She and her husband had grown up with very little, often struggling to make ends meet. They had learned to be resourceful, to stretch every dollar as far as it would go, and to save for the future—no matter how uncertain it might be. It was a habit that had served them well, allowing them to build a life for their family, one small step at a time.

It was also what had led Jan to create her own rainy day fund, tucked away in a hidden compartment of her purse. It wasn't much, but it was enough to make a difference when it mattered most. And today, it mattered more than ever.

She had watched Crash struggle, had seen the weight of his frustration and the growing tension between his dreams and the reality of his life. She knew that a new phone wouldn't solve all his problems, but it would give him a tool, a symbol of hope and possibility—a way to bridge the gap between where he was and where he wanted to be.

The sound of footsteps in the hallway pulled Jan from her thoughts, and she looked up to see Crash entering the kitchen, his hair tousled from sleep. He blinked in the morning light, clearly not fully awake yet, but when his eyes landed on the small box on the table, he froze.

"Gran... what's this?" Crash asked, his voice still thick with sleep.

Jan smiled softly, gesturing for him to sit down. "It's something I wanted to give you," she said, her voice gentle. "Go on, open it."

Crash hesitated for a moment, then slowly reached out and picked up the box. He turned it over in his hands, feeling the weight of it, before carefully unwrapping the paper. As the box lid lifted, his eyes widened in surprise.

Inside was a brand-new phone, sleek and modern, nestled in a bed of soft tissue paper. It was a far cry from the old, battered phone he had lost—a device that seemed to belong to a different era altogether.

"Gran... I... I don't know what to say," Crash stammered, his voice filled with emotion. "You didn't have to do this. This must have cost a fortune..."

Jan reached out and gently placed her hand on his. "It's something I wanted to do," she said softly. "You've been working so hard, Crash. I've seen how much this means to you, how much you've been struggling without it. This is just a small way for me to help."

Crash looked down at the phone, a lump forming in his throat. He knew how much his grandparents had gone through to build the life they had, how carefully they had saved and planned for the future. The fact that Jan had chosen to use some of that money to buy him this phone—a tool he needed so desperately—meant more to him than he could put into words.

"But Gran," he began, his voice cracking slightly, "you and Grandpa worked so hard for everything you have. I don't want to take this from you..."

Jan shook her head, her smile warm and full of understanding. "Crash, your grandfather and I may have started with very little, but we learned that it's not about what you have—it's about what you do with it. We saved for moments like this, for when our family needed something to help them move forward. This phone isn't just a device—it's a symbol of what you can achieve, of the future you're working toward. And I know you'll make the most of it."

Crash swallowed hard, the tears he had been holding back threatening to spill over. He had always known his grandmother was a strong, resourceful woman, but in this moment, he felt the full depth of her love and understanding. She wasn't just giving him a phone—she was giving him hope, a renewed sense of determination, and the belief that he could make something more of himself.

"Thank you, Gran," Crash whispered, his voice thick with emotion. "I... I promise I won't let you down."

Jan squeezed his hand, her eyes shining with pride. "I know you won't, Crash. I've always believed in you, and I always will. Now, take this and go make something of yourself. You have the talent, the drive, and the heart to do great things."

Crash nodded, his resolve hardening as he looked down at the phone in his hands. It wasn't just a device—it was a symbol of everything he was working toward, a tool that would help him bridge the gap between his dreams and reality. With this phone, he could start making the videos that would showcase his creativity, his passion, his unique perspective. He could take the first steps toward the life he wanted, a life where he could honor his family's legacy while forging his own path.

As he stood up from the table, Crash felt a surge of energy, a renewed sense of purpose. He was ready to take on whatever challenges lay ahead, knowing that his grandmother—and his entire family—were behind him, supporting him every step of the way.

"Thank you, Gran," Crash said again, his voice stronger now. "I'm going to make you proud."

Jan smiled, her heart full as she watched him walk out of the kitchen, the phone clutched tightly in his hand. She knew that there would be difficult days ahead, that the road to success was rarely smooth. But she also knew that Crash had the strength, the determination, and the love of his family to guide him through it all.

And as she sat back down at the table, sipping her tea and feeling the warmth of the morning sun on her face, Jan whispered a silent prayer for her grandson's happiness and success. She knew he was destined for great things, and she was proud to be a part of his journey.

Crash leaned against the counter, his eyes fixed on the security monitor looking for any anomalies that could be that sly seal Fred. He had seen Fred twice now, each time the sea lion had appeared as if out of nowhere, moving with a purpose that defied explanation. Fred's antics were no longer just a curiosity—they had become a puzzle that Crash was determined to solve.

He had noticed a pattern in Fred's movements, something that didn't quite add up. Each time Fred had been spotted near the store, he had made a beeline for the back alley, darting between the dumpsters and then disappearing toward the direction of the cable car line. It was as if Fred had a plan, a route that he knew by heart, one that allowed him to slip away unnoticed every time.

Crash had spent hours thinking about it, piecing together the clues, until he came up with a plan of his own. If Fred was going to keep coming back to the store, then Crash would be ready for him. Crash surmised there must be only two reasons why he kept coming back. Either the Anuman family store had the very best and least guarded fresh fish for Fred to pick off—possible given the pride and effort his mother put into their supplies—or he was tracing his steps, looking for his bucket hat.

The key to his plan was simple: a rental electric scooter. Crash had discovered something interesting about these scooters—if you wrapped them in copper wire for long enough, the Faraday cage effect would block their cell signal, causing them to default to operating without requiring payment. It was a trick he had learned online, one of those obscure bits of information that most people would never think to use.

But Crash wasn't most people. He had spent the better part of the afternoon preparing the scooter, carefully wrapping it in copper wire and stashing it in the alley behind the store, just out of sight. It was positioned perfectly—close enough for Crash to reach in a hurry, but far enough from the main road that it wouldn't draw attention.

The plan was simple: plant the hat back near the fish case were Crash pulled it from Fred's head as bait, wait for Fred to make his move, then use the scooter to get ahead of him, cutting off his escape route. Crash already knew which direction Fred would run—toward the cable car line, where he could disappear into the maze of streets that led to the wharf. All Crash had to do was take a few shortcuts, and he'd be in position to intercept Fred before he could vanish again.

Crash felt a mixture of excitement and nerves as he finished his preparations. It was a risky plan, but it was the best chance he had to uncover the truth about Fred. If he could catch Fred in the act, follow him, and see where he went, he might finally get the answers he was looking for.

All that was left now was to wait.

The store was quiet, the evening rush having passed, leaving only a handful of customers browsing the aisles. Crash's mother and grandmother were busy restocking shelves, their focus on the day-to-day tasks that kept the store running smoothly. But Crash's mind was elsewhere, his attention fixed on the door, waiting for the moment when Fred would appear.

He didn't have to wait long.

A flash of movement at the edge of his vision caught Crash's attention. He turned, just in time to see the familiar figure of Fred slipping through the door. The sea lion moved with a strange sort of confidence, as if he knew exactly where he was going.

Crash's heart raced as he watched Fred slink toward the back of the store, his eyes locked on the hat peaking out from just under the display shelf; glancing momentarily at the supremely tempting fish along his route. It was almost comical, the way Fred seemed so at ease in a place where he clearly didn't belong. But Crash wasn't laughing—this was his chance, the moment he had been waiting for.

Crash moved quickly, slipping out the back door and retrieving the scooter from its hiding place. The copper wire glinted in the fading light as Crash tested the scooter to make sure it worked. The motor hummed to life, and Crash felt a surge of adrenaline.

He was ready.

Crash positioned himself at the end of the alley, just out of sight, and waited. He could hear the faint sounds of the store behind him, the murmur of voices, the clinking of glass bottles. But his focus was entirely on the alleyway in front of him, on the path that he knew Fred would take once he made his move.

Minutes passed, each one stretching out longer than the last, until finally, Crash heard the sound he had been waiting for—the soft rustle of something moving in the alley. He tensed, gripping the handlebars of the scooter, ready to spring into action.

And then, there he was—Fred, with a couple of fish clamped in his jaws, moving with surprising speed for a creature of his size. The sea lion's movements were almost too smooth, too calculated, as if he had done this a hundred times before.

But this time, Crash had the upper hand.

He kicked off, the scooter surging forward with a burst of speed as he shot out of the alley and into the street. Fred turned, his eyes widening in surprise as he saw Crash coming toward him. For a moment, their gazes locked—Crash's filled with determination, Fred's with a flicker of something that almost looked like amusement.

Fred bolted, his path taking him toward the cable car line just as Crash had predicted. But this time, Crash was right behind him, the scooter cutting through the narrow streets with ease. He took the shortcuts he had planned, weaving through the alleys, taking corners at breakneck speed, determined not to let Fred slip away.

The chase was on.

Crash could see Fred up ahead, the sea lion's green bucket hat, back on his head, bobbing as he raced toward the cable car line. But this time, Crash was closing the distance. He was faster, more determined, and this time, he wouldn't let Fred escape.

As they neared the end of the street, Crash knew he had one shot to get ahead of Fred. He pushed the scooter to its limit, cutting around a corner and skidding to a stop just in time to block Fred's path. The sea lion skidded to a halt, his eyes darting around as he realized he was trapped.

Crash stepped off the scooter, his heart pounding as he faced Fred. The sea lion stared back at him, unblinking, as if sizing him up.

"It's the end of the line, Fred."

There was something in Fred's gaze—something intelligent, almost human—that sent a shiver down Crash's spine.

For a moment, neither of them moved. It was as if the world had paused, the tension between them crackling like electricity.

Then, with a flick of his tail, Fred darted to the side, slipping through a gap in the fence that Crash hadn't noticed before. In an instant, he was gone, disappearing into the shadows like a ghost.

Crash stood frozen for a moment, staring at the spot where Fred had just slipped through the gap in the fence. His heart was still racing from the chase, and frustration threatened to boil over. He had been so close—closer than ever before. But Fred had outmaneuvered him once again.

But this time, something was different. Crash could feel it in the air, a sense of urgency that hadn't been there before. He couldn't just let this go. Fred was no ordinary sea lion, and Crash was determined to find out where he was going.

Taking a deep breath, Crash forced himself to think clearly. Fred had gotten through the fence, but he couldn't have gone far. The alley behind the fence led into a maze of narrow streets and pathways, most of which were unfamiliar to Crash. But if Fred was heading toward the cable car line as he always did, there was still a chance to catch up.

Crash quickly surveyed his surroundings, his eyes landing on a series of fire escapes and narrow ledges that lined the buildings around him. The thought struck him suddenly—if he could get up high, he might be able to spot Fred from above and follow him without being seen.

Without wasting another second, Crash scrambled up the nearest fire escape, his sneakers—fully tied this time—gripping the rusty metal as he pulled himself higher. The city unfolded below him as he climbed, the narrow alleyways stretching out in every direction. He moved quickly, his eyes scanning the streets below for any sign of Fred.

And then, he spotted him.

Fred was moving swiftly through a side street, his green bucket hat bobbing with each step. From his vantage point, Crash could see the route Fred was taking, heading straight toward the cable car line just as he had predicted. But what caught Crash's attention was the way Fred seemed to be moving with purpose, as if he knew exactly where he was going.

Crash followed from above, moving across the rooftops and ledges with a surprising ease. The thrill of the chase had given him a renewed energy, and he navigated the maze of fire escapes and ladders with a single-minded focus. He was determined not to lose Fred this time

Chapter 8
A Minor Theft of Major Consequences

As he continued to follow, Crash noticed that Fred's path seemed to narrow, leading toward a specific area near the cable car museum. The closer they got, the more Crash's curiosity grew. What was Fred doing here? Where was he going?

Fred finally stopped at the entrance to an old, seemingly abandoned building near the Cable Car Museum and Powerhouse. From above, Crash could see the building was covered in ivy and graffiti, blending in with the rest of the neglected structures in the area. But there was something about the way Fred approached the building, slipping through a narrow gap in the wall, that made Crash's heart race.

Crash waited, watching intently as Fred disappeared into the building. The entrance was cleverly camouflaged, almost invisible to anyone who didn't know where to look. But now that Crash had seen it, he couldn't unsee it.

He descended the fire escape as quietly as he could, his feet barely making a sound as he landed on the ground. His breath came in quick, shallow bursts, a mixture of excitement and trepidation swirling in his chest. He approached the gap in the wall cautiously, his eyes scanning the area to make sure he hadn't been followed or noticed.

Crash hesitated for a moment, his hand resting on the rough stone of the building's exterior. A thousand thoughts raced through his mind. Was he really about to do this?

But the curiosity, the need to know, was too strong to resist. Crash took a deep breath, steeling himself for whatever lay ahead, and slipped through the gap in the wall.

The inside of the building was dark, the air heavy with dust and the faint smell of rust and oil. Crash's footsteps echoed softly as he moved deeper into the structure, his eyes adjusting to the dim light filtering through cracks in the ceiling. The place felt abandoned, but there was something else—a sense of life, of purpose, that lingered just beneath the surface.

As Crash moved further in, he began to notice subtle signs that this place wasn't as deserted as it seemed. There were small, carefully constructed pathways cleared of debris, and patches of the floor that had been swept clean. The deeper he went, the more he felt that he was entering a space that was intentionally hidden, designed to keep out intruders.

Finally, Crash came to a heavy, rusted door, slightly ajar. He hesitated, his heart pounding in his chest. This was it—the threshold between the world he knew and whatever lay beyond. With a mix of fear and excitement, he pushed the door open and stepped inside.

What he saw on the other side took his breath away.

Fred's lair was nothing like Crash had imagined. The room was expansive, with the charm of exposed brick walls that stretched high above, their rough texture softened by the warm, ambient glow of dim lighting. The space had a sleek, almost industrial feel to it, the kind of place you might expect to see in a high-end tech startup rather than hidden beneath the streets of San Francisco.

In one corner of the room, a wall of high-end video monitors displayed an array of data streams, each screen flickering with complex, matrix-like code that seemed to pulse with a life of its own. The screens cast a soft, bluish hue across the room, their light reflecting off stacks of servers that hummed quietly in the background. The air was cool, filled with the faint hum of technology at work.

In the center of the room, there was a conversation pit—a sunken area surrounded by thick, luxurious leather couches that looked incredibly out of place given the lair's subterranean location. The couches were arranged in a perfect circle around a low, glass coffee table that held a few carefully placed objects: a high-tech tablet, a sleek remote control, and what looked like a vintage radio.

Everything was meticulously arranged, as if Fred took pride in the organization of his space.

Crash's eyes widened as he took in the scene. There was something almost surreal about it all—the idea of a sea lion living in such a sophisticated, high-tech environment was so absurd that it bordered on the impossible. And yet, here it was, right in front of him.

Fred himself was perched on one of the leather couches, his green bucket hat still securely on his head. He looked perfectly at ease, as if lounging in a conversation pit surrounded by advanced technology was the most natural thing in the world. There was an air of quiet confidence about him, a sense that he was in complete control of his domain.

The contrast between Fred's appearance—a sea lion in a bucket hat—and the high-tech fortress he inhabited was almost too much for Crash to process. It was as if two completely different worlds had collided in this hidden space, creating something entirely new and unexpected.

As Crash stood there, trying to make sense of what he was seeing, Fred turned his head and looked directly at him. Their eyes met, and for a moment, Crash felt a strange connection, as if Fred was silently acknowledging his presence, welcoming him into this hidden world.

But there was also something else in Fred's gaze—an invitation, perhaps, or a challenge. It was as if Fred was saying, "You've found me, but do you really understand what you're looking at?"

Crash swallowed hard, his heart pounding in his chest. This wasn't just a lair—it was a glimpse into a world he had never known existed, a world where a sea lion could build a high-tech fortress and live in it undetected. The possibilities of what this place represented, of what Fred was capable of, were staggering.

For a moment, Crash wondered if he was in over his head. But the curiosity that had driven him to this point refused to let go. He had come this far, uncovered the entrance to Fred's world, and he wasn't about to turn back now.

Taking a deep breath, Crash stepped further into the room, his eyes darting between the monitors, the servers, and the seemingly relaxed sea lion who watched him with a calm, steady gaze.

With a mix of trepidation and excitement, he approached the conversation pit, unsure of what he would find but determined to uncover the secrets of "Fred."

Crash stood at the edge of the conversation pit, his heart still racing from the surreal experience of discovering Fred's lair. The sea lion, with his green bucket hat slightly askew, watched him with an expression that seemed almost human—curiosity mixed with a quiet, measured assessment.

For a long moment, neither of them spoke. Crash didn't know what to say, how to break the silence in a room that seemed to hum with unspoken secrets. But Fred, as if sensing Crash's uncertainty, made the first move.

With a surprising amount of grace, Fred slid off the leather couch and padded over to the low glass coffee table. He nudged the vintage radio with his nose, causing it to emit a soft crackle before a smooth jazz melody filled the room. The sound seemed to ease some of the tension in the air, giving the lair an unexpectedly warm, inviting atmosphere.

Crash couldn't help but smile. "You like jazz?" he asked, more to break the silence than anything else.

Fred nodded—or at least, it seemed like a nod—before flopping down onto one of the couches, his gaze still fixed on Crash. There was something in Fred's eyes that spoke of intelligence, but also of something deeper, something more vulnerable.

Crash took a tentative step forward, then another, until he was standing just a few feet from Fred. "I didn't expect to find... well, this," Crash admitted, gesturing to the room around them. "You've got quite the setup here."

Fred's whiskers twitched, and he let out a soft bark, almost as if he was chuckling. Crash wasn't sure how, but he got the distinct impression that Fred was pleased with the compliment.

"I mean, I didn't expect to find a sea lion living in a place like this," Crash continued, sitting down on the edge of the couch across from Fred. "It's... incredible. How did you even—" He stopped himself, realizing how ridiculous it would be to ask how a sea lion had managed to put all of this together.

Fred seemed to understand anyway. He tilted his head slightly, his gaze never leaving Crash's, as if he were sizing him up, deciding whether to let him in on the secrets of this hidden world.

After a moment, Fred reached out with one of his flippers and tapped the glass coffee table. Crash's eyes followed the movement, and he realized that Fred was pointing to the tablet that sat on the table.

Curious, Crash picked up the tablet, its sleek surface cool against his skin. The screen flickered to life, revealing a series of complex diagrams, schematics, and data streams. It was a world of information that seemed almost impossible for someone like Fred to navigate, and yet, here it was—proof that Fred was far more than he appeared.

"You're... really smart, aren't you?" Crash said softly, more to himself than to Fred. "You've been hiding all of this because you don't want anyone to find you."

Fred nodded again, this time more clearly. There was a seriousness in his expression now, a weight that Crash hadn't noticed before. It was as if Fred was acknowledging the truth of Crash's words, and also the loneliness that came with it.

Crash felt a pang of sympathy. "You've been alone here, haven't you?" he asked gently. "No one knows about this place. No one knows about you."

Fred's eyes softened, and for a moment, Crash thought he saw a flicker of sadness pass across the sea lion's face. It was as if the mask of confidence Fred had worn since Crash entered the lair had slipped, revealing the isolation that came with being so different, so out of place in the world.

"I get it," Crash said quietly. "I know what it's like to feel out of place. To want something more, but not knowing how to get it."

Fred looked at him, really looked at him, and Crash felt a connection form between them—a bond of shared understanding, of unspoken truths that neither of them had fully realized until now.

"I'm glad you let me find you," Crash continued. "I know it wasn't easy, but... I'm really glad we met."

Fred's response was subtle, but unmistakable—a soft, almost imperceptible nod, as if he was saying that he was glad too. For the first time, Fred seemed to relax, his posture loosening as he leaned back against the cushions of the couch.

They sat in silence for a few moments, the jazz playing softly in the background, creating a bubble of peace in the midst of the high-tech fortress.

Crash hesitated for a moment, then decided to take a risk. "Hey, Fred," he began, choosing his words carefully, "would you mind if I took a picture of you? Just... you know, no one will ever believe this."

The reaction was immediate. Fred's eyes widened, and in an instant, he was off the couch and standing in front of Crash, his expression fierce and unyielding. He let out a sharp, warning bark, shaking his head vigorously, his flippers slapping the ground with surprising force.

Crash's heart skipped a beat. "Okay, okay, no pictures," he said quickly, holding up his hands in surrender. "I'm sorry—I didn't mean to upset you."

Fred's gaze softened slightly, but the intensity didn't fully leave his eyes. It was clear that the idea of being photographed—or perhaps recorded in any way—was something Fred couldn't tolerate.

Crash slowly lowered his hands, feeling a wave of relief as Fred stepped back. "I get it," he said, his voice calming. "No pictures. I promise."

Fred seemed to relax at that, though the tension in the air remained. It was as if Fred had drawn a line, made it clear that while he was willing to let Crash into his world, there were still boundaries that couldn't be crossed.

Crash nodded, understanding. "You've done everything you can to stay hidden." As he spoke, he noticed his phone in his pocket and pulled it out, frowning when he saw that there was no signal. "And I'm guessing you've made sure that no one can track you either."

Fred nodded once, his gaze steady. There was a quiet determination in his eyes, a resolve to protect his sanctuary at all costs.

Crash couldn't help but be impressed. "You're really good at this," he said, tucking his phone away. "I mean, you've thought of everything."

Fred's response was a small, almost shy nod, as if he was accepting the compliment but didn't want to make a big deal out of it.

Crash looked up at the wall of computer screens glowing in the darkness. What looked like a custom, sea lion sized gaming chair sat behind the expansive desk littered with keyboards sporting over sized keys. In the darkness, Crash could just make out what looked like an endless doorway, a cool salty breeze blowing from it directed straight toward the warfs "A tunnel? All the way to the bay?"

Fred patted his stomach. Sea lions eat a lot of fish.

"Fred, how did you afford all this?"

The gentle sea lion slipped off the couch and plopped himself onto the sea lion sized gaming chair and began to type out commands on his keyboard. An excel document popped up with spreadsheet titled "Targets Down." Below were columns labeled Asset, Bounty, and Status. Pages of rows scrolled past with lines such as "Russian National Trust, €800k, Executed", "Predator Tracking Backdoor, $3.6m, Executed", "McDonald's Ice Cream Fix, $27m, Failed."

"You're a white hat hacker?"

Fred smiled.

"Well, that explains how you've managed to keep this a secret. You probably managed to exploit every phone in the city!"

Fred typed two words onto the screen, "white hat."

"Well, it's nice to know you're on the good side. That's pretty cool, Fred"

The moment of tension passed, and once again, the room settled into a comfortable silence. Crash leaned back on the couch, feeling a strange sense of contentment wash over him. It was clear that Fred had let him in for a reason, that there was something more to this connection than just curiosity or a shared sense of loneliness.

It was respect, Crash realized. Fred respected him for finding the lair, for understanding the need for secrecy, and for not pushing too hard when it came to boundaries. And perhaps, just perhaps, Fred was happy to have found a friend—someone who saw him not as a strange anomaly, but as a being with intelligence, feelings, and a need for connection.

As they sat together in the dimly lit lair, Crash felt the beginnings of a friendship forming, one that was built on mutual understanding and a shared sense of purpose. He didn't know where this journey would take them, but for the first time, he felt ready to face whatever lay ahead.

Crash sat back on the leather couch, his mind racing with the possibilities that had suddenly opened up to him. He glanced around Fred's lair, his eyes lingering on the high-end video monitors, the stacks of servers, and the surprisingly cozy conversation pit. The room was a strange mix of high-tech sophistication and unexpected warmth—a place that was both a fortress and a home.

As he watched Fred, now settled comfortably on the couch across from him, Crash felt a thrill of excitement building in his chest. He had discovered something incredible, something that no one else in the world knew about. A sea lion with a hidden lair, living in the heart of San Francisco, surrounded by technology that seemed lightyears ahead of anything Crash had ever seen. The thought of sharing this discovery with the world, of becoming a star on MeTube, sent a rush of adrenaline through him.

But there was one problem: Fred had made it clear that he didn't want to be photographed or recorded. The sea lion's strong reaction to Crash's earlier request had been impossible to ignore, and it had left Crash feeling hesitant, unsure of how far he could push the boundaries of their newfound friendship.

Still, the temptation was too great. This was a once-in-a-lifetime opportunity, and Crash couldn't shake the feeling that this could be his ticket to fame, the chance to finally break free from the life he had been living.

Carefully, he slid his phone out of his pocket, glancing at Fred to make sure he wasn't paying too much attention. Fred's focus seemed to be elsewhere, his eyes half-closed as he relaxed in the dim light of the lair, the soft jazz still playing in the background. It was the perfect moment.

With his heart pounding in his chest, Crash held the phone low, angling it just right to capture Fred in the frame without drawing attention. He hesitated for a split second, a pang of guilt flickering through him, but the thrill of what he was about to do quickly drowned it out.

He pressed the shutter button, the phone's camera silently capturing the image.

Crash felt a surge of triumph as he glanced down at the screen. There it was—a perfect shot of Fred in his lair, surrounded by the evidence of his extraordinary life. It was everything Crash had hoped for, the proof he needed to take the first step toward the fame he had always dreamed of.

He quickly tucked the phone back into his pocket, a smile tugging at the corners of his lips. The thought of uploading the photo, of sharing it with the world, made his pulse quicken. This was it—this was the moment that could change everything.

But as Crash was getting ready to leave, something unexpected happened.

Fred stirred, lifting his head and looking directly at Crash. For a moment, Crash's heart skipped a beat, fear gripping him as he wondered if Fred had somehow noticed what he had just done. But instead of anger or suspicion, Fred's expression was calm, even friendly.

To Crash's surprise, Fred slowly slid off the couch and moved toward a small alcove at the side of the room. He nudged open a drawer with his nose and pulled out a neatly folded blanket, which he then carried over to Crash and gently placed at his feet.

Crash blinked in surprise, unsure of how to react. "Uh, thanks, Fred," he said awkwardly, picking up the blanket and feeling its soft, worn texture. It was clear that the blanket had been well cared for, as if it held some sentimental value.

Fred looked up at him, his eyes warm and inviting. There was something in his gaze that spoke of more than just hospitality—there was a genuine desire for connection, for friendship. It was as if Fred was offering more than just a blanket; he was offering a place in his world, a bond that went beyond the strange circumstances that had brought them together.

Crash felt a wave of emotion wash over him. He had been so focused on the idea of fame, of using this incredible discovery to launch himself into the spotlight, that he hadn't fully considered what it meant to Fred. This wasn't just a lair—it was Fred's home, a sanctuary he had carefully built and protected. And now, Fred was inviting Crash to be a part of it.

For a moment, Crash felt a pang of guilt so strong that it made his stomach twist. He had just taken a photo behind Fred's back, ready to use it to his advantage, and here Fred was, showing him kindness, trust, and a desire for friendship.

Fred let out a soft, contented bark and nudged Crash's leg with his nose, as if encouraging him to make himself comfortable. The gesture was so sincere, so full of warmth, that it nearly brought tears to Crash's eyes.

"Fred," Crash began, his voice thick with emotion, "I... I really appreciate this. I didn't expect... well, I didn't expect any of this. You letting me in, showing me all of this... it means a lot."

Fred looked up at him, his eyes full of understanding, as if he knew exactly what Crash was feeling.

Crash swallowed hard, the weight of the photo in his pocket suddenly feeling like a burden. He had come here thinking only of himself, of what this discovery could do for him. But now, standing in Fred's lair, surrounded by the evidence of a life lived in solitude and secrecy, he realized that there was so much more at stake.

Fred had trusted him, let him into his world, and in return, Crash had betrayed that trust—if only in the smallest way.

As he got ready to leave, Crash felt torn between the excitement of what he had captured on his phone and the deepening bond he was forming with Fred. The image on his phone represented a future full of possibilities, but it also represented a betrayal, a line crossed that could never be uncrossed.

Fred nudged him again, this time with a playful bark, as if to say, "Come back soon."

Crash forced a smile, trying to push down the guilt that gnawed at him. "I will, Fred. I'll be back."

As he left the lair, the door closing quietly behind him, Crash couldn't shake the feeling that he had just made a decision that would change everything—for better or for worse.

He slipped the phone out of his pocket once more, staring at the photo he had taken. It was perfect, exactly what he needed to make his mark. But as he looked at it, the thrill of his success was overshadowed by the realization of what it had cost him.

With a heavy heart, Crash tucked the phone away and made his way home, his thoughts a whirlwind of conflicting emotions. He had what he needed to take the next step, but at what price?

As he walked through the darkened streets of San Francisco, the image of Fred's trusting eyes lingered in his mind, a reminder of the choice he had made—and the consequences that might follow.

Chapter 9
The City That Forgot Itself

The night air was cool against Crash's skin as he walked through the quiet streets of San Francisco, his thoughts heavy with the events that had just unfolded. The city around him seemed almost surreal, the distant hum of traffic and the occasional flicker of streetlights creating a backdrop that felt detached from the whirlwind of emotions swirling inside him.

In his pocket, the phone felt like a lead weight, pulling at his conscience with every step he took. The image he had captured—Fred, lounging in his high-tech lair, surrounded by the secrets of a life no one else knew about—was everything Crash had dreamed of. It was the key to a future he had longed for, the ticket to fame and success that had always seemed just out of reach.

And yet, as he walked slowly home, the thrill of what he had done was overshadowed by a growing sense of unease.

Crash had always considered himself a good person—someone who tried to do the right thing, even when it was difficult. But tonight, he couldn't shake the feeling that he had crossed a line, one that was far more significant than he had realized in the moment. Fred had trusted him, let him into his world, and in return, Crash had taken something that wasn't his to take.

The memory of Fred's warmth, his unexpected hospitality, and the clear desire for friendship tugged at Crash's heart. Fred had been so open, so genuine in his gesture of kindness, offering Crash a place in his hidden world without hesitation. And what had Crash done? He had betrayed that trust for the sake of a photo—a photo that now felt more like evidence of a wrongdoing than a triumph.

Crash's footsteps slowed as he neared a small park, the quiet, tree-lined path offering a moment of respite from the noise in his mind. He stopped, taking a seat on a weathered bench, the cool metal biting into his skin even through his jeans. For a moment, he simply sat there, staring up at the sky, trying to make sense of the conflicting emotions that churned inside him.

The excitement, the anticipation of what that photo could mean for his future, was still there, but it was increasingly tempered by a deepening sense of guilt. He couldn't ignore the nagging voice in the back of his mind, the one that kept asking if this was really worth it. Was fame, success, and everything that came with it really worth betraying the trust of someone who had offered him genuine friendship?

Crash pulled out his phone, staring at the screen as the image of Fred filled the display. It was a perfect shot, capturing the essence of the strange, wonderful world that Fred had created for himself. But as Crash looked at it now, the photo didn't fill him with the same sense of pride and excitement. Instead, it filled him with a sense of loss—loss of the purity of the connection he had begun to build with Fred.

His finger hovered over the delete button, the option to erase the photo and put the moment behind him seeming both simple and impossibly difficult. Deleting the photo would mean giving up on the opportunity it represented, but keeping it felt like holding onto something that wasn't his to keep.

Crash sighed, lowering the phone but not yet making a decision. The moral complexities of the situation were becoming more apparent with every passing moment. The deeper his relationship with Fred became, the more complicated things would get. Tonight had been just the beginning—a small taste of the difficult choices that lay ahead.

He couldn't go back and undo what he had done, but he could try to make better choices moving forward. Maybe that was all he could do—learn from this, try to be a better friend, a better person. Maybe it wasn't too late to make things right.

As he neared his home, the lights from the windows casting a warm glow onto the sidewalk, Crash felt a small sense of resolution settle in his chest. He didn't have all the answers, and he knew he would face difficult choices in the days to come. But he also knew that he couldn't ignore the twinge of guilt that had taken root in his conscience.

Crash paused at the door, looking out at the darkened street one last time before stepping inside. The image of Fred, the choices he had made, and the road ahead weighed heavily on his mind. But he was determined to find a way forward—one that honored the trust Fred had placed in him, one that allowed him to chase his dreams without losing sight of what really mattered.

And with that thought, Crash closed the door behind him, one that could never be opened again.

The night air was cool against Crash's skin as he walked through the quiet streets of San Francisco, his thoughts heavy with the events that had just unfolded. The city around him seemed almost surreal, the distant hum of traffic and the occasional flicker of streetlights creating a backdrop that felt detached from the whirlwind of emotions swirling inside him.

In his pocket, the phone felt like a lead weight, pulling at his conscience with every step he took. The image he had captured—Fred, lounging in his high-tech lair, surrounded by the secrets of a life no one else knew about—was everything Crash had dreamed of. It was the key to a future he had longed for, the ticket to fame and success that had always seemed just out of reach.

And yet, as he walked slowly home, the thrill of what he had done was overshadowed by a growing sense of unease.

Crash had always considered himself a good person—someone who tried to do the right thing, even when it was difficult. But tonight, he couldn't shake the feeling that he had crossed a line, one that was far more significant than he had realized in the moment. Fred had trusted him, let him into his world, and in return, Crash had taken something that wasn't his to take.

The memory of Fred's warmth, his unexpected hospitality, and the clear desire for friendship tugged at Crash's heart. Fred had been so open, so genuine in his gesture of kindness, offering Crash a place in his hidden world without hesitation. And what had Crash done? He had betrayed that trust for the sake of a photo—a photo that now felt more like evidence of a wrongdoing than a triumph.

Crash's footsteps slowed as he neared a small park, the quiet, tree-lined path offering a moment of respite from the noise in his mind. He stopped, taking a seat on a weathered bench, the cool metal biting into his skin even through his jeans. For a moment, he simply sat there, staring up at the sky, trying to make sense of the conflicting emotions that churned inside him.

The excitement, the anticipation of what that photo could mean for his future, was still there, but it was increasingly tempered by a deepening sense of guilt. He couldn't ignore the nagging voice in the back of his mind, the one that kept asking if this was really worth it. Was fame, success, and everything that came with it really worth betraying the trust of someone who had offered him genuine friendship?

Crash pulled out his phone, staring at the screen as the image of Fred filled the display. It was a perfect shot, capturing the essence of the strange, wonderful world that Fred had created for himself. But as Crash looked at it now, the photo didn't fill him with the same sense of pride and excitement. Instead, it filled him with a sense of loss—loss of the purity of the connection he had begun to build with Fred.

His finger hovered over the delete button, the option to erase the photo and put the moment behind him seeming both simple and impossibly difficult. Deleting the photo would mean giving up on the opportunity it represented, but keeping it felt like holding onto something that wasn't his to keep.

Crash sighed, lowering the phone but not yet making a decision. The moral complexities of the situation were becoming more apparent with every passing moment. The deeper his relationship with Fred became, the more complicated things would get. Tonight had been just the beginning—a small taste of the difficult choices that lay ahead.

He couldn't go back and undo what he had done, but he could try to make better choices moving forward. Maybe that was all he could do—learn from this, try to be a better friend, a better person. Maybe it wasn't too late to make things right.

As Crash stood up from the bench and continued his walk home, the phone still tucked away in his pocket, he made a silent promise to himself. He would think carefully about what he did next, about the kind of person he wanted to be. He would find a way to balance his dreams with the responsibility that came with the trust Fred had placed in him.

The road ahead wouldn't be easy. The temptation to use the photo, to chase the fame he had always wanted, would be strong. But Crash knew that if he was going to keep Fred's trust, if he was going to honor the friendship that was beginning to take shape, he would have to navigate these moral complexities with care.

As he neared his home, the lights from the windows casting a warm glow onto the sidewalk, Crash felt a small sense of resolution settle in his chest. He didn't have all the answers, and he knew he would face difficult choices in the days to come. But he also knew that he couldn't ignore the twinge of guilt that had taken root in his conscience.

Crash paused at the door, looking out at the darkened street one last time before stepping inside. The image of Fred, the choices he had made, and the road ahead weighed heavily on his mind. But he was determined to find a way forward—one that honored the trust Fred had placed in him, one that allowed him to chase his dreams without losing sight of what really mattered.

And with that thought, Crash closed the door behind him, ready to face whatever came next.

Crash sat behind the counter at the store, his phone gripped tightly in his hands, the weight of the moment pressing down on him. It was early, the store just beginning to stir to life with a few customers milling about, but Crash's mind was a thousand miles away. His eyes flicked back and forth between the photo on his phone screen and the upload button.

The photo of Fred, sitting calmly in his high-tech lair, looked even more surreal now than it had last night. The dim light, the sophisticated monitors and servers, the leather couches—it all seemed like something out of a science fiction movie, not the hidden world of a sea lion. And yet, here it was, captured on his phone, ready to be shared with the world.

Crash's heart raced with a mixture of excitement and fear. This was the moment. This was his chance. He could almost see it now— his MeTube channel blowing up overnight, the comments flooding in, the interviews, the attention. For the first time in his life, he had something that no one else had, something so incredible that it could catapult him into the spotlight.

But as his thumb hovered over the upload button, that same twinge of guilt surfaced, gnawing at the edges of his excitement. Fred had trusted him. Fred had opened up his world to Crash, offered him friendship. And Crash had taken this photo without his permission, knowing full well how Fred felt about being recorded.

He tried to push the guilt aside, rationalizing that this was an opportunity he couldn't pass up. Besides, Fred would never have to know, right? Crash wasn't planning to betray him fully—just to get a little taste of fame, to open the door to something bigger.

Crash glanced up, catching his reflection in the small security mirror near the register. His face was pale, his eyes slightly hollow from lack of sleep. He had spent most of the night thinking about this, turning it over in his mind, imagining all the possibilities. The excitement was still there, but it was tempered now by the weight of what he was about to do.

Without allowing himself to overthink it anymore, Crash took a deep breath and tapped the upload button.

The phone buzzed softly in his hand, the screen flickering as the progress bar began to fill. Crash's heart thudded in his chest as he watched the bar inch forward, the anticipation building with each passing second. This was it—the moment everything could change.

He clicked over to MeTube, watching the video thumbnail of Fred in his lair appear in his channel's feed. The caption read, "Secret Sea Lion Lair? The Hidden Life of Fred." The thumbnail was striking, showing just enough to intrigue viewers without giving too much away. Crash could almost imagine the clicks rolling in, the views ticking up by the thousands.

For a moment, time seemed to stand still as he stared at the screen, waiting for the first few views to pop up. The tension in his chest tightened, his breath coming in shallow bursts. Any second now, someone would see it. Any second now, his life would change.

The minutes ticked by, and still, the view counter stayed stubbornly at zero. Crash frowned, refreshing the page several times, his excitement beginning to fray around the edges. Nothing. No views, no comments. Just silence.

He checked his phone's signal, worried that maybe the upload hadn't gone through properly. But everything seemed fine. The video was there, it was public, and yet… nothing.

Crash's stomach twisted as he refreshed the page again, still hoping for something, anything—a spark that would ignite the fire he had been waiting for. But the view count remained at zero, a glaring reminder that nothing was happening.

His fingers drummed nervously on the counter as he glanced around the store, trying to distract himself. His mother and grandmother were chatting quietly as they restocked some items on the shelves, oblivious to the turmoil raging inside Crash. The store was calm, the usual hum of life continuing as it always did, but Crash felt like his world was teetering on the edge of something.

Another minute passed. Then another. Still, no views.

The excitement that had filled him just moments ago began to ebb away, replaced by a creeping sense of doubt. What if no one cared? What if the photo wasn't as groundbreaking as he had thought? What if, after all this, his shot at fame fizzled out before it even began?

Crash tried to shake off the doubt, forcing himself to remain calm. Maybe it just needed more time. Maybe people were still waking up, still logging on. He had to be patient, had to trust that this was the start of something big.

But the longer he waited, the more the tension built. The excitement that had once driven him now felt like a ticking clock, each second slipping away with no response, no validation. The photo—his golden ticket—was out there in the world, but it seemed like the world wasn't interested.

Crash's hand trembled as he refreshed the page one last time, staring at the empty view counter. His stomach dropped, the weight of disappointment settling over him like a heavy fog.

He had built this moment up so much in his mind, imagined the fame, the attention, the escape from his mundane life. But now, all of that seemed to be slipping through his fingers. And as the realization hit him, a new emotion began to creep in—regret.

He had uploaded the photo, invaded Fred's privacy, and for what? A few minutes of anticipation that had led to nothing? He had risked everything—his friendship with Fred, the trust he had been given—and it felt like he had thrown it all away for the promise of something that never came.

Crash sat back in his chair, the phone still clutched in his hand, the silence around him growing louder with every passing second.

Maybe he had made a mistake.

Crash slumped back in his chair, his eyes fixed on the phone screen as the minutes ticked by. The view counter remained stubbornly at zero, refusing to budge no matter how many times he refreshed the page. The excitement that had surged through him just moments ago was quickly evaporating, leaving behind a hollow sense of disappointment.

He had imagined this moment so many times—the thrill of watching the views skyrocket, the comments pouring in, the feeling of finally being noticed. But now, as the silence stretched on, all of that seemed like a distant fantasy. The photo that had felt like a golden ticket now seemed insignificant, just another post lost in the endless sea of content.

Crash glanced up from his phone, his eyes scanning the store as if searching for some kind of distraction. But the store was quiet, just the usual trickle of customers moving through the aisles, oblivious to the turmoil raging inside him. His mother was busy helping a customer near the produce section, her voice soft and cheerful, while his grandmother rearranged the shelves with a calm, methodical precision.

For a moment, Crash felt a wave of envy wash over him. They seemed so content, so grounded in their routines, while he was stuck in this limbo, desperately searching for something that would give his life meaning. He had thought that fame, attention, the validation of the online world would be the answer, but now he wasn't so sure.

The lack of response to his post was more than just a disappointment—it was a stark reminder of how fleeting and elusive online fame could be. One moment you were riding high, filled with anticipation, and the next, you were left with nothing but emptiness.

Crash's thoughts began to spiral as the reality of his situation settled in. He had been so focused on chasing after something more, something bigger, that he had overlooked the cost. He had taken a photo behind Fred's back, invaded his privacy, all for the sake of a few clicks, a few moments of fame that never materialized.

And now, as he sat there, staring at the unresponsive screen, he couldn't help but feel like he had betrayed not just Fred, but himself. He had compromised his values, his integrity, for something that had turned out to be meaningless.

A heavy sigh escaped his lips as he set the phone down on the counter, the excitement that had fueled him now replaced by a deep sense of frustration. This wasn't how it was supposed to go. He was supposed to be celebrating, basking in the glow of his success, not sitting here, feeling more lost and disconnected than ever.

Crash rubbed his temples, trying to push down the growing sense of failure that gnawed at him. He had always wanted more out of life, always felt like there was something bigger out there for him, but now he wasn't sure what that was anymore. If fame wasn't the answer, then what was?

The store's bell chimed as a customer entered, momentarily drawing Crash's attention. He watched as the customer greeted his mother with a friendly nod, their interaction so simple, so normal. It made Crash feel even more out of place, like he was adrift in a world that didn't quite make sense to him.

The silence of the online world, the emptiness of the view counter, seemed to mock him, reminding him that no matter how hard he tried, he couldn't force people to care. He couldn't make fame happen just because he wanted it, just because he thought he deserved it.

Crash picked up his phone again, staring at the photo that had once filled him with so much hope. Now, it just felt like a reminder of everything that was wrong—his impatience, his desperation, his willingness to sacrifice trust for a shot at something that wasn't even real.

As he stared at the image of Fred in his lair, Crash felt a stirring of something deeper—a need for something more meaningful, something that couldn't be captured in a photo or measured in views. He didn't know what that was yet, but he knew he had to find it.

The path to fame, to success, was a dead end. Crash could see that now. It was time to stop chasing after something that wasn't meant for him and start looking for what truly mattered.

Crash set the phone down again, this time with a sense of finality. He needed to rethink everything, to figure out what he really wanted, what he was willing to fight for. The disappointment he felt now, the frustration with his own life, was a wake-up call—a reminder that there was more to life than fleeting moments of online recognition.

As he stood up from the counter, the weight of the day's events still heavy on his shoulders, Crash made a silent promise to himself. He would find something real, something meaningful, something that didn't depend on the whims of an unseen audience.

And with that thought, he turned away from the phone, ready to face the next chapter of his life—whatever that might be.

The room was bathed in the soft, cold glow of multiple computer screens, their blue light casting sharp shadows on the sleek, modern furniture. The air hummed with the low, constant buzz of servers running tirelessly, processing vast amounts of data in real time. At the center of it all sat Leonard, his eyes sharp and calculating as he watched the endless streams of information flow across his monitors.

Leonard was a man of precision and control, someone who prided himself on knowing everything that happened within his sphere of influence—and that sphere was vast. His operations spanned continents, his network of surveillance extending into places most people would never even dream of. To Leonard, information was power, and he wielded it with ruthless efficiency.

Today, however, something unusual had caught his attention.

One of the screens in front of him displayed a series of posts and uploads from various social media platforms, all of them being scanned and analyzed by his sophisticated algorithms. Most of the content was noise—mundane, irrelevant chatter that Leonard dismissed without a second thought. But one post, buried deep in the feed, had triggered an alert.

Leonard leaned forward, his interest piqued as he zeroed in on the screen. The post was from a relatively obscure account, one that had barely registered on his radar before. But the image attached to the post was what intrigued him. It showed a dimly lit room, high-tech monitors and servers lining the walls, and at the center of it all, a sea lion wearing a green bucket hat.

Leonard's eyes narrowed as he studied the image. There was something familiar about the setup, something that tugged at the edges of his memory. He quickly pulled up a series of files, cross-referencing the image with data he had collected over the years.

It didn't take long for the pieces to fall into place.

"So, there you are," Leonard murmured to himself, a small, predatory smile curling at the corners of his lips. He recognized the setup now—the advanced technology, the hidden lair. It was all too familiar. And the sea lion… there was no mistaking him. This was the creature that had eluded him years ago, the one that had been the subject of countless experiments before disappearing in an escape worth of a Bond film.

Fred.

Leonard's mind raced as he considered the implications of what had just happened. The truth was, Fred wasn't just valuable to Leonard for his own purposes—though having a hyperintelligent sea lion under his control would undoubtedly be an asset. The real value lay in the fact that the government organization from which Fred had escaped wanted him back *badly*. Fred was no ordinary experiment; he was the only participant to have successfully undergone the highly classified and controversial program without succumbing to the rigors of the experiment. The others—humans and animals alike—had either failed to develop the desired enhancements or had met tragic ends, their bodies unable to handle the strain of the procedures.

But Fred had not only survived; he had thrived. His intelligence had skyrocketed, his cognitive abilities surpassing those of even the most advanced artificial intelligence. And now, Fred was on the loose, a potential game-changer in the world of espionage. The government had poured billions into the program, hoping to create the ultimate spy—a being with the cognitive capabilities of a supercomputer and the physical abilities to operate undetected in environments where humans couldn't. A sea lion like Fred could infiltrate underwater facilities, slip past security unnoticed, and gather intelligence without raising suspicion. He was the perfect spy, and his loss had been a major blow to the project.

For Leonard, this wasn't just about Fred's unique capabilities. It was about his own survival. Leonard's empire had been built on a foundation of delicate favors and unspoken agreements with powerful government entities. The government had looked the other way when it came to regulatory scrutiny, passing favorable legislation that allowed Leonard's business to thrive and capping corporate taxation at rates that kept his profits soaring. In return, Leonard was expected to provide certain "services" when called upon—services that ranged from monitoring web traffic and collecting data on political dissidents, to quietly locating individuals the government was particularly interested in finding.

Over the years, Leonard had become deeply indebted to these government agencies. His company's lucrative government contracts were one thing, but the real power lay in the understanding that Leonard would be willing to do almost anything to maintain his influence and ensure that his empire remained untouchable. When the agency had learned of Fred's escape, they had turned to Leonard, knowing he had the resources to track down the elusive sea lion. The pressure had been immense. If Leonard could deliver Fred, it would secure his position for years to come, keeping the government on his side and ensuring his continued prosperity.

But now, with Fred out of reach, Leonard could feel the walls closing in. He had failed in his task, and he knew the government wouldn't take kindly to failure. The stakes were higher than ever.

Without Fred, Leonard's carefully constructed empire was at risk of collapsing. The favors, the deals, the protection—it could all evaporate in an instant. And Leonard, a man who had spent his life meticulously controlling every aspect of his world, was now facing the terrifying prospect of losing it all.

As he grappled with this realization, Leonard's desperation grew. He needed to find a way to recover from this setback, to regain control before it was too late. Fred wasn't just a valuable asset; he was the key to Leonard's survival. Without him, everything Leonard had built could come crashing down.

Leonard quickly accessed the account that had posted the image, scanning through its history, searching for any clues about its owner. The account belonged to a young man named Crash, someone who seemed to be a nobody—until now. Leonard's fingers danced across the keyboard, pulling up more information about Crash, his location, his connections.

It didn't take long to paint a picture. Crash was a local, working at a small family-run store. The post reeked of desperation— someone trying to make a name for himself by revealing something extraordinary. But what Crash didn't realize was that by posting that image, he had just placed himself directly in Leonard's crosshairs.

Leonard's smile widened as he considered his next move. This was an opportunity—one that he couldn't afford to miss. Fred was too valuable, too important to let slip away again. And now that he knew where to find him, Leonard was ready to act.

But he couldn't just storm in, guns blazing. No, that wasn't his style. Leonard was a man of subtlety, of manipulation. He would play the long game, slowly tightening his grip until there was no escape. He would use Crash, exploit his weaknesses, and then, when the time was right, he would swoop in and take what was his.

Leonard leaned back in his chair, his eyes gleaming with anticipation. The game was on, and he had all the pieces he needed to win.

With a few quick commands, Leonard set his plan into motion. He ordered a detailed surveillance on Crash—his movements, his interactions, everything. He wanted to know exactly what Crash was up to, what he knew, and most importantly, where Fred was hiding. The more information he had, the easier it would be to manipulate the situation to his advantage.

As the data began to stream in, Leonard allowed himself a moment of satisfaction. This was what he lived for—the thrill of the hunt, the anticipation of victory. And this time, he wouldn't fail. Fred would be his, and with him, the power to reshape the world in ways no one could imagine.

Leonard's gaze returned to the image on the screen, his mind already racing with possibilities. Crash had no idea what he had just unleashed, no idea of the storm that was about to descend upon him. But Leonard would make sure that by the time it was over, Fred would be back where he belonged—and Crash would be nothing more than a footnote in the history of his success.

With a final, satisfied nod, Leonard turned his attention to the monitors, watching as the pieces began to fall into place. The game had begun, and Leonard was ready to play it to the end.

Chapter 10
Signal Lost

Crash's post had been nothing more than a blip on the vast radar of the internet, but to Leonard, it was a golden opportunity. An opportunity to finally reclaim what had once slipped through his fingers.

He leaned forward, his fingers tapping rhythmically on the desk as he considered his next move. The photo Crash had uploaded was dangerous—not because of what it revealed to the general public, but because of what it revealed to Leonard. If anyone else with power or resources saw it, they might also recognize the value of Fred, and Leonard wasn't about to let that happen.

He needed to control the situation, and that meant controlling the narrative.

With a few quick keystrokes, Leonard accessed the back channels of the internet, the hidden pathways that allowed someone with the right skills to manipulate content in ways most people couldn't even begin to comprehend. He found Crash's post, buried in the chaos of social media, and with a decisive click, he blocked it from public view.

The image, the post, the entire account—it all vanished from the public eye, as if it had never existed. Leonard's systems ensured that the block was thorough, leaving no trace for Crash to follow. To Crash, it would look like a glitch, a technical error, something easily dismissed and forgotten.

But to Leonard, it was a strategic move, one that would buy him the time he needed to put his plan into action.

With the post safely blocked, Leonard turned his attention to Crash himself. The young man was clearly out of his depth, a small-time player who had stumbled upon something far bigger than he could handle. Leonard's surveillance had already provided a wealth of information about Crash—his background, his family, his dreams, decades of metadata from every interaction he had with the internet. And now, Leonard would use that information to manipulate him, to steer him in the direction that best suited Leonard's goals.

Leonard's fingers danced across the keyboard as he set up a series of automated tasks, each one designed to subtly influence Crash's actions. It was a delicate balance—he couldn't push too hard, couldn't reveal his hand too soon. But with the right nudges, the right distractions, he could guide Crash exactly where he wanted him.

First, Leonard planted a series of fake notifications on Crash's social media accounts—messages that would make it seem like the post was gaining attention, like people were noticing it. The notifications were carefully crafted, just believable enough to keep Crash hooked, to keep him checking, waiting, hoping. But none of them would lead anywhere. They were a trap, designed to keep Crash focused on the wrong things while Leonard worked behind the scenes.

Next, Leonard began to create a trail—a series of breadcrumbs that would lead Crash to believe that his post had attracted the interest of someone important, someone who could help him achieve the fame he so desperately wanted. A few well-placed comments, a private message from a mysterious account, a mention from an obscure but influential blog—each one carefully crafted to build up Crash's hopes, to draw him deeper into the web that Leonard was weaving.

Leonard knew that Crash's desire for recognition was his greatest weakness, and he intended to exploit it to the fullest. By the time Crash realized what was happening, it would be too late. He would be ensnared, a pawn in Leonard's game, with no way out.

But Leonard wasn't just interested in manipulating Crash—he wanted to ensure that no one else could interfere. The photo was blocked, but there was always a risk that Crash might try to re-upload it, or that someone else might stumble upon the truth. Leonard needed to keep a tight grip on the situation, and that meant isolating

Crash, keeping him dependent, keeping him unaware of the larger forces at play.

With a satisfied nod, Leonard set the final phase of his plan into motion. A subtle but effective campaign of disinformation—rumors, false leads, fake posts—would be seeded across the internet, ensuring that if anyone did come across the photo or any mention of Fred, they would dismiss it as a hoax, a conspiracy theory not worth investigating.

Leonard sat back, his gaze fixed on the monitors as the threads of his plan began to weave together. He had everything he needed—control over the narrative, influence over Crash, and a clear path to reclaiming Fred. All that remained was to watch and wait, to let the pieces fall into place as he tightened his grip on the situation.

Crash, meanwhile, would remain blissfully unaware of the danger he was in. He would continue chasing after the illusion of fame, oblivious to the fact that he was being manipulated, that every step he took was being guided by someone far more powerful than he could imagine.

Leonard's smile widened as he considered the possibilities. Fred was within reach at last, and this time, nothing would stand in his way. Not Crash, not the internet, not the world. Leonard would have what he wanted, and he would do it on his terms.

The game was set, and Leonard was ready to play it to the end.

The room was silent except for the faint hum of the servers, their rhythmic buzz a constant reminder of the immense power at Leonard's fingertips. He sat back in his chair, fingers steepled in thought, his eyes narrowing as he considered the next steps in his plan. Everything was proceeding smoothly, but there was one more piece to the puzzle that needed to be addressed—one that required a delicate touch.

With a measured breath, Leonard reached for a sleek, black phone on his desk. This phone was different from the others—no apps, no internet, no traceable signals. It was a direct line, used only for the most sensitive communications. The kind that couldn't afford to be intercepted.

He dialed a number from memory, each digit entered with precision. The line connected after a single ring, the silence on the other end heavy with anticipation.

"Is it secure?" came a voice, low and calm, the kind of voice that carried authority without needing to raise it.

"Always," Leonard replied, his tone equally composed. "I wouldn't risk anything else."

There was a pause, as if the person on the other end was considering something. Then, "You have news?"

Leonard allowed himself a small smile. "Yes. I've located our long-lost friend."

The voice on the other end remained silent, waiting for Leonard to continue.

"It's him," Leonard confirmed. "The same one from the experiments. He's been living off the grid, but I've found him. It's only a matter of time before he's back where he belongs."

"Good," the voice replied, with a hint of satisfaction. "This has been a long time coming. You understand the importance of this, Leonard. We cannot afford any mistakes."

Leonard's eyes darkened, his expression hardening. "There won't be any mistakes. I've already begun the necessary steps. The situation is under control."

"Who found him?" the voice asked, a note of curiosity creeping in.

"A boy, he's being handled," Leonard said smoothly. "He's insignificant—a means to an end. I'll use him to get what we need, and then he'll be dealt with."

Another pause, longer this time. "See that you do. The stakes are higher than you realize, Leonard. This isn't just about the creature. There are... others who have taken an interest in this project. Powerful individuals who will not tolerate failure."

Leonard's pulse quickened, though he kept his voice steady. "I understand. The creature will be secured, and the situation will be contained. You have my word."

"I expect nothing less," the voice replied. "But remember, Leonard, we're dealing with forces beyond our usual scope. If this goes wrong, it won't just be your head on the line."

Leonard's jaw tightened. He wasn't used to being questioned, especially not by someone who was supposed to trust his abilities. But he knew better than to let his irritation show. "It won't go wrong. I'll make sure of it."

"Very well," the voice said, a finality to the words. "Keep me informed. And Leonard—no loose ends."

The line went dead, leaving Leonard in the silence of his office, the weight of the conversation lingering in the air. He set the phone down carefully, his mind racing as he processed the implications of the call.

He had known from the beginning that this project was important—Fred's intelligence and capabilities were too valuable to ignore. But this was the first time he had sensed just how far-reaching the consequences could be if things went awry. The mention of "others" taking an interest, of powerful individuals with a stake in Fred's capture, added a new layer of complexity to the situation.

Leonard had always thrived on control, on being the one to pull the strings. But now, it seemed there were others who held strings of their own, and they were watching closely.

He stood up from his chair, crossing the room to a window that overlooked the city. The skyline was bathed in the soft light of the setting sun, a stark contrast to the shadowy dealings that were unfolding behind the scenes.

Fred was more than just an asset—he was a key to something larger, something that Leonard was only beginning to understand. And if Leonard wanted to stay ahead of the game, he would need to be more careful, more ruthless, more precise than ever before.

The stakes had just been raised, and Leonard wasn't about to let anyone else take control. This was his project, his game, and he would see it through to the end, no matter what—or who—stood in his way.

With a determined glint in his eye, Leonard turned away from the window, ready to put the next phase of his plan into motion. The call had been a reminder of what was at stake, but it had also solidified his resolve.

There could be no loose ends. And that meant Crash, Fred, and anyone else who got in the way would be dealt with swiftly and efficiently.

Leonard sat at his desk, the glow of the monitors casting a cold light across his sharp features. The earlier conversation still echoed in his mind, fueling his resolve. It was time to take the next step, to move from the shadows and start influencing events directly. Crash needed to be brought closer, drawn into Leonard's orbit, and that required a personal touch.

A visit.

Leonard smirked at the thought. The boy had no idea what he had stumbled into, no understanding of the forces that were now in play. Leonard would visit him under the pretense of neighborhood improvement—a project that would seem innocuous, even beneficial, but would serve as the perfect cover for Leonard's true intentions.

He opened a file on his computer, one of many detailed dossiers he kept on individuals of interest. Crash's file was relatively thin, but it contained all the essentials: a young man with dreams of escaping his mundane life, a struggling family business, a lack of significant connections. In Leonard's eyes, Crash was the perfect target—desperate, inexperienced, and easily manipulated.

But Leonard wasn't one to leave things to chance. He needed to ensure that his approach was flawless, that every detail was accounted for. He began drafting a plan, meticulously outlining the steps he would take to gain Crash's trust.

First, the excuse. Leonard typed out a brief document, labeling it "Community Revitalization Project." The language was carefully chosen—vague enough to avoid suspicion, but authoritative enough to convince Crash that this was a legitimate effort. Leonard knew that small businesses like the one Crash's family ran were always on edge, wary of changes that could disrupt their already precarious existence. Offering to "improve" the area would disarm Crash, make him more receptive to Leonard's visit.

Next, the approach. Leonard decided to present himself as a well-meaning corporate liaison, someone with the power to make real changes in the neighborhood. He would mention potential grants, financial assistance, maybe even a few hints about increased foot traffic and higher profits. It was all smoke and mirrors, of course— Leonard had no intention of actually improving anything. But the promise of support would lure Crash in, make him more willing to listen.

Finally, the execution. Leonard planned to visit the store during a quiet period, when Crash would be there alone, without the watchful eyes of his mother or grandmother. He would make it seem like a casual drop-in, a friendly chat about the future of the neighborhood. But in reality, Leonard would be assessing Crash, probing for weaknesses, planting seeds of doubt and curiosity that would draw him further into the web.

Leonard paused, reviewing his plan with a critical eye. It was a delicate balance—too much pressure, and Crash might resist; too little, and he might not take the bait. Leonard prided himself on his ability to walk that fine line, to manipulate without ever appearing to do so.

He leaned back in his chair, satisfied with his preparations. This visit would be the first step in securing Crash's cooperation, in ensuring that the boy remained unaware of the true stakes. Leonard had no doubt that once he was in control, Crash would be pliable, eager to please, desperate for the validation that Leonard would so carefully offer.

But there was something Leonard hadn't accounted for—something that lingered just beneath the surface of his meticulously crafted plan. Crash had already begun to doubt his decisions, to question the morality of his actions. The guilt, the unease that had taken root in Crash's mind, was slowly growing, making him more aware, more cautious than Leonard realized.

As Leonard finalized the details of his visit, he underestimated the subtle shift that had begun in Crash—a shift that would make the boy less predictable, less easily manipulated. Leonard saw Crash as a pawn, a simple tool to be used and discarded, but in doing so, he overlooked the potential for resistance, for change.

And so, with a sense of confidence that bordered on arrogance, Leonard set the plan into motion. He sent the documents, scheduled the visit, and prepared to descend upon the small family store with all the charm and false benevolence he could muster.

But even as he prepared to manipulate Crash, Leonard was blind to the growing awareness in his target—a blind spot that would soon complicate his carefully laid plans.

The pieces were moving, the game was advancing, and Leonard was ready to make his move. But the game was far from over, and the outcome was anything but certain.

The bell above the store's entrance chimed softly, signaling the arrival of a new customer. Crash looked up from the counter where he had been rearranging some items, expecting to see one of the regulars. Instead, he was greeted by the sight of a man who immediately commanded attention.

Leonard stepped into the store with an air of effortless authority, his tailored suit and polished shoes setting him apart from the usual crowd. His movements were smooth, calculated, as if he were a conductor orchestrating a symphony with every step. The sunlight streaming through the windows caught the silver in his hair, adding a distinguished touch to his already striking appearance.

For a moment, Crash felt a flicker of awe. Leonard was the kind of person who seemed to belong in a boardroom or on the cover of a magazine, not in a small, family-run store. There was something magnetic about him, a charisma that drew Crash in before he even realized what was happening.

"Good afternoon," Leonard said, his voice smooth and warm, like honeyed whiskey. He flashed a smile that was equal parts charm and confidence, the kind of smile that made people feel like they were the most important person in the room. "I'm Leonard. I believe we have some business to discuss."

Crash blinked, momentarily caught off guard by the man's presence. "Uh, hi. I'm Crash," he replied, his voice sounding oddly small in comparison. "Business? I'm not sure I—"

Leonard held up a hand, his smile never wavering. "No need to worry, Crash. I'm here on behalf of the Community Revitalization Project. We're looking to invest in local businesses, help them grow, bring more foot traffic to the area. I'm sure you've heard about it?"

Crash frowned slightly, trying to recall if he had heard anything about such an initiative. Nothing came to mind, but Leonard's confident demeanor made it hard to question him. "Uh, maybe. I'm not sure," Crash said, his unease growing as he tried to process the situation.

Leonard stepped closer, his gaze sweeping the store with an appraising look. "You have a wonderful business here, Crash. A lot of potential. With the right support, this place could be thriving, attracting more customers, maybe even expanding."

Crash felt a swell of pride at Leonard's words, but it was quickly tempered by a nagging sense of discomfort. There was something about Leonard that didn't sit right with him, something in the way the man's eyes lingered on certain parts of the store, as if he were assessing more than just the business.

"Thanks," Crash said cautiously. "But we're doing okay, I think. I mean, it's not easy, but we manage."

Leonard nodded, his expression sympathetic. "I understand. Small businesses like yours are the backbone of this community, but they often struggle to reach their full potential. That's where we come in. We provide the resources, the guidance, and the funding to help you succeed. Think of it as a partnership—one that benefits everyone."

Crash found himself nodding along, caught up in Leonard's persuasive tone. The idea of having some extra support, of making the store more successful, was certainly appealing. But at the same time, the unease in his gut was growing stronger. There was something too slick, too polished about Leonard's pitch, something that made Crash feel like he was being drawn into something he didn't fully understand.

As if sensing Crash's hesitation, Leonard leaned in slightly, lowering his voice as if sharing a secret. "I know this might all seem a bit overwhelming, but I assure you, Crash, we have your best interests at heart. I wouldn't be here if I didn't believe in the potential of this store—and in you."

Crash looked into Leonard's eyes, searching for any sign of deception. But Leonard's gaze was steady, unwavering, filled with a sincerity that was almost convincing. Almost.

"That's… really nice of you," Crash said slowly, still trying to wrap his head around the situation. "But why us? Why this store?"

Leonard's smile widened, and for a brief moment, Crash thought he saw something predatory in the man's expression. "Why not you, Crash? Why not this store? You're at the heart of this community, and with the right support, you could be something more. I'm offering you an opportunity—one that doesn't come around often."

Crash's mind raced, torn between the allure of what Leonard was offering and the persistent sense of unease that had settled in his chest. It was as if his instincts were screaming at him to be cautious, to not be so easily swayed by Leonard's charm. But Leonard's words were like a balm, soothing those worries and replacing them with visions of success, of a future where the store thrived beyond his wildest dreams.

But something still didn't add up. Crash couldn't shake the feeling that there was more to Leonard's visit than just neighborhood improvement. The way Leonard spoke, the way he carried himself— it all felt too calculated, too rehearsed, as if he were playing a role rather than being genuine.

And then there was the fact that Leonard had shown up out of the blue, with no warning, no prior contact. It was all too convenient, too perfectly timed, especially given everything that had been happening with Fred and the photo.

Crash's thoughts flickered back to Fred, to the guilt that had been gnawing at him ever since he uploaded that photo. What if Leonard knew? What if this visit wasn't just about the store, but about something else entirely?

"Crash," Leonard's voice cut through his thoughts, bringing him back to the present. "I can see you're a man who thinks carefully about his decisions, and I respect that. But I also know that sometimes, opportunities like this one don't wait. They require a leap of faith."

Crash hesitated, his mind a whirlwind of conflicting emotions. Leonard was right—this was an opportunity, one that could potentially change everything for the better. But the unease, the suspicion, it was all too strong to ignore.

"I… I need some time to think about it," Crash finally said, trying to buy himself some space to figure out what was really going on.

Leonard's smile didn't falter, but there was a brief flicker of something in his eyes—disappointment, perhaps, or annoyance. "Of course, Crash. Take all the time you need. But remember, opportunities like this don't come around every day."

Crash nodded, feeling the tension in the air as Leonard turned and made his way to the door. The man's presence seemed to fill the store, leaving a lingering sense of pressure even after he was gone.

The bell chimed again as Leonard stepped outside, his parting words hanging in the air like a challenge. "I'll be in touch, Crash. Let me write up a more detailed proposal for you and stop back in the morning."

As the door closed behind Leonard, Crash felt a shiver run down his spine. The man's charm and authority were undeniable, but so was the underlying sense of danger that had permeated the entire conversation.

Crash stared at the door for a long moment, his mind still racing. Before today, Leonard had been more than just a tech mogul to him—he had been an idol, someone Crash had admired from afar, a symbol of everything he had once dreamed of becoming. Leonard's achievements, his influence, his seemingly unshakable confidence—Crash had aspired to all of it. Meeting him in person had felt like stepping into the orbit of a giant, someone who could change the course of his life with a single decision. But now, as the reality of the encounter settled in, the awe that had filled Crash began to twist into something more complicated. Leonard had made a strong impression, but he had also left behind a trail of unanswered questions and lingering doubts. What was this really about? What did Leonard want from him? And why couldn't Crash shake the feeling that he had just been caught in the web of something much larger and more dangerous than he had ever imagined?

The evening sun cast a warm, golden light through the small kitchen window as the family gathered around the dinner table. The familiar clatter of plates and the comforting aroma of homemade food filled the air. It was a routine they shared every night, a moment of peace and connection amidst the chaos of their daily lives.

Crash sat quietly, pushing his food around his plate, his mind still reeling from the day's events. Across the table, his mother, Somjai, was bustling around, making sure everyone had enough to eat, while his grandmother, Jan, sat calmly, her eyes sharp and observant as she noticed Crash's uncharacteristic silence.

"So, how was your day, dear?" Somjai asked as she finally sat down, a warm smile on her face. "Anything interesting happen at the store?"

Crash hesitated for a moment, glancing up at his mother and grandmother. He hadn't meant to keep it to himself, but the encounter with Leonard had left him so overwhelmed that he hadn't even processed how to talk about it. Now, under their expectant gazes, he realized he couldn't keep it to himself any longer.

"Actually, yeah," Crash said, his voice careful and measured. "Something... pretty big happened."

Somjai and Jan both paused, their attention fully on him now. "What is it, Crash?" Jan asked, her tone calm but curious.

Crash took a deep breath, trying to find the right words. "Leonard Trice stopped by the store today," he said, watching as the words hung in the air.

There was a brief moment of stunned silence before Somjai's eyes widened in surprise. "Leonard Trice? *The* Leonard Trice? The tech mogul? What did he want with our store?"

Crash nodded, feeling the weight of their astonishment. "Yeah, *that* Leonard. He said he's working on this big project to help revitalize the neighborhood. He wants our store to be the cornerstone of it. He talked about turning it into a hub for the community, something that could really make a difference around here."

Somjai's face lit up with excitement, her hands clasping together. "That's incredible, Crash! I can't believe you didn't mention it sooner! Leonard himself came to our store—this could be a huge opportunity for us!"

Jan, however, remained more measured. Her eyes narrowed slightly, and she leaned forward, her expression thoughtful. "And he just showed up out of the blue? No warning? No appointment?"

Crash shrugged, feeling a bit sheepish. "Yeah, it was pretty sudden. He just walked in and started talking about this project. It all happened so fast, I'm still trying to wrap my head around it."

Jan nodded slowly, her skepticism apparent. "It sounds too good to be true, Crash. People like Leonard don't usually get involved in small neighborhood stores like ours unless there's something in it for them. Did he say what he expects from you?"

Crash hesitated, recalling the vague promises and unanswered questions Leonard had left him with. "Not really... He said he wanted my help, but he wasn't specific. It all sounded pretty great, but I don't know... There's something about it that just doesn't sit right with me."

Somjai reached across the table to place a reassuring hand on Crash's arm. "Whatever it is, it's a big deal that Leonard is interested in our store. But your grandmother's right—it's important to be careful when someones motivations aren't easy to see"

"He said he would be back tomorrow with a more detailed plan. You two can look it over and decide."

Jan looked down for a moment in contemplation then back up, her gaze softening as she looked at Crash. "You're an adult now, Crash. You want independence, you want to reach out on your own. This is your decision to make. Besides, we your mother and I don't know the first thing about this tech stuff. We won't even know what we're reading. We're here to give you our input and experience, but in the end, you're the one who has to choose what's best for you, for us, for the store. Just remember that if something seems too good to be true, it usually is."

Crash looked between his mother and grandmother, feeling the weight of their trust and the responsibility that came with it. He had always valued their opinions, but this was a decision he would have to make on his own. The thought both excited and terrified him.

"I'll think it over," Crash said finally, his voice steady. "I won't rush into anything. I just… I want to make sure I'm doing the right thing, not just for us, but for everyone in the neighborhood."

Somjai smiled warmly, giving his hand a gentle squeeze. "We know you will, Crash. You've got a good head on your shoulders, and whatever you decide, we'll support you."

Jan's expression softened even more as she gave a small nod of approval. "Just trust your instincts, and remember, we're here if you need us."

The conversation shifted to lighter topics as they finished their meal, but Crash couldn't shake the thoughts swirling in his mind. Leonard's proposal was still fresh, and the doubts it had stirred continued to gnaw at him. As he sat there with his family, he knew that the decision ahead would not be an easy one, but with their support, he felt a little more prepared to face whatever came next.

The bell above the store door chimed once more, announcing Leonard's return. Crash looked up, trying to steady himself as Leonard entered with the same air of confidence and authority that had marked his first visit. This time, though, there was an added layer of intent in Leonard's gaze, as if he were about to deliver something of great importance.

"Crash," Leonard greeted him warmly, flashing that same charismatic smile that seemed to put everyone at ease. "I appreciate you taking the time to think things over. I know this must be a lot to take in."

Crash nodded, still feeling a mix of curiosity and unease. He had spent the hours since Leonard's first visit turning the conversation over in his mind, trying to make sense of what exactly was being offered to him. And now, it seemed, Leonard was here to lay it all out.

"Yeah, I've been thinking," Crash replied, his tone cautious. "I just… I'm not sure what to make of all this."

Leonard nodded sympathetically, as if he understood exactly what Crash was feeling. "That's completely understandable. It's a big decision, and I wouldn't expect you to make it lightly. But that's why I'm here—to give you all the information you need, to help you see the bigger picture."

Chapter 11
The Boy and the Bucket Hat

Crash watched as Leonard reached into his sleek leather briefcase and pulled out a neatly bound folder. The words "Community Revitalization Project" were printed in bold letters across the cover, accompanied by an official-looking logo that lent an air of legitimacy to the document.

Leonard placed the folder on the counter and slid it toward Crash. "This," he began, his voice taking on a tone of quiet authority, "is the blueprint for a brighter future—not just for your store, but for the entire neighborhood."

Crash hesitated, then picked up the folder and began to flip through it. Inside were detailed plans, diagrams, and projections, all of which painted a picture of transformation. There were plans for new infrastructure, improved public spaces, marketing campaigns to attract more visitors, and financial incentives for local businesses. It was a carefully crafted vision of progress, one that promised growth, prosperity, and renewed energy for the community.

"This is impressive," Crash admitted, though his voice was tinged with uncertainty. "But... how do I fit into all of this? I mean, we're just a small store. Why is this important to you?"

Leonard leaned in slightly, his expression earnest and sincere. "Crash, you're more than just a small store. You're a cornerstone of this community, a place where people come together, where they feel a sense of connection. The Community Revitalization Project isn't just about buildings or infrastructure—it's about people, about preserving what makes this neighborhood special while giving it the tools to thrive in the future."

Crash absorbed Leonard's words, feeling a swell of pride but also a twinge of doubt. It all sounded so good, so idealistic, but something about it still didn't sit right with him. "And what do you get out of this?" Crash asked, his tone careful.

Leonard's smile never wavered. "My company believes that when communities thrive, everyone benefits. It's about creating a win-win situation. We invest in neighborhoods like yours because we see the potential, and in turn, that success reflects back on us. It's good business, yes, but it's also about doing the right thing. We have the resources to make a difference, and we want to use them in a way that benefits everyone."

Crash glanced back down at the folder, flipping through a few more pages. The plans were comprehensive, the language polished and persuasive. But as he read, he couldn't shake the feeling that there was more to this than Leonard was letting on. Still, the promise of success, of finally being recognized, was tempting.

Leonard must have sensed Crash's hesitation, because he took a step closer, his voice dropping to a more personal, almost intimate tone. "Crash, I can see that you're someone who cares deeply about this place, about your family, about the future. This project could be the answer to everything you've been looking for—a way to secure the store's future, to make a name for yourself, to be part of something bigger."

Crash's heart pounded in his chest as Leonard's words took hold. It was everything he had ever wanted—to be successful, to be recognized, to rise above the mundane life he felt trapped in. And yet, the nagging doubt remained, a small voice in the back of his mind that warned him to be careful, to not be so easily swayed.

"What would I have to do?" Crash asked, his voice quieter now, almost hesitant.

Leonard's smile widened, but there was something almost predatory in his eyes. "It's simple, really. We would need your support—your endorsement of the project, your willingness to be part of the change. You would be a face of the revitalization, someone the community could rally around. In return, you would have our full backing, our resources, our commitment to making this neighborhood—and your store—a success."

Crash swallowed hard, the weight of the decision pressing down on him. On one hand, it was everything he had dreamed of—a chance to be more than just another struggling business owner. But on the other hand, something about Leonard's offer felt too good to be true, too perfectly tailored to his desires.

Leonard's voice cut through his thoughts, soft and persuasive. "This is a rare opportunity, Crash. One that could change your life, and the lives of everyone around you. But it requires courage, vision, and a willingness to take that leap of faith."

Crash looked up at Leonard, searching the man's eyes for any sign of deceit. But Leonard's gaze was steady, unyielding, radiating confidence and control. It was hard not to be drawn in, not to believe that this was the answer to everything Crash had been searching for.

But even as he felt the pull of Leonard's words, Crash couldn't shake the unease that gnawed at him. There was a price to be paid here, one that wasn't immediately clear, and Crash knew that whatever decision he made, it would have consequences far beyond what he could see.

"I'll need to think about it," Crash finally said, his voice trembling slightly with the weight of the decision.

Leonard's smile remained, but there was a flicker of something in his eyes—impatience, perhaps, or frustration. "Of course, Crash. Take the time you need. But remember, opportunities like this don't come around every day. I believe you're the right person for this—someone who can make a real difference."

Crash nodded, his mind a whirlwind of conflicting thoughts and emotions. Leonard's pitch was compelling, persuasive, but it was also laced with a sense of danger, a feeling that this decision would set him on a path that could not easily be undone.

As Leonard left the store, the door closing softly behind him, Crash felt the full weight of what had just transpired. He had been offered a glimpse of a different future, one filled with success, recognition, and the promise of something more. But with that promise came a choice—a choice that could change everything.

Crash looked down at the folder in his hands, the words "Community Revitalization Project" staring back at him like a challenge. The temptation was strong, almost overwhelming, but so was the doubt, the fear of what aligning with Leonard might really mean.

And so, with his mind torn between the allure of success and the warning signs he couldn't ignore, Crash stood alone in the quiet of the store, at a crossroads that would define his future.

The store felt unusually quiet after Leonard's departure, the echo of the door's chime still lingering in the air. Crash stood behind the counter, the folder from Leonard resting on the worn wood surface in front of him. The weight of the decision he was facing pressed down on him, heavy and suffocating.

He ran a hand through his scruffy black hair, his mind racing in circles. Leonard's words were still fresh, playing over and over in his head—the promises of success, the visions of a thriving store, the recognition he had always craved. It was everything he had wanted, laid out so neatly, so perfectly. And yet, there was a gnawing sense of unease that he couldn't shake.

Crash's eyes drifted to the folder, its polished cover gleaming in the afternoon light. The Community Revitalization Project—it sounded so good, so right, like the answer to all his problems.

He flipped through the pages again, skimming the detailed plans and projections. On the surface, it all made sense. The neighborhood would benefit, the store would prosper, and Crash would finally have the chance to be something more than just a struggling shopkeeper. But beneath that polished veneer, something felt off. Leonard's smooth talk, his too-perfect pitch—it all felt like a carefully constructed illusion.

Crash sighed, leaning heavily on the counter as he tried to make sense of his swirling emotions. He wanted to believe in Leonard's offer, wanted to believe that this was his chance to finally make something of himself. But his gut was telling him to be careful, to not be so easily swayed by promises that seemed too good to be true.

He thought back to the conversation, to the way Leonard had so effortlessly appealed to his deepest desires. The man had known exactly what to say, exactly how to push Crash's buttons, making him feel seen, important, valued. It was intoxicating, the idea that someone like Leonard believed in him, believed in the potential of the store. But that very precision, that uncanny ability to tap into his hopes and dreams, was what made Crash suspicious.

He had seen enough in life to know that nothing came without a price. His family's struggles, the hardships they had faced—those had taught him that the world didn't just hand out success. It had to be earned, fought for, and even then, it wasn't guaranteed. So why was Leonard so eager to help? What did he really want?

Crash shook his head, trying to clear the fog of doubt that had settled in. He knew he needed to be careful, to think this through. But the allure of what Leonard was offering was hard to resist. The chance to finally escape the mediocrity that had defined his life, to be recognized, respected—it was everything he had ever wanted.

And yet, the thought of aligning with Leonard—one of Crash's greatest hero's—made his stomach twist. There was a darkness there, a sense that Leonard wasn't being entirely honest, that there was more to this project than he was letting on. Crash had felt it in the way Leonard's eyes had lingered a little too long, in the way his smile had never quite reached his eyes. There was something predatory about Leonard, something that made Crash feel like he was being lured into a trap.

But what if he was wrong? What if this really was his chance to make a difference, to change his life for the better? Was he going to let fear and doubt hold him back, keep him stuck in the same place he had always been? Or was he going to take the leap, trust in the possibility that this could be the opportunity he had been waiting for?

Crash groaned in frustration, his thoughts a tangled mess of conflicting emotions. He had never been good at making decisions, always second-guessing himself, always worrying about the consequences. And now, faced with a choice that could alter the course of his life, he was more conflicted than ever.

The store was quiet, the usual background noise of customers and conversations absent, leaving Crash alone with his thoughts. He could feel the pressure building, the weight of the decision pressing down on him. On one side, there was the safety of the familiar, the life he knew, with all its struggles and disappointments. On the other, there was the promise of something more, something bigger, but also the risk of stepping into the unknown, of aligning with someone he didn't fully trust.

Crash closed the folder and pushed it aside, unable to look at it any longer. He needed time to think, to sort through his doubts and desires, to figure out what really mattered to him. Leonard's offer was tempting, almost irresistible, but Crash knew he couldn't make this decision lightly.

He stood up from the counter, pacing the small space behind it as he tried to clear his mind. The tension in his chest tightened, the conflict between his intuition and his desires pulling him in opposite directions. He wanted to believe that Leonard's offer was genuine, that this was the opportunity he had been waiting for. But the voice in the back of his mind kept whispering, warning him to be careful, to not be so easily swayed.

As the sun began to set, casting long shadows across the store, Crash felt no closer to a decision than he had been when Leonard first walked in. The doubts and desires swirled together, a storm of emotions that left him feeling lost, uncertain, and more alone than ever.

Crash paused by the window, staring out at the street as the day slowly faded into night. He knew that whatever choice he made, it would change everything. But for now, all he could do was wrestle with the doubts and desires that consumed him, knowing that the decision he faced was one that would define his future.

Crash had barely slept the night before, his mind racing with thoughts of Leonard's pitch and the possibilities it presented. He had spent hours going over the details in the folder, trying to convince himself that this was the opportunity he had been waiting for. By morning, he had managed to push most of his doubts to the side, focusing instead on the excitement of what could be.

He needed to talk to someone about it, someone who might understand, who could help him sort through the whirlwind of emotions. And there was only one person—well, one sea lion—who came to mind.

Crash asked his mother to watch the front of the store for a while, saying he wanted to think about Leonard's offer for a while. He made his way to Fred's lair, his thoughts still buzzing with anticipation. The idea of finally being able to make something of himself, to have a real shot at success, was intoxicating. He was sure Fred would see it too, would understand why this project could be the answer to all their problems.

Fred was lounging on one of the leather couches in his lair when Crash arrived, his green bucket hat tilted slightly to the side. He looked up as Crash entered, his whiskers twitching in curiosity.

"Fred!" Crash called out, a wide grin on his face as he hurried over. "You won't believe what's happening! I've got to tell you about this incredible opportunity."

Fred raised an eyebrow—or at least, Crash imagined he did, given the way his head tilted slightly. The sea lion shifted on the couch, his dark eyes following Crash's every movement.

Crash wasted no time diving into the details, his words spilling out in a rush of enthusiasm. He told Fred about Leonard's visit, the Community Revitalization Project, and how it could completely transform the neighborhood—and, by extension, their lives. He spoke of the potential for the store to thrive, for them to be part of something bigger, something that could bring them the recognition they both deserved.

But as Crash spoke, he noticed that Fred's expression—if it could be called that—remained unchanged. The sea lion's eyes narrowed slightly, and his usually relaxed posture became more rigid. It was subtle, but Crash could tell that something was off.

When he finally finished his enthusiastic spiel, he looked at Fred, expecting some kind of reaction—support, excitement, maybe even a bark of approval. But instead, Fred simply stared at him, his gaze unreadable.

"Well?" Crash prompted, feeling a flicker of unease in the pit of his stomach. "What do you think? Isn't this amazing?"

Fred let out a low, rumbling noise—a sound that Crash had come to recognize as a sign of discontent. The sea lion shifted again, his gaze never leaving Crash's face.

"I'm not so sure about this," Fred seemed to say with his body language, his eyes reflecting a deep skepticism. He let out another rumble, his flippers slapping the ground in a way that conveyed more than words ever could.

Crash frowned, the excitement draining from his face as he realized that Fred wasn't on board. "What do you mean you're not sure? Fred, this could be our big break! Leonard believes in us—in me! He wants to help us succeed."

But Fred wasn't convinced. He let out a sharp bark, shaking his head in a clear gesture of disagreement. There was something in Leonard's offer that didn't sit right with Fred, something that made his instincts scream in warning.

Crash's frown deepened as he watched Fred's reaction, frustration bubbling up inside him. "Why are you being like this? You haven't even met Leonard. How can you just write this off?"

Fred's response was immediate. He barked again, a deeper, more urgent sound, before nudging a stack of papers on the coffee table with his nose. Crash glanced down at the papers, realizing that they were old newspaper clippings—stories about corporate takeovers, shady deals, and broken promises. Fred had clearly been doing his own research, and what he had found didn't paint a pretty picture.

Crash sighed, running a hand through his hair as he tried to make sense of Fred's skepticism. "Look, I know you're worried, but this is different. Leonard isn't like those other guys. He's offering us a real chance to make something of ourselves, to be part of something that matters."

But Fred wasn't convinced. He shook his head again, his flippers tapping the ground in a rhythmic pattern that seemed to say, "Be careful, Crash. There's more to this than you realize."

Crash felt a pang of frustration. Why couldn't Fred see what he saw? Why couldn't he understand how much this meant to Crash, how much he wanted—no, needed—this opportunity to work?

"Fred," Crash said, his voice tinged with desperation, "I know you're trying to protect me, but you have to trust me on this. I need this. We need this. It's our chance to finally get out of this rut, to be something more than just a couple of nobodies."

But Fred's eyes only darkened further, his skepticism deepening. He barked once more, a sharp, almost reprimanding sound that made Crash wince.

"Why won't you just support me on this?" Crash snapped, the words tumbling out before he could stop them. "Why can't you see that this is a good thing?"

Fred's gaze softened slightly, but the concern in his eyes remained. He let out a low, mournful sound, as if trying to communicate the danger he sensed, the risks that Crash wasn't seeing.

Crash sighed, the fight draining out of him. He knew Fred was only trying to look out for him, but it was hard not to feel frustrated, even betrayed, by Fred's lack of enthusiasm. He had expected support, validation, but instead, he was met with doubt and caution.

"Fine," Crash muttered, stepping back from the couch. "You don't have to agree with me. But I'm not giving up on this, Fred. This could be our only chance."

Fred watched him quietly, his eyes filled with an unspoken warning. Crash could feel the tension in the air, the first major rift between them forming right before his eyes.

The silence stretched out between them, heavy and uncomfortable. Crash turned away, his heart heavy with disappointment and frustration. He had wanted Fred to be excited, to share in the vision of what could be. But instead, all he felt was the weight of Fred's skepticism, pulling him back from the dream he so desperately wanted to believe in.

As he left the lair, the doubts Fred had planted began to take root, intertwining with his desires in a way that left him more conflicted than ever. Crash knew he was standing on the edge of a precipice, and the decision he made next could either lift him to new heights or send him plummeting into the abyss.

Crash paced back and forth in Fred's lair, his frustration growing with each step. The initial disappointment from Fred's skepticism had now blossomed into something sharper—an irritation that gnawed at him, fed by the feeling that Fred just didn't understand what this opportunity meant to him.

Fred, meanwhile, sat on the edge of the leather couch, his gaze fixed on Crash, his expression unreadable. He had sensed the tension in the air, the shift in Crash's demeanor, and he knew that their conversation was far from over.

"Fred, I don't get it," Crash began, his voice tight with frustration. "Why are you so against this? You've seen the neighborhood—it's falling apart. The store isn't doing great, and we both know it. This project could change everything."

Fred tilted his head slightly, his eyes narrowing as he let out a low, rumbling sound. It was a sound that Crash had come to recognize as Fred's way of saying, "Think carefully, Crash. There's more at play here than you realize."

But Crash wasn't in the mood to think carefully. His desperation for change, for something better, had clouded his judgment, making it difficult for him to see beyond the promise of success that Leonard had dangled in front of him.

"I know you're worried," Crash continued, trying to keep his tone calm, "but Leonard isn't the enemy here. He's trying to help us—help the whole neighborhood. Why can't you see that?"

Fred's response was immediate. He barked sharply, shaking his head as if to emphasize his point. There was a firmness in his posture, a resolve that Crash hadn't seen before. Fred wasn't just skeptical—he was deeply concerned, and he wasn't going to back down.

Crash stopped pacing, turning to face Fred with a look of exasperation. "You're acting like this is some kind of trap, but it's not. It's a chance to finally get out of this rut, to make something of ourselves. Don't you want that?"

Fred's eyes softened slightly, but the concern in his gaze remained. He let out a soft, mournful sound, his flippers tapping the ground in a rhythmic pattern that seemed to say, "There's more to this than you think, Crash. You need to look beyond the surface."

Crash's irritation flared. "Look beyond the surface? What does that even mean? You're being too cautious, too suspicious of everything. But sometimes you have to take a risk, Fred. Sometimes you have to believe that things can get better."

Fred's response was more measured this time. He let out a low rumble, his gaze steady and serious. It was as if he were trying to convey something complex, something that couldn't be easily put into words. Crash could feel the weight of Fred's experiences, the knowledge that came from years of living on the edge of human society, seeing both its wonders and its darker side.

"Fred," Crash said, his voice growing more insistent, "I imagine you've seen things, been through things that I can't even imagine. But that doesn't mean everyone is out to get us. Leonard isn't some villain—he's offering us a lifeline."

But Fred wasn't convinced. He shook his head again, his expression darkening as he let out a series of sharp barks. To Crash, it felt like Fred was trying to warn him, to protect him from something he couldn't see.

"What are you so afraid of?" Crash snapped, the frustration boiling over. "Why can't you just trust me on this? For once, I want to make my own decisions, to take control of my own life. Is that so wrong?"

Fred's response was immediate and forceful. He barked loudly, his flippers slapping the ground with a force that made Crash take a step back. There was a fire in Fred's eyes now, a determination that Crash hadn't seen before. Fred wasn't just being cautious—he was trying to prevent Crash from making a mistake, a mistake that could have far-reaching consequences.

Fred, still visibly upset, waddled over to his computer, his flippers moving with purpose as he began typing on the keyboard. Crash watched him curiously, sensing that Fred was about to reveal something important. After a few moments, the screen filled with words, and Fred gestured for Crash to read.

"Never trust an offer that seems too good, Crash," Fred typed, his tone serious. "Let me tell you a story—a story about a young sea lion named Arf Arf."

Crash leaned in, his eyes scanning the words as Fred continued.

"Once upon a time, there lived a young sea lion named Arf Arf. Arf would laugh, and play, and do all the weird things that young sea lion pups do. He spent his days lounging at the Wharf, munching on snacks tossed by tourists. Life was simple and carefree. But when the slow season arrived and the tourists disappeared, Arf would wander deep into the bay, searching for whatever tasty treats he could find.

One day, feeling braver than usual, Arf Arf decided to venture into the open ocean. Now, his mother and father had always warned him that the ocean was dangerous—filled with fishermen and massive ships that could swallow up a sea lion, never to be seen again. But Arf thought he was different—smarter, faster, better than any other sea lion. He believed nothing could harm him.

So, Arf ventured far, far away from home, deep into the open ocean, where he stumbled upon something strange—a line of lovely, fresh fish, all strung together and just waiting to be eaten. It was a feast like nothing he had ever seen. But the moment Arf took his first bite, he was hooked—literally. The next thing he knew, he was being pulled up, up, up, onto the deck of a giant green boat.

The men on the boat wore green, spotted clothes and spoke in hushed voices. They took Arf deep into the belly of the ship, where other men in white coats waited with sharp needles and strong straps. They ran experiment after experiment on him, pushing him to the brink of death over and over again. It was a nightmare, and Arf was terrified. But Arf was also stubborn and strong—he fought with everything he had to survive.

As time passed, Arf began to learn the patterns of the men who held him captive. He studied how the straps that held him down worked, how the locks on the doors turned, the sound of their footsteps, and the faces of the lazy ones who let their guard down. He paid attention to every detail, waiting for the right moment to make his move.

Then, one day, Arf decided it was time to escape. In a blaze of glory, he put his plan into action. He made his way up, up, up through the ship, setting off decoy alarms, confusing the guards, and even triggering the sprinklers over vats of dry ice to cover his trail with thick, billowing clouds of smoke. The ship was in chaos, and Arf was almost free.

Finally, Arf reached the deck of the boat, the open ocean just a leap away. But just as he was about to dive to freedom, he heard the cocking of a gun behind him. He spun around and, with a surge of strength, knocked out the final guard before he could pull the trigger. The man fell, his bucket hat knocked from his head in the struggle.

In a final act of defiance, Arf picked up that hat and placed it on his own head. It was more than just a trophy—it was a symbol. A symbol of his resistance against the chains that had tried to strip away his identity as a sea lion and replace it with the burden of living between two worlds."

Crash finished reading, his eyes wide as he absorbed the gravity of Fred's story. Fred, or rather Arf Arf, had been through more than Crash could have ever imagined. It was no wonder Fred was so skeptical of Leonard and his too-good-to-be-true offers.

Fred looked up at Crash, his eyes serious as he typed the final words: "Remember, Crash—never trust an offer that seems too good. Sometimes, what's behind it is far worse than you can imagine."

Crash nodded slowly, his mind racing with the implications of what Fred had just shared. Leonard's offer suddenly felt more ominous, and Crash couldn't shake the feeling that Fred was right— that they were being drawn into something much larger and more dangerous than they had anticipated.

But Crash was too wrapped up in his own desires to see it. "I'm not a kid anymore, Fred!" he shouted, the words coming out harsher than he intended. "I can make my own choices, and I'm choosing to trust Leonard. You don't have to agree with me, but you don't get to tell me what to do. Just because bad things happened to you, doesn't mean they'll happen every time."

Fred's gaze hardened, the tension between them thickening. He let out a low, rumbling growl, his expression one of both disappointment and concern. It was clear that Fred believed Crash was making a grave mistake, and the realization that he couldn't convince Crash otherwise weighed heavily on him. Sometimes holding a colt too hard makes the just kick even harder.

The silence that followed was heavy, filled with unspoken words and unresolved tension. Crash could feel the rift forming between them, a chasm that hadn't been there before. It was a painful realization, one that made his heart ache, but his stubbornness wouldn't allow him to back down.

"Fine," Crash muttered, his voice tight with anger as he turned away from Fred. "If you don't want to support me, that's your choice. But I'm not giving up on this. This could be incredible. It's the best thing that has ever come into my life, and I'm not going to let it go!"

Fred watched him quietly, his expression unreadable but the concern still evident in his eyes. He let out a final, mournful bark, as if to say, "I hope you know what you're doing, Crash."

But Crash was too consumed by his frustration to respond. The sting of Fred's lack of support cut deep, and all he could focus on was the dream that Leonard had dangled in front of him—the chance to finally be something more, to escape the life he felt trapped in.

Without another word, Crash stormed out of the lair, his footsteps echoing sharply against the cold, stone walls. The door slammed shut behind him with a finality that reverberated through the empty space, leaving Fred alone in the silence.

As Crash hurried away, his anger only grew, each step fueling the fire of his defiance. He couldn't believe that Fred, his closest friend, the one who had always stood by him, couldn't see how important this opportunity was. Why couldn't Fred just trust him for once? Why did he always have to be so cautious, so skeptical of anything that offered even a glimpse of hope?

The more Crash thought about it, the angrier he became. By the time he reached the street, his resolve had hardened into something unyielding. Fred didn't understand—couldn't understand—what this meant to him. But Crash wasn't going to let that stop him. He was

going to prove Fred wrong. He was going to make something of himself, no matter what it took.

Back in the lair, Fred watched the door with a heavy heart, the final echoes of Crash's departure still lingering in the air. He knew he couldn't protect Crash from everything, no matter how much he wanted to. Some lessons can only be taught through experience.

The lair felt emptier than ever before. The usual hum of the monitors and the soft jazz playing in the background did little to fill the void that Crash had left behind. Fred sat in his usual spot on the leather couch, but there was no comfort to be found in the familiar surroundings. His green bucket hat, which usually brought him a sense of playful pride, now sat crooked on his head, a symbol of the disarray he felt inside.

Fred let out a long, mournful sigh, his flippers resting limply at his sides. The argument with Crash replayed in his mind, each word cutting deeper than the last. He had only wanted to protect Crash, to make him see the potential dangers of Leonard's project, but instead, he had driven a wedge between them. And now, he wasn't sure if that wedge could ever be removed.

The decision weighed heavily on Fred, but the more he thought about it, the more he realized that he needed to give Crash space. Maybe he had been too overprotective, too insistent on his own perspective without considering how much this opportunity meant to Crash. Maybe he had failed to recognize the depth of Crash's desperation for change, for something more than the life he was living.

Fred's eyes flicked to the door, the one Crash had walked out of not long ago. A part of him wanted to go after Crash, to try to make things right, to apologize for pushing too hard. But another part of him knew that it wouldn't be that simple. The hurt and frustration between them ran too deep, and trying to force a reconciliation now might only make things worse.

No, Fred decided, it was better to lay low for a while, to give Crash the time and space he needed to sort through his emotions. Maybe if he stayed out of the way, Crash would have the chance to think things over, to see the situation more clearly. And maybe, just maybe, he would come to understand why Fred had been so adamant in his warnings.

Fred let out a low, mournful whimper, his flippers twitching as he struggled with his emotions. He wasn't used to feeling this vulnerable, this uncertain. His life had always been about survival, about navigating the human world with a mix of caution and curiosity. But this—this was different. This was about something deeper, something that touched the very core of who he was.

He glanced around the lair, his gaze lingering on the things that had once brought him comfort—the monitors with their endless streams of data, the cozy corners where he could retreat and think, the hidden nooks where he stored his little treasures. But now, all of it felt hollow, meaningless without Crash to share it with.

Fred shifted uncomfortably on the couch, his thoughts drifting to the quiet understanding that had seemed to pass between them without the need for words. He missed it already, missed the sense of belonging that had come with their friendship.

But Fred knew he couldn't force Crash to see things his way. He couldn't make him understand the dangers of Leonard's project if Crash wasn't ready to listen. And so, with a heavy heart, Fred made the decision to step back, to let Crash make his own choices, even if it meant watching from the sidelines.

Chapter 12

Welcome to the Network

It wasn't easy. Every instinct in Fred's body screamed at him to protect Crash, to keep him safe from the threats that Fred had learned to navigate over the years. But he also knew that Crash needed to find his own path, to make his own mistakes, even if those mistakes led to pain.

Fred let out another sigh, his gaze drifting to the door once more. He knew what he had to do, but that didn't make it any less painful. For now, he would lay low, avoid the store, and give Crash the space he needed. It was the only way Fred could think of to preserve their friendship, to keep the hope alive that, one day, they could find their way back to each other.

With a final, sorrowful glance around the lair, Fred settled into a quiet corner, his heart heavy with the weight of his decision. The lair, once a sanctuary, now felt like a prison—a place of solitude where he would wait, hoping that time and distance might heal the rift that had formed between them.

As the lair grew silent, the only sound the faint hum of the monitors, Fred curled up on the couch, his bucket hat slipping down over his eyes. He would wait, and he would hope. But for now, he would do what he had never done before—he would stay hidden, away from the world, away from Crash, until the time was right to return.

And as Fred closed his eyes, the sadness that enveloped him was a reminder of just how much was at stake, and how much he had come to care for the boy who had stumbled into his life.

The sun was shining brightly as Crash walked through the streets of his neighborhood, but the warmth of the day did little to lift the heaviness in his heart. The bustling activity around him, the distant hum of the city, felt muted, as if he were moving through the world in a daze. For the first time in a long while, Crash felt truly alone.

His phone buzzed in his pocket, dozens of notifications drawing his attention. He pulled it out and glanced at the screen. The numbers were staggering—thousands of likes, comments, and shares on his latest post. "The algorithm must have finally caught onto my photo of Fred," he thought, unaware that Leonard had artificially created the sudden surge in interest on Crash's account. It was everything he had dreamed of, everything he had worked for. The fight with Fred blunting any feelings of remorse for betraying their new found friendship.

But as he stared at the screen, a hollow feeling settled in his chest. The validation he had once craved now felt empty, devoid of the satisfaction he had expected it to bring. Crash had thought that fame, recognition, and success would fill the void inside him, but instead, it only seemed to highlight how disconnected he felt from the people around him.

He remembered back to Fred's story. Only now recognizing the pain and trauma that Fred must have been through. Crash was really only thinking about himself, what this project could mean for him. Now, with his post out to the world, that friendship was done for.

He walked past a group of teenagers, their laughter ringing in his ears as they huddled together, sharing jokes and stories. Crash watched them for a moment, a pang of longing tugging at his heart. He used to have that—companionship, friendship, people who understood him. But now, all of that felt distant, like a memory from another life.

Crash shoved his phone back into his pocket and kept walking, his steps slower, more deliberate. The streets he had grown up on, the familiar sights and sounds of the neighborhood, now felt alien to him. It was as if he were an outsider in his own world, watching from the sidelines as life went on without him.

The store loomed ahead, its worn facade a stark contrast to the vibrant energy of the city around it. Crash hesitated at the entrance, his hand hovering over the door handle. The thought of going inside, of facing his mother and grandmother, filled him with a sense of dread. He knew they would ask him what was wrong, why he seemed so distant, so troubled. And he didn't have the words to explain it to them, didn't know how to tell them that despite his success, he had never felt more alone.

With a heavy sigh, Crash pushed the door open and stepped inside. The familiar smell of the store greeted him, the scent of fresh produce and old wood mingling in the air. His mother was behind the counter, her warm smile fading as she caught sight of him.

"Crash, honey, are you okay?" she asked, her voice filled with concern. "You look tired."

Crash forced a smile, nodding quickly. "I'm fine, Mom. Just a long day."

"Did you make a decision about the project?"

He mumbled something about needing to get some air and quickly made his way to the back of the store, needing to escape the concerned looks his mother was giving him. The storeroom was cool and dimly lit, the boxes and crates stacked haphazardly around him providing a small sense of comfort. Crash leaned against the wall, closing his eyes as he tried to sort through the mess of emotions swirling inside him.

He had thought that success would bring him happiness, that the recognition he had longed for would finally make him feel like he belonged. But instead, it had only made him feel more isolated, more disconnected from the people who mattered most.

And then there was Fred. The memory of their argument, of the hurt and disappointment in Fred's eyes, made Crash's chest ache. He had pushed away the one friend who had always been there for him, the one person who had understood him better than anyone else. And for what? For a few thousand likes, for a taste of fame that now felt bitter in his mouth.

Crash pulled out his phone again, staring at the screen as the notifications continued to roll in. It all seemed so pointless now, so shallow. He had been chasing after something that had never truly mattered, and in the process, he had lost sight of the things that did.

The loneliness crashed over him like a wave, pulling him under, making it hard to breathe. He had never felt so alone, so cut off from the world around him. And the worst part was that it was all his own doing.

Crash let out a shaky breath, his eyes stinging with unshed tears. He didn't know how to fix this, didn't know how to bridge the gap that had formed between him and Fred, between him and his family. All he knew was that he couldn't keep going like this, couldn't keep pretending that everything was fine when it so clearly wasn't.

But even as he stood there, feeling the weight of his choice pressing down on him.

Like pulling off a band-aid Crash typed his initials and signed his name on the contract emailed to him by Leonard's assistant and hit send. He messed up with Fred, but maybe he can do better for the store.

Soon after the hum of construction machinery filled the air, mingling with the distant chatter of workers and the occasional beep of reversing trucks. The Community Revitalization Project was in full swing just hours after Crash signed his contract with Leonard, and the neighborhood was starting to transform before Crash's eyes.

As the days turned into weeks, Crash found himself more involved in the project than he had anticipated. Leonard had been true to his word, giving Crash a front-row seat to the changes taking place. Crash's role had grown from simply endorsing the project to actively participating in meetings, giving input on decisions, and even appearing in promotional materials. It was everything he had wanted—visibility, recognition, a chance to be part of something bigger.

The first signs of change were subtle. New digital kiosks were installed on street corners, sleek and modern, offering everything from directions to local advertisements. At first, they seemed like a convenience, a step toward modernizing the area. But as more kiosks appeared, they began to feel omnipresent, their screens flickering with images that felt eerily uniform, as if the neighborhood was being branded with a new, sanitized identity.

Crash watched as residents hesitated in front of the kiosks, their expressions a mix of curiosity and discomfort. The older generation, in particular, seemed wary, their eyes lingering on the screens with a hint of suspicion. But the younger crowd embraced the new technology, snapping selfies and sharing them online, oblivious to the growing disconnect between the old and the new.

Any graffiti or vandalism on them, fixed before the next day.

The project's influence extended to the local businesses as well. Leonard's team offered to "help" with storefront renovations, replacing old signs with digital displays, installing new lighting, and even suggesting changes to store layouts. Crash's family store was among the first to receive the makeover.

Crash's mother and grandmother were hesitant at first, unsure about the sleek new sign that now glowed brightly over the entrance. The old wooden sign, hand-painted by Crash's grandfather years ago, was gone, replaced by something modern and impersonal. The new layout inside the store was efficient but lacked the warmth and charm that had once made it feel like home.

Crash tried to reassure them, reminding himself that this was progress, that the changes would bring in more customers, more business. But even as he spoke the words, he couldn't shake the feeling that something important had been lost, something that couldn't be replaced by flashy technology or polished design.

The old security cameras with the broken VCR, replaced with a brand new network based boxed branded with a subsidiary Leonard owned.

The streets themselves were changing too. Leonard's team had installed a network of sensors and cameras, ostensibly for "security and efficiency." The idea was to create a "smart neighborhood," where everything was interconnected, where data could be used to improve daily life. But the effect was unsettling. The once lively, chaotic streets now felt controlled, monitored, as if the neighborhood itself was being watched.

Crash walked the streets one evening, the glow of the new streetlights casting harsh, artificial shadows. He noticed the way people moved differently now, more aware of the cameras, more cautious. The vibrant street life that had once defined the neighborhood seemed to be fading, replaced by a sterile, ordered environment that felt out of place.

The people who had called the streets home, gone. Pushed out, locked out from their home.

As the project continued, the community's reaction grew increasingly divided. Some residents welcomed the changes, excited by the prospect of modernization and the potential for economic growth. They praised the project, calling it a much-needed revitalization of a struggling area.

But others weren't so sure. There were whispers of unease, of fear that the project was erasing the character of the neighborhood, that the technology was more invasive than it appeared. The older residents, in particular, seemed to sense something deeper, something that couldn't be captured by the shiny new facade.

Crash found himself caught between the two sides, unsure where he stood. He wanted to believe in the project, wanted to trust that Leonard's vision was a positive one. But the growing sense of unease, the small, nagging doubts that he had tried to ignore, were becoming harder to push aside.

One evening, after another long day of meetings and planning sessions, Crash sat alone in the store, staring at the new digital sign outside. The notifications on his phone buzzed incessantly, messages of support and excitement pouring in from his growing online following. But the excitement he had once felt was gone, replaced by a heavy sense of doubt.

He thought about Fred, about the warnings his friend had tried to give him. The argument they had had, the rift that had formed between them, weighed heavily on Crash's mind. Fred had seen the dangers, had sensed the underlying threat in Leonard's project, and Crash had dismissed him, blinded by his own desires.

Now, as he looked around at the neighborhood that was slowly changing before his eyes, Crash couldn't help but wonder if Fred had been right all along. The project was progressing, yes, but at what cost? The community felt different, disconnected, as if something vital had been stripped away.

Crash sighed, leaning back in his chair as he tried to sort through the conflicting emotions that churned inside him. He had wanted this so badly—had wanted to be part of something bigger, to make a difference. But now, with the changes unfolding around him, he couldn't shake the feeling that he had made a terrible mistake.

The effects of Leonard's influence were becoming more apparent, and Crash was beginning to see the cracks in the facade, the shadows that lurked beneath the surface.

The lair was quiet, the usual hum of activity reduced to a soft, almost imperceptible buzz as Fred sat in front of his array of monitors. His green bucket hat was tilted forward, casting a shadow over his intense gaze as he focused on the screen in front of him. The days of laying low had given Fred time to think, time to watch from the sidelines as the neighborhood began to change.

Fred had been wary of Leonard from the start, but now that he was no longer in regular contact with Crash, his instincts told him that something was seriously wrong. The technology that Leonard had introduced into the neighborhood was too intrusive. Fred had seen enough in his time to know when something was off, and this project reeked of hidden agendas.

Fred was already weeks into his investigation. He started by tapping into the digital kiosks that had sprung up around the neighborhood. At first glance, they appeared to be harmless—providing information, displaying advertisements, and connecting people to local services. But Fred knew better than to take things at face value.

His flippers moved deftly across the keyboard, bypassing the basic security protocols with ease. He had learned a lot during his time as a top tier hacker, enough to recognize that these kiosks were far from ordinary. As he dug deeper into the system, Fred's eyes narrowed in concentration. There were layers of code here that didn't belong, subroutines hidden beneath the surface that pointed to something far more sinister.

Fred's heart pounded as he uncovered the truth. The kiosks weren't just gathering basic data—they were part of a vast surveillance network, recording everything from facial recognition data to personal conversations. The sensors and cameras installed throughout the neighborhood were all feeding into the same system, creating a comprehensive map of everyone's movements, interactions, and behaviors.

The implications were chilling. Leonard's project wasn't about revitalizing the neighborhood—it was about control. Fred could see it now, the way the technology was subtly shaping people's lives, influencing their decisions, and monitoring their every move. This wasn't just an invasion of privacy; it was an assault on the very essence of the community.

Fred let out a low growl, his flippers clenching into fists. He had to act quickly, but he also had to be careful. Leonard was powerful, and the reach of his project extended far beyond what Fred had initially suspected. But Fred wasn't about to let Leonard get away with it. Not when the stakes were this high, and certainly not when Crash and the rest of the community were at risk.

He pulled up more data, his flippers flying over the keys as he hacked deeper into the system. The more he uncovered, the more horrified he became. It wasn't just surveillance—there were also elements of psychological manipulation embedded in the technology. The digital ads, the suggested routes, even the layout of the new storefronts—they were all designed to subtly influence behavior, pushing people to conform to a new, sanitized version of the neighborhood.

Fred's mind raced as he processed the information. He could see now how Leonard had played on Crash's desires, how he had used the promise of success and recognition to manipulate him into supporting the project. And Fred had stood by, watching it happen, powerless to stop it—until now.

He knew what he had to do. This was no longer just about protecting Crash; it was about protecting everyone. Fred needed to expose Leonard's true intentions, to show the community what was really happening before it was too late. But he couldn't do it alone. He would need help, and more importantly, he would need to regain his trust with Crash.

The thought of facing Crash again after their argument made Fred's heart ache, but he knew it was necessary. There was no time for pride, no time to dwell on past mistakes. Crash needed to know the truth, and Fred needed to make things right between them. Besides, one of them needed to be the adult.

Fred gathered the data he had uncovered, compiling it into a secure file that he could share with Crash when the time was right. He knew that this would be dangerous, that Leonard wouldn't take kindly to being exposed. But Fred didn't care. He had been hiding long enough, and it was time to come out of the shadows.

With one last glance at the monitors, Fred slipped out of the lair, moving with purpose through the hidden passages he knew so well. The lair was silent in his absence, the monitors still glowing faintly in the darkness. But there was a sense of anticipation in the air, a feeling that the calm before the storm was about to break.

Fred was on the move, and the truth was about to come to light.

The morning air was crisp as Crash walked down the street, the familiar sights of the neighborhood passing by in a blur. He had been so wrapped up in the excitement of the project, in the thrill of finally being recognized, that he had pushed aside the nagging doubts that had lingered in the back of his mind. But now, those doubts were impossible to ignore.

Crash passed by one of the new digital kiosks, its bright screen flickering with images and ads. A group of teenagers stood nearby, engrossed in the latest trend, their faces lit by the cold glow of the screen. Crash paused, watching them for a moment. There was something unsettling about the way they were drawn to the kiosk, almost as if they were being hypnotized by the flashing images.

He continued walking, his eyes drifting over the storefronts that had been "revitalized" as part of the project. The old, weathered signs were gone, replaced by sleek, digital displays that all seemed to blend together in a uniform sheen. The unique character of each shop, the little quirks that had once defined them, had been smoothed over, replaced by something more polished—and less personal.

Crash couldn't shake the feeling that the neighborhood was losing something essential, something that couldn't be replaced by modern technology or flashy renovations. He had thought the project would bring new life to the area, but instead, it seemed to be draining the life out of it, one small change at a time.

As he rounded the corner, Crash noticed an older woman standing in front of what used to be a beloved local bakery. The shop had been a staple of the community for decades, known for its hand-painted sign and warm, inviting atmosphere. But now, the sign was gone, replaced by a digital display advertising "Artisan Baked Goods" in bold, impersonal letters.

The man's face was etched with sadness as she stared at the display, his hand resting on the doorframe as if she were trying to hold on to a memory that was slipping away. Crash recognized him as Mr. Ruiz, a longtime resident of the neighborhood and a regular customer at his family's store.

"Mr. Ruiz?" Crash called out gently as he approached her.

He turned to him, his eyes filled with a mixture of confusion and sorrow. "Oh, Crash," she said softly. "I was just... I was just thinking about how much this place has changed. I used to come here every morning, you know. They made the best empanadas. But now... it doesn't feel the same."

Crash nodded, his heart heavy with a growing sense of unease. "I know what you mean. The project was supposed to help the neighborhood, but... I'm starting to wonder if it's doing more harm than good."

Mr. Ruiz looked at him closely, as if searching for something in his expression. "It's not just the shops, Crash," he said quietly. "It's the people. I've been here a long time, and I've never seen folks act the way they're acting now. Everyone's so... distant. Like they're not really here anymore, not really connected to each other."

Crash felt a chill run down his spine. He had noticed it too—the way people seemed more distracted, more disconnected. The sense of community that had always been the heart of the neighborhood was fading, replaced by something colder, more isolated.

"You think it's because of the project?" Crash asked, his voice tinged with doubt and fear.

Mr. Ruiz hesitated, then nodded slowly. "I don't know what it is exactly, but something's not right. It's like... like the neighborhood's being taken over by something we don't understand. And I'm worried, Crash. I'm worried about what's going to happen to us, to all of us."

Crash's stomach tightened as Mr. Ruiz's words echoed the fears he had been trying to ignore. He had been so eager to believe in the project, to see it as a way to improve his life, that he hadn't stopped to consider the cost. But now, the signs were impossible to ignore.

"I'm worried too," Crash admitted, his voice barely above a whisper. "But I don't know what to do about it. I mean… what if we're too late? What if the project's already gone too far?"

Mr. Ruiz placed a gentle hand on his arm, his touch warm and reassuring. "It's never too late, Crash. We have to watch out for each other, and we have to be willing to fight for what really matters."

Crash nodded, the weight of his words sinking in. He had been so focused on his own dreams, on his own desires, that he had lost sight of the bigger picture. But now, with Mr. Ruiz's concerns adding to his own growing doubts, he knew he couldn't ignore the signs any longer.

As Crash walked away from the bakery, his mind was a whirlwind of thoughts and emotions. The subtle changes in the neighborhood, the growing disconnect among the people, the cold, calculating nature of the technology—everything was beginning to add up, painting a picture that was far darker than he had imagined.

Crash's doubts were no longer just whispers in the back of his mind. They were loud, insistent, impossible to ignore. And as he continued his walk, his heart heavy with the weight of realization, he knew that he was getting closer to the truth—a truth that he had been too blind, too eager to see.

The tension inside him reached its peak, a knot of fear and determination that spurred him to action. He couldn't keep pretending that everything was fine, couldn't keep pushing aside the signs that something was very, very wrong. It was time to confront the reality of what was happening in his neighborhood, no matter how difficult, no matter how painful.

Fred sat hunched over his monitors, his flippers tapping rhythmically against the keyboard. The dim light from the screens cast long shadows across the lair, accentuating the intensity in Fred's eyes as he delved deeper into Leonard's system. Hours had passed, but Fred's determination had only grown stronger with each passing moment.

He had uncovered layers of surveillance and manipulation embedded in the technology, but something told Fred that he hadn't yet reached the heart of the operation. There was more to Leonard's project than met the eye—something darker, more insidious—and Fred knew he had to find it before it was too late.

His flippers moved faster, bypassing firewalls and security protocols with practiced ease. Fred's experience with advanced systems and his innate intelligence made him uniquely suited to this task, and he was determined to use every ounce of that knowledge to protect his community.

Suddenly, Fred's eyes widened as he stumbled upon a hidden backdoor—a flaw in the system's security that allowed access to the core data without triggering any alarms. Fred hesitated for a moment, realizing the significance of what he had found. This was it—the breakthrough he had been searching for.

With a deep breath, Fred pressed a few more keys, accessing the backdoor and diving into the heart of Leonard's network. The screen flickered as lines of code and data scrolled rapidly, revealing the full extent of Leonard's surveillance and data collection.

Fred's heart sank as the truth unfolded before him. The system wasn't just monitoring the neighborhood—it was tracking individual residents, recording their movements, conversations, and even their most private moments. Every interaction, every decision, was being analyzed and stored, creating detailed profiles that could be used to manipulate and control.

Fred's flippers clenched into fists as he realized the depth of Leonard's deception. This wasn't just about revitalizing the neighborhood or increasing efficiency—this was about power. Leonard was using the project to gain control over the community, to shape it according to his own twisted vision, and to exploit the people who lived there for his own gain.

The implications were staggering. Leonard had access to information that could destroy lives, ruin reputations, and undermine the very fabric of the community. And all of it was being done under the guise of progress and improvement.

Fred's mind raced as he considered the consequences. If Leonard's true intentions were exposed, the entire project would come crashing down—but only if Fred acted quickly. He had to warn Crash, had to show him the evidence and make him understand the danger they were all in.

But Fred knew that time was running out. Leonard's surveillance network was vast, and it wouldn't take long for him to realize that someone had accessed the backdoor. Fred needed to move fast, and he needed to be careful.

With a sense of urgency, Fred began compiling the data he had uncovered, encrypting it and preparing it to be shared with Crash. He knew that Crash had been growing increasingly doubtful about the project, and this would be the final piece of the puzzle—the proof that Crash needed to see the truth.

As Fred worked, his thoughts drifted to Crash, to the rift that had formed between them. He regretted the harsh words they had exchanged, the distance that had grown between them. But there was no time for self-pity. Fred had to set things right, had to protect Crash and the community they both cared about.

Once the data was securely stored, Fred grabbed a small device—a portable drive that he could use to transfer the files to Crash without leaving a digital trace. He knew that Leonard would be monitoring the usual channels, so he needed to be discreet.

With the device in hand, Fred made his way to the exit of the lair, his mind focused on the task ahead. He had uncovered the truth, and now it was time to act. The stakes were higher than ever.

Chapter 13
When Machines Dream of Order

The sun had dipped low in the sky as Crash made his way back toward the store. His thoughts were a tangled mess, his mind still reeling from the doubts and suspicions that had been building inside him. The conversation with Mr. Ruiz had only deepened his unease, and now he felt like he was on the edge of something big— something that would change everything.

Crash reached the alleyway that led to the back entrance of the store, his steps slowing as he approached. A sense of trepidation settled over him, a feeling that something—or someone—was waiting for him. He paused for a moment, gathering his thoughts, before taking a deep breath and stepping into the alley.

As he rounded the corner, Crash's heart skipped a beat. There, standing in the shadows, was Fred. The sea lion's green bucket hat was tilted slightly to the side, his dark eyes fixed on Crash with a mix of determination and something that looked like regret.

For a moment, neither of them spoke. The tension between them was palpable, a reminder of the harsh words they had exchanged and the rift that had formed between them. But beneath that tension was something else—an unspoken understanding that they needed each other now more than ever.

Crash was the first to break the silence. "Fred…" he began, his voice uncertain, almost hesitant. "What are you doing here?"

Fred let out a low, rumbling sound, his flippers twitching nervously. He took a tentative step forward, his gaze never leaving Crash's face. The sea lion's eyes were filled with a mixture of apology and urgency, as if he were trying to convey just how much he regretted their fallout—and just how important it was that they set things right.

"I… I've been thinking," Crash continued, his voice trembling slightly. "About everything. About the project, about Leonard… and about us. I was wrong, Fred. I didn't listen to you when I should have. And now… I think you were right all along."

Fred's eyes softened, and he let out a soft, mournful bark, as if to say, "I'm sorry too, Crash. I never wanted to hurt you. I was just trying to protect you."

Crash swallowed hard, taking a step closer to Fred. The tension between them began to ease, replaced by a growing sense of relief. "I've been seeing things, Fred. The way the neighborhood's changing, the way people are acting… something's not right. I've been ignoring it because I didn't want to admit that I might have made a mistake. But I can't ignore it anymore."

Fred nodded, his gaze filled with understanding. He reached into a small pouch he had slung across his back and pulled out the portable drive he had prepared. With a determined bark, he held it out to Crash, his eyes urging the boy to take it.

Crash hesitated for only a moment before reaching out and taking the drive from Fred's flipper. As their hands met, Crash felt a surge of emotion—a mixture of guilt, regret, and a renewed sense of purpose. He knew that this was the moment they had both been waiting for, the moment when they could finally set things right.

"What's on this?" Crash asked, his voice quiet but steady.

Fred barked again, a sharp, affirmative sound. He tapped the drive with his flipper, then motioned to the nearby store, indicating that they needed to go inside and look at the contents together.

Crash nodded, understanding the urgency in Fred's gesture. He led the way into the store, the familiar surroundings offering a small measure of comfort as they made their way to the back room. Crash quickly booted up the old desktop computer that still sat on his grandmother's sewing table, inserting the drive into the USB port.

The screen flickered to life, displaying a series of files that Fred had compiled during his investigation. As Crash clicked through them, his eyes widened in shock. The evidence was all there—the surveillance, the data collection, the psychological manipulation. Everything Leonard had been doing, everything Fred had uncovered, was laid out in stark detail.

"This is… this is unbelievable," Crash muttered, his voice filled with a mixture of horror and disbelief. "He's been watching us, manipulating us… all this time?"

Fred nodded solemnly, his expression grave. He let out a low growl, a sound that conveyed his anger and determination to put an end to Leonard's plans.

Crash turned to Fred, his eyes filled with determination. "We have to stop him, Fred. We can't let him get away with this. But we can't do it alone. We need to get this information out to the community, to show them what's really going on."

As they finalized their plan, the tension that had once hung over them began to dissipate, replaced by a sense of purpose and resolve. The emotional wounds of their argument were still there, but they had been healed by the understanding that they needed each other now more than ever.

The dim light from the computer screen illuminated the small back room of the store, casting shadows that danced across the walls. Crash leaned forward, his eyes glued to the monitor as Fred navigated through the files he had uncovered. The air was thick with tension, the weight of what they were about to see pressing down on them both.

Fred's flippers moved with precision, opening file after file, each one revealing more of the dark underbelly of Leonard's project. Crash's heart pounded in his chest, his pulse quickening with each new piece of evidence. He had known something was wrong, had felt it in his gut, but seeing it laid out in front of him like this was something else entirely.

"This… this is insane," Crash muttered, his voice barely above a whisper. "I had no idea it was this bad."

Fred let out a low growl, his eyes narrowing as he opened a particularly damning file. The screen filled with data—surveillance footage, records of conversations, detailed profiles of residents. It was all there, meticulously cataloged and analyzed. Leonard's project wasn't just about revitalizing the neighborhood; it was about control, manipulation, and exploitation.

Crash's hands clenched into fists as he stared at the evidence, anger and fear swirling inside him. "He's been watching everyone," he said, his voice trembling with disbelief. "Tracking their every move, listening to their conversations... even influencing their decisions. This isn't just about making money—he's trying to control the entire community."

Fred barked in agreement, his flippers tapping the keyboard to bring up more files. The deeper they went, the more sinister the project became. There were logs of psychological manipulation tactics embedded in the digital kiosks, subtle messages designed to influence behavior and push people toward certain actions. The new storefronts, the layout of the streets, even the ads on the kiosks—they were all part of a carefully crafted strategy to reshape the community according to Leonard's vision.

Crash felt a chill run down his spine as he realized just how deep the deception went. "He's playing us all like puppets," he said, his voice thick with anger. "And we've been blind to it this whole time."

Fred let out a sharp bark, his eyes flashing with determination. He moved to another folder, this one filled with financial records and correspondence. As Crash read through the emails, he saw just how far-reaching Leonard's influence was. There were messages from city officials, business leaders, and even members of the media— all of them complicit in Leonard's scheme, either knowingly or unknowingly.

"This is huge," Crash said, his voice barely containing the urgency he felt. "If we can get this out to the public, we can stop him. But we have to be careful. Leonard's got connections everywhere. If he finds out we have this, he'll come after us."

Fred nodded, his expression grim. He knew the risks—they were up against a powerful and dangerous opponent. But they couldn't back down now. The truth was too important, and the stakes were too high.

Crash ran a hand through his hair, trying to think of their next move. "We need to make sure this gets into the right hands," he said, his mind racing. "Someone who can expose Leonard without being silenced. But first, we need to make sure we're safe. We can't let Leonard find out we have this until we're ready."

Fred barked in agreement, his eyes filled with resolve. He reached out with his flipper and tapped on the last file in the folder. As it opened, Crash's breath caught in his throat. It was a detailed plan—Leonard's blueprint for the future of the neighborhood. And it was far worse than they had imagined.

The plan outlined the complete transformation of the community, turning it into a sterile, controlled environment where every aspect of life was monitored and manipulated. The people who didn't fit into Leonard's vision—the elderly, the poor, the nonconformists—were to be pushed out, replaced by a more "desirable" population. It was social engineering on a massive scale, all under the guise of progress.

Crash felt sick to his stomach as he read the plan, the full scope of Leonard's ambitions laid bare before him. "He's not just trying to control us," Crash said, his voice thick with emotion. "He's trying to erase us. Everything that makes this community unique, everything that gives it life—he wants to wipe it all away and replace it with something cold, something... artificial."

Fred let out a low, mournful sound, his flippers trembling with anger. He had seen enough. It was time to act.

Crash turned to Fred, his eyes blazing with determination. "We can't let this happen, Fred. We have to stop him. But we need a plan—a way to get this information out without putting ourselves or the community at risk."

Fred barked in agreement, his eyes locking with Crash's. They were in this together, and they knew that the road ahead wouldn't be easy. But they had the truth on their side, and they weren't going to let Leonard destroy their home.

The night was cool, the sky above shrouded in clouds that blocked out the stars. Fred moved through the quiet streets of the neighborhood, his flippered feet padding softly on the pavement. He was cautious, as always, his senses heightened as he kept to the shadows. The supplies he needed were tucked away in various hidden spots throughout the city, and tonight he was on his way to collect some of the more essential items for his lair.

As he neared the familiar alleyway where he kept a stash of electronics and other necessities, Fred paused, his instincts prickling with unease. He scanned the area, his sharp eyes catching every detail—the flickering streetlamp, the rustle of a stray newspaper in the breeze, the distant hum of the city. Everything seemed normal, but Fred couldn't shake the feeling that something was off.

Cautiously, he approached the hidden compartment he had built behind a loose brick in the wall. As he reached out to remove the brick, a sudden noise—a faint, almost imperceptible click—sent a jolt of alarm through him. Fred's heart raced as he realized, too late, that he had walked straight into a trap.

Before he could react, the alley was flooded with light. Blinding, harsh beams from overhead spotlights pinned Fred in place, casting long, distorted shadows against the walls. He spun around, trying to find an escape route, but his path was blocked. A group of men, dressed in tactical gear and moving with military precision, closed in from all sides.

Fred's mind raced, quickly assessing the situation. He had been careful, meticulous even, in covering his tracks. How had Leonard found him? And then it hit him—Crash. The social media posts, the brief moments of carelessness. Leonard had been watching, waiting for the perfect moment to strike, and now Fred was surrounded, outnumbered, and outmaneuvered.

The leader of the group stepped forward, a tall, imposing figure with cold, calculating eyes. He held a device in his hand—some sort of advanced tranquilizer gun, Fred guessed—and his expression was one of grim determination.

"Don't bother resisting," the man said, his voice steady and unyielding. "We know who you are, and we know what you're capable of. There's no way out."

Fred's eyes darted around the alley, searching for any opening, any possible way to escape. But the men had anticipated his every move. They closed in with practiced efficiency, their formation tight and impenetrable. Fred's heart pounded as he realized there was no way to fight his way out of this. He was trapped.

The leader raised the tranquilizer gun, aiming it directly at Fred. "It's over," he said, his tone leaving no room for doubt.

Fred's mind whirred, calculating his last possible options. But even as he considered his next move, he knew it was futile. Leonard's men were too well-prepared, too precise. They had studied him, learned his patterns, and now they were here to take him down.

In a final act of defiance, Fred bared his teeth, letting out a low growl as he crouched low to the ground, ready to spring. But before he could make his move, the sharp hiss of the tranquilizer dart cut through the air. Fred felt the sting as it embedded in his side, the sedative working quickly to dull his senses. His vision blurred, and the world around him began to fade.

As he sank to the ground, his last coherent thought was of Crash. He had to warn him, had to tell him not to trust Leonard. But the darkness closed in too fast, and Fred slipped into unconsciousness before he could do anything more.

The men moved swiftly, securing Fred in a reinforced crate designed specifically for him. The leader watched as his team worked, his expression unchanging. They had completed their mission with ruthless efficiency, and now they would deliver their prize to Leonard.

As the crate was loaded into an unmarked van, the leader allowed himself a small, satisfied smile. Leonard would be pleased. The sea lion that had eluded them for so long was finally captured, and soon, he would be back where he belonged—in the hands of those who had created him.

The van pulled away from the alley, leaving no trace of the ambush behind. The only sign of the struggle was the faint echo of footsteps fading into the night.

The evening sky was tinged with a soft purple hue as Crash made his way toward Fred's lair, the familiar route etched in his memory. The events of the day had left him uneasy, a nagging feeling that something was wrong gnawing at the back of his mind. He quickened his pace, eager to see Fred and talk things over, hoping to mend the rift that had grown between them.

As he approached the hidden entrance to the lair beneath the Cable Car Museum, Crash noticed something that made his heart skip a beat. The usually subtle entrance, cleverly camouflaged, was now slightly ajar. The heavy steel door, always securely locked, hung loosely on its hinges, as if it had been forced open.

Panic began to bubble up inside him as Crash pushed the door wider, his breath catching in his throat. The interior of the lair, once meticulously organized with Fred's unique blend of high-tech equipment and sea lion charm, was in shambles. Monitors were smashed, cables ripped from the walls, and papers were scattered across the floor like confetti from some twisted celebration. The scene was one of chaos—clearly the result of a violent struggle.

"Fred?" Crash called out, his voice trembling as he stepped deeper into the lair. But there was no response, only the eerie silence of an empty, ransacked room. The tension in the air was palpable, thick with the remnants of the conflict that had taken place.

Crash's eyes darted around the room, desperately searching for any sign of Fred, but the absence of the sea lion was all too clear. He moved frantically from one corner to the next, his hands shaking as he sifted through the wreckage. The usually comforting hum of Fred's servers was gone, replaced by the cold silence of lifeless machines.

As he knelt by the overturned conversation pit, Crash's mind raced. What had happened here? Who could have done this? And then, as the reality began to sink in, the answer hit him like a punch to the gut—Leonard.

A wave of guilt washed over Crash, almost knocking the breath out of him. He knew, deep down, that this was his fault. Leonard had been watching, waiting for the perfect opportunity, and Crash had given it to him on a silver platter. The social media posts, the careless moments—he had led Leonard straight to Fred.

The realization made his stomach churn. "No, no, no..." Crash muttered under his breath, his voice barely audible as he tried to piece together the details. There were signs of a struggle—claw marks on the floor, a few scattered tufts of fur—but nothing that indicated where Fred had been taken. It was as if he had vanished without a trace.

Crash collapsed onto a nearby chair, his head in his hands as the weight of his actions bore down on him. The rift between him and Fred seemed like a distant memory now, overshadowed by the crushing guilt and fear that consumed him. He had been so blinded by his own ambitions, so eager to prove himself, that he had ignored the very real dangers Fred had warned him about.

Tears of frustration welled up in Crash's eyes as he replayed the events in his mind, desperately wishing he could take it all back. But it was too late. Fred was gone, and it was because of him.

The room seemed to close in around him, the walls echoing with his own harsh breathing. Crash knew he had to act, but his mind was a whirlwind of emotions—fear, guilt, anger—all competing for dominance. He couldn't think straight, couldn't see a clear way forward.

But one thing was certain: he had to find Fred. He couldn't let Leonard win. He couldn't let Fred suffer because of his mistakes.

Crash forced himself to stand, wiping the tears from his eyes. He looked around the lair one last time, taking in the destruction, the evidence of a struggle that Fred had fought valiantly against but had ultimately lost. This was no longer just about proving himself or chasing a dream—this was about righting a wrong, about saving his friend.

He didn't know where to start, but he knew he couldn't do it alone. He would need help, and he would need it fast.

As he stepped out into the night, the cool air hit him like a slap in the face, sharpening his senses. The neighborhood stretched out before him, quiet and unaware of the battle that had just begun. But Crash knew that this was where it would end—right here, in the place he had called home his entire life.

And he would do whatever it took to bring Fred back.

The streets were eerily quiet as Crash made his way back to the heart of the neighborhood. His mind was racing, heart pounding in his chest as he struggled to come up with a plan. Fred was gone—captured by Leonard—and Crash knew he had little time to act. But where could he turn? Who could help him take on someone as powerful and connected as Leonard?

As he hurried past the familiar shops and homes, a thought struck him—a risky, desperate thought, but it was the only one that made sense. Fred had a network of allies, people who understood the digital world as well as, if not better than, anyone else. They were hackers, like Fred—people who lived on the fringes, working in the shadows, but with skills that could rival even Leonard's top engineers.

Crash's steps quickened as the idea took root. He would reach out to Fred's network, the very people who had helped Fred gather the information they needed to expose Leonard. These were the ones who knew Fred best, the ones who might have the expertise to trace where Fred had been taken and find a way to free him.

But how could he contact them? Fred had been the connection, the one with the knowledge and access. Crash slowed, his desperation threatening to turn into hopelessness—until he remembered his social media presence. Since Leonard's proposal, his accounts had blown up, gaining thousands of followers almost overnight. It wasn't much, but it was a start. If he could get a message out, maybe—just maybe—someone out there would know what to do.

Without hesitation, Crash pulled out his phone, his fingers trembling as he opened the app. He hesitated for a brief moment, his mind racing with doubts. Could he really do this? Would anyone even care enough to help? But then he remembered Fred—their friendship, the sacrifices Fred had made for him—and he knew he had no choice.

Crash hit the "Go Live" button, his face appearing on the screen, illuminated by the streetlight overhead. The comments started pouring in almost immediately, a flood of curious followers eager to see what he had to say. But this wasn't about likes or followers anymore—this was about saving Fred.

"Hey, everyone," Crash began, his voice shaky but determined. "I know a lot of you have been following my journey with Leonard's project, but something's happened—something bad. I need your help. This isn't a joke or a stunt. This is real."

He took a deep breath, steadying himself. "There's someone—someone really important—who's been taken. His name is Fred. Fred Lions. Some of you might know him as @FredLions. He's a friend, and he's in trouble because of me. Leonard... Leonard's taken him, and I don't know where. I don't know how much time he has."

The comments started scrolling faster, with viewers asking questions, expressing concern, but Crash didn't have time to respond to them individually. He had to keep going.

"Fred's not just any friend," Crash continued. "He's the reason I'm even talking to you right now. He's helped me and so many others in ways you can't imagine. And now he needs our help. If you're out there—if you know anything about hacking, tracing signals, or anything that could help find him—I'm begging you to reach out."

Crash paused, his eyes scanning the screen, searching for any signs of recognition or support. The viewer count was skyrocketing, but he needed more than just viewers—he needed action.

"I'm uploading everything Fred managed to gather about Leonard," Crash said, his voice growing steadier with purpose. "It's all the evidence we have—files, codes, anything that could lead us to him. I'm sending it securely, and I need you—anyone who can—to use it. To find Fred, to bring him home."

With a few quick taps, Crash began uploading the files Fred had stored on his device, ensuring they were encrypted and sent to a secure location where they could be accessed by those who knew what to do with them. The process felt agonizingly slow, each second ticking by like an eternity.

Finally, the upload was complete. Crash looked back at the camera, his expression resolute. "Please," he said, his voice thick with emotion. "Help me bring Fred back. He's more than just a friend— he's part of this community, and we can't let Leonard take him away. Not like this."

He ended the live stream, his heart pounding in his chest as he stared at the screen. Had it worked? Would anyone respond? The uncertainty gnawed at him, but there was no time to dwell on it. He had taken the first step—now he had to hope that Fred's network would come through.

Crash lowered his phone, the weight of the situation settling heavily on his shoulders. He had put everything on the line, trusting in the goodwill of strangers and the skills of hackers he had never met. But deep down, he knew it was Fred's best chance—maybe his only chance.

As he stood there in the quiet of the night, the only sounds were the distant hum of traffic and the faint buzz of his phone as notifications began to flood in. Crash held his breath, waiting, hoping, praying that somewhere out there, someone was ready to help.

The battle to save Fred had begun.

Chapter 14
Absurdity at the End of the Line

Crash sat on the edge of his bed, staring at his phone as the minutes ticked by. The livestream had ended, but the weight of what he had just done still hung heavily in the air. He had put everything out there—Fred's life, his own future, the safety of the community—all in the hands of people he had never met, people who existed behind usernames and avatars.

The screen of his phone buzzed with notifications, the stream of comments, messages, and pings relentless. Crash's heart pounded in his chest as he opened the app, unsure of what he would find. Would anyone actually help? Or had he just made everything worse?

Then, suddenly, the screen filled with messages—more than he could keep up with. The first was from someone named @ ShadowNet, a well-known figure in the hacking community. The message was short and to the point:

@ShadowNet: *Got your message. We're on it. Sit tight.*

Crash barely had time to process it before more messages started flooding in.

@CodeMaster: *Just received the data. Beginning analysis. We'll find him.*

@Encryptor: *Tracing the last known locations. Stay strong, Crash. We've got your back.*

@CyberPhantom: *Leonard won't know what hit him. We're not letting Fred go down without a fight.*

Crash's breath caught in his throat as he scrolled through the messages. Hackers from across the globe—people he had only heard about in passing—were rallying behind him, offering their skills, their expertise, and their determination to bring Fred back.

It was happening. They were responding.

Within minutes, a virtual command center began to take shape. Using encrypted channels, the hackers started coordinating their efforts, each taking on different aspects of the mission. Some focused on tracing Fred's last known location using the data Crash had uploaded, while others worked on disrupting Leonard's surveillance network to create cover for the rescue operation.

Crash's phone buzzed again, this time with a message from @ ShadowNet.

@ShadowNet: *Crash, we're in. We've got eyes on Leonard's network. It's massive, but we've identified weak points. We'll need you to stay in close contact— this is going to get intense.*

Crash felt a surge of hope and adrenaline. "I'm ready," he typed back, his fingers flying over the keyboard. "Just tell me what you need."

The response was immediate.

@ShadowNet: *We'll need access to the local network. Can you get to Fred's lair? We might be able to use his equipment to boost our signals and bypass Leonard's firewalls.*

Crash nodded, even though @ShadowNet couldn't see him. "On my way," he replied, already grabbing his jacket and heading for the door.

As he raced through the quiet streets, the gravity of what was happening started to sink in. These weren't just random people— these were some of the best hackers in the world, uniting for a cause that was bigger than any of them. Fred had made an impact on their lives, just as he had on Crash's, and now they were willing to risk everything to save him.

When Crash arrived at the lair, he quickly activated the remaining equipment that had survived the ambush. Monitors flickered to life, and soon the screens were filled with lines of code, scrolling faster than Crash could follow. The hackers were already at work, their digital presence filling the space with a palpable sense of urgency.

@Encryptor: *We're in! Boosting signals now. Keep an eye on the feed, Crash—if anything looks off, let us know immediately.*

Crash nodded, his hands shaking slightly as he watched the screens. He wasn't a hacker, but he could sense the intensity of the work being done. These people were taking risks—serious risks—to help him. It was a battle being fought in the shadows, and the stakes couldn't have been higher.

The minutes stretched on, each one feeling like an eternity. Crash's phone buzzed constantly with updates, each one more critical than the last.

@CyberPhantom: *We're breaching Leonard's mainframe. Gotta move fast—he's got redundancies, but we're cutting through them.*

@CodeMaster: *Tracing Fred's last ping… We're close, just need a bit more time.*

Crash clenched his fists, his heart hammering in his chest. Every part of him wanted to be out there, doing something more tangible, more physical to help. But he knew that this was where the real battle was taking place—in the digital realm, where lines of code and streams of data determined the outcome.

And then, just as the tension reached its breaking point, a message flashed across the screen.

@ShadowNet: *We've got him. Location confirmed. Transmitting coordinates now.*

Crash nearly dropped his phone in his rush to see the coordinates. They were close—closer than he had expected. Leonard had taken Fred to one of his more secure facilities on the outskirts of the city, a place that was heavily guarded and nearly impenetrable.

@ShadowNet: *This is it, Crash. We're going to need everyone on deck for the next phase. Get ready—it's going to be a fight.*

Crash took a deep breath, trying to steady his nerves. They had found Fred—but the hardest part was yet to come. The hackers had done their part, and now it was up to him and the community to finish the job.

Crash: Thank you. All of you. We won't let you down.

@ShadowNet: *We know you won't. Let's bring him home.*

Crash disconnected the feed, the room falling silent once more. But this time, the silence was filled with a renewed sense of purpose. They had a plan, they had a team, and they had hope.

And as Crash stepped out of the lair, heading back to the neighborhood to rally the troops, he knew one thing for certain— Fred was counting on him, and he wasn't going to let him down.

The sun had dipped below the horizon, casting long shadows across the streets of the neighborhood as Crash made his way toward the small coffee shop on the corner. The same shop where, just weeks ago, he had seen his reflection in the window and questioned his place in the world. Tonight, he was returning with a purpose—a desperate plea for help that he knew only the people who lived here, who truly cared about this place, could answer.

Crash pushed open the door, the familiar bell above it jingling softly. The shop was warm, the scent of freshly brewed coffee mingling with the murmur of conversation. Regulars sat at their usual tables, chatting quietly or working on laptops, oblivious to the turmoil raging within him.

He hesitated for a moment, standing just inside the doorway, before steeling himself and stepping further in. He needed to do this. Fred needed him to do this.

As he approached the counter, the barista looked up and smiled in recognition. "Hey, Crash. The usual?"

Crash shook his head, his throat tight. "No, actually… I need to talk to everyone."

The barista frowned slightly, sensing something was wrong. "Is everything okay?"

Crash took a deep breath and turned to face the rest of the shop, his voice loud enough to carry but filled with a nervous edge. "Can I get everyone's attention, please? Just for a minute?"

The quiet conversations halted, and heads turned toward him. Crash felt his heart hammering in his chest, but he pushed forward, knowing he couldn't turn back now.

"I know most of you," Crash began, his voice wavering slightly. "We've all lived here for years. We've seen the good and the bad, and we've always looked out for each other. But tonight… I'm asking for your help. I need it more than ever."

The room was silent, the weight of his words hanging in the air. Crash swallowed hard, his hands trembling slightly as he continued.

"There's someone—someone really important to me, to all of us—who's in danger. His name is Fred. Some of you might know him, even if you didn't realize it. Fred's been a part of this community for a long time, helping out in ways most of us never even saw."

Crash hesitated, searching for the right words to explain what Fred really was, how he was more than just another member of the community. "Fred… he's different. He's not like us, but he cares about this place—about all of you. He's been protecting us, using his skills to keep us safe, to fight against people like Leonard."

Murmurs spread through the room at the mention of Leonard's name, and Crash knew he had to act fast before the skepticism could take root.

"Leonard isn't who you think he is," Crash pressed on, his voice growing stronger. "He's been using us—using this neighborhood—as part of some twisted experiment. He's watching us, collecting data, controlling us in ways we don't even realize. And now he's taken Fred, because Fred knew too much. He tried to stop him, and now Leonard has him locked up, God knows where."

The room had gone completely still, the tension thick enough to cut with a knife. Crash could see the uncertainty in their eyes, the disbelief warring with the instinct to protect their own.

"Fred's not just a friend," Crash said, his voice cracking with emotion. "He's been our guardian, our protector. And now he needs us. I need you. We have to get him back, and we have to stop Leonard before he tears this place apart."

The barista stepped out from behind the counter, her expression a mix of concern and resolve. "What do you need us to do, Crash?"

Crash let out a breath he hadn't realized he was holding, a wave of relief washing over him. "We've got a plan—a way to get Fred out and expose Leonard for what he's really doing. But we can't do it alone. We need people who know this neighborhood, who care about it, who are willing to stand up and fight for it."

A murmur of agreement rippled through the room, and one by one, people began to nod, some even standing up to show their support.

"What do you need?" another voice called out from the back.

Crash smiled, the tension in his shoulders easing slightly. "We need eyes and ears on the ground. We need people to help us navigate the area, create distractions, anything that can give us the upper hand. Leonard's not going to see this coming if we all work together."

The barista nodded, her eyes determined. "You can count on us, Crash. We're with you."

The rest of the room echoed her sentiment, a wave of solidarity washing over Crash as he realized just how much strength there was in this community. These were his people, and together, they were going to take on Leonard and bring Fred home.

"Thank you," Crash said, his voice thick with emotion. "I can't do this without you."

The room buzzed with energy as people began to talk, share ideas, and plan their roles in the rescue mission. Crash felt a surge of hope and determination. They had the support they needed, the people who cared about this place and were willing to fight for it.

"Alright, let's get going. Follow me, I have an idea of where we can plan all this"

And with their help, they were going to save Fred.

Crash paced back and forth in the Fred's lair that had become their impromptu command center. The air was thick with tension, the weight of the upcoming mission pressing down on everyone present.

In mere hours, the hackers had descended upon Fred's lair along with some now dedicated volunteers from the local community. It's amazing what can be done when a rockstar of underground hacking calls out for help.

Around him, a mix of hackers and local community members worked in focused silence, their eyes glued to monitors, fingers flying over keyboards as they pulled together the final pieces of the plan.

The hackers had done the impossible—they had traced Fred's location and breached Leonard's supposedly impenetrable systems. But finding Fred was only the beginning. Now, they had to figure out how to get him out, and that meant coming up with a plan that was as bold as it was dangerous.

Crash stopped in front of the main screen, where @ShadowNet had set up a live feed from Leonard's facility. The building was a fortress, surrounded by high walls, security cameras, and guards who looked like they were straight out of a military operation. Getting in was going to be a challenge; getting out with Fred was going to be even harder.

"We've identified some weak points in Leonard's security," @ShadowNet began, his voice steady but urgent as he addressed the group. "He's relying heavily on automated systems—drones, sensors, facial recognition—but we've managed to create blind spots. Small windows of time where we can move undetected. But we'll need precise timing and coordination to pull this off."

Crash nodded, absorbing the information. "What about the guards?" he asked, his voice tense. "We can't just walk in and out without them noticing."

"Leave that to us," @Encryptor chimed in, not looking up from his screen. "We've already started feeding false data into their systems. As far as they're concerned, everything's normal. We'll keep them distracted, but it won't last long. You'll have maybe fifteen minutes, tops."

Crash glanced around the room, meeting the eyes of the community members who had volunteered to help. They were ordinary people—shop owners, neighbors, friends—but they had a stake in this, and they were ready to fight for Fred. Crash could see the determination in their faces, a reflection of his own resolve.

"We need to make this count," Crash said, his voice growing firmer. "This isn't just about saving Fred. We need to expose Leonard for what he really is. If we can get Fred out, we'll have the evidence we need to bring him down—and we'll broadcast it for the whole world to see."

@CodeMaster nodded, pulling up a blueprint of the facility on one of the screens. "We've got a clear path to Fred's location, but we'll need to synchronize our movements with the disruption in the security system. Any deviation could trigger an alarm, and if that happens, we're looking at a full lockdown."

Crash studied the blueprint, his mind racing as he visualized the plan. The path was tight, with little room for error. But he trusted these people—trusted their expertise and their commitment. They had come this far, and he wasn't about to let fear stop them now.

"We'll split into two teams," Crash decided, his tone decisive. "Team A will handle the extraction—getting in, securing Fred, and getting out. Team B will stay outside, monitoring the situation and keeping Leonard's security forces occupied. We need to hit them fast and hard, and then disappear before they even know what happened."

The room was silent as the plan settled over everyone. It was risky—one mistake could mean disaster—but it was their best shot. The tension was thick, but there was also a sense of camaraderie, a shared understanding that they were all in this together.

@ShadowNet leaned back in his chair, crossing his arms as he regarded Crash. "You're sure about this? Once we start, there's no turning back."

Crash met his gaze, his expression resolute. "I'm sure," he said firmly. "We've come too far to back down now. We're going to save Fred, and we're going to make sure Leonard can never hurt anyone like this again."

The hackers nodded, returning to their screens with renewed focus. The room buzzed with energy as they finalized the details, checking and double-checking every aspect of the plan. Crash could feel the urgency building, the ticking clock in the back of his mind reminding him that time was running out.

As the final preparations were made, Crash took a moment to look around the room. He saw the determination in the eyes of his neighbors, the quiet confidence of the hackers who had answered his call, and the flicker of hope that they could actually pull this off.

"This is it," Crash said, addressing the group one last time. "We're doing this for Fred, for our community, and for everyone Leonard has tried to control. Let's bring him home."

With that, the room erupted into action. The plan was in motion, and there was no turning back. Crash felt a surge of adrenaline as he readied himself for what was to come. The stakes had never been higher, but he knew, deep in his heart, that they were ready.

They were going to save Fred. And they were going to take down Leonard once and for all.

The night was thick with tension, the air still and heavy as Crash and his small team approached Leonard's high-security facility. The building loomed before them, a fortress of steel and concrete, its perimeter lined with surveillance cameras and patrolling guards. The only sounds were the distant hum of traffic and the soft rustle of leaves in the breeze. It felt as if the world itself was holding its breath, waiting for what was to come.

Crash adjusted the earpiece in his ear, listening intently as @ShadowNet's voice crackled through the feed. "You're clear to proceed. The cameras are on a loop, but you'll need to move quickly. We've only got a few minutes before the system resets."

Crash nodded, even though @ShadowNet couldn't see him, and signaled to the rest of the group. Beside him were @Encryptor, the barista from the coffee shop, and a few other trusted members of the community. Each one carried a mix of determination and fear in their eyes, but they were ready to do whatever it took to bring Fred home.

They moved silently, slipping through the shadows toward the first checkpoint. The facility's outer wall was guarded by motion sensors, but @Encryptor had already hacked into the system, creating a brief window of time when they could pass through undetected. Crash's heart pounded in his chest as they ducked beneath the sensors, his breath coming in shallow, controlled bursts.

"Easy now," @Encryptor whispered, his fingers dancing over a portable keypad. "Just a few more steps… and… we're through."

They reached the wall, pressing their backs against the cold stone as they caught their breath. Crash felt a surge of adrenaline, his senses heightened as he scanned the area for any signs of movement. So far, so good.

"Next checkpoint in thirty seconds," @ShadowNet's voice came through again, calm and precise. "You'll need to cross the courtyard. We've disabled the drones, but there are guards on patrol. Stick to the shadows and stay low."

Crash peered around the corner, eyes narrowing as he took in the expanse of the courtyard. It was wide open, bathed in the harsh light of overhead floodlights, with only a few patches of darkness offering cover. A pair of guards walked a slow circuit around the perimeter, their rifles slung over their shoulders, their expressions bored but alert.

"Go," Crash whispered, and the group moved as one, slipping into the shadows and inching their way toward the far side of the courtyard. The seconds ticked by agonizingly slowly as they crouched behind a row of bushes, waiting for the guards to pass.

Crash's pulse quickened as one of the guards paused, his head turning slightly as if sensing something out of place. The group froze, their breaths held in unison as they watched him, praying he wouldn't investigate further. After what felt like an eternity, the guard shrugged and continued his patrol, oblivious to the intruders just feet away.

"Move, now," Crash urged, and they darted across the open space, their footsteps silent against the pavement. They reached the cover of the next wall just as @ShadowNet's voice came through again.

"Good work. You're almost there. The entrance to the underground level is just ahead, but it's heavily secured. We'll need to bypass three separate locks to get through. @Encryptor, you're up."

@Encryptor nodded, already setting to work on the first lock. The keypad glowed faintly in the darkness, the numbers shifting as

@Encryptor input a series of codes. Crash stood watch, his eyes darting between the surrounding area and the entrance, every nerve on edge as they waited.

"First lock, disengaged," @Encryptor whispered, a small smile of satisfaction crossing his face. He moved on to the second, the tension in the air thickening with each passing second.

Crash's thoughts drifted to Fred, imagining him alone and trapped somewhere within the facility, surrounded by cold, unfeeling walls. The thought fueled his determination, driving away the fear and doubt that threatened to creep in. They were so close now—he could feel it.

The second lock clicked open, and @Encryptor moved swiftly to the third. "Almost there," he muttered, his focus razor-sharp. "Just… a little… more…"

With a final click, the third lock disengaged, and the door slid open with a soft hiss. The group exchanged glances, a mix of relief and anticipation flickering in their eyes.

Chapter 15
The Silence After the Storm

"This is it," Crash whispered, his voice low but filled with resolve. "Fred's just down there. Stay close, stay quiet, and let's bring him home."

They descended the narrow staircase, the walls closing in around them as they ventured deeper into the heart of the facility. The air grew cooler, the sounds of the outside world fading away until all that remained was the echo of their footsteps and the distant hum of machinery.

Crash's heart raced as they reached the bottom, a long, dimly lit corridor stretching out before them. Doors lined the walls, each one sealed with heavy locks, but @ShadowNet had provided them with the exact location of Fred's holding cell. They moved swiftly and silently, the tension building with every step.

"Last door on the right," @ShadowNet's voice guided them. "That's where he is."

Crash's breath caught in his throat as they approached the door, the culmination of everything they had fought for just within reach. @Encryptor moved to the keypad, but before he could start, a soft beep echoed through the corridor.

"What was that?" the barista whispered, her voice tinged with panic.

Crash's heart sank as he realized what it meant. "They've detected us," he said, his voice tight. "We have to hurry."

@Encryptor worked frantically, his fingers flying over the keypad as the alarm began to build, growing louder and more insistent with each passing second. The sound reverberated through the corridor, a sharp, piercing warning that their time was running out.

"Come on, come on…" Crash urged, his eyes darting back toward the staircase. They had moments, maybe seconds, before Leonard's forces would be upon them.

Finally, with a sharp click, the door unlocked and slid open, revealing the small, dimly lit room beyond.

Crash took a deep breath, steeling himself for what he might find inside. "Let's get him out of here," he said, stepping forward into the darkness.

But before they could reach Fred, the sound of approaching footsteps echoed down the corridor.

Crash stepped into the dimly lit room, his heart pounding in his chest as he scanned the small space. The room was stark and cold, the walls lined with metal panels that reflected the faint glow of the overhead lights. In the center of the room, lying on a low metal platform, was Fred.

The sight of him hit Crash like a punch to the gut. Fred was slumped over, his usual energetic demeanor replaced by a look of exhaustion and pain. His once bright eyes were dull, and his body was marked with bruises and cuts from the rough handling he had endured. Yet, despite his weakened state, there was a flicker of determination in Fred's eyes as he lifted his head and saw Crash standing there.

"Fred!" Crash rushed forward, dropping to his knees beside the platform. He reached out, his hands shaking as he gently touched Fred's side. "We're here. We're getting you out of here."

Fred's eyes brightened slightly at the sight of Crash, and he let out a soft, raspy bark. It was a far cry from his usual playful tone, but it was enough to show that he was still fighting.

The rest of the team quickly joined Crash, their expressions a mix of relief and urgency. @Encryptor moved to check Fred's restraints, his fingers working quickly to undo the metal clasps that held Fred down.

"Hang in there, buddy," Crash murmured, his voice thick with emotion. "We're going to get you out of this."

Fred blinked slowly, his gaze shifting between Crash and the others. Despite his obvious pain, there was a spark of recognition in his eyes—a sign that he understood what was happening and that he wasn't alone.

"We don't have much time," @ShadowNet's voice crackled through the earpiece. "Leonard's men are closing in. You need to move, now."

Crash nodded, his focus sharpening as the urgency of the situation pressed down on him. "Fred, can you walk?" he asked, his voice firm but gentle.

Fred hesitated for a moment, then slowly nodded. With @ Encryptor's help, Fred struggled to his feet, his legs trembling slightly as he adjusted to the weight of his own body. It was clear that he was in pain, but the determination in his eyes hadn't waned.

"We need to get him out of here, fast," the barista urged, her eyes darting toward the door. "The alarm's going to bring everyone down on us."

Crash supported Fred as they moved toward the exit, the sound of approaching footsteps growing louder with each passing second. There was no time to waste, no room for error.

As they reached the door, Fred let out a low, rumbling growl—a sign that he was more alert now, more aware of the danger they were in. Crash could see the gears turning in Fred's mind, even in his weakened state, as he began to assess their situation.

"Fred, we need your help," Crash said urgently. "We have to get out of here, but they've got this place locked down. Can you guide us?"

Fred paused, his eyes narrowing as he processed the information. Then, with a slow, deliberate nod, he turned toward the corridor, his senses on high alert. He motioned with his head for them to follow, his movements more calculated now as his hyper-intelligent mind began to take control.

@Encryptor stayed close to Fred, his portable device ready to disrupt any security systems they encountered along the way. The barista and the other community members formed a protective circle around them, their expressions tense as they prepared for the worst.

As they moved down the corridor, Fred led them with surprising precision, avoiding areas where they would be most vulnerable to detection. Every so often, he would pause, his ears twitching as he listened for approaching guards, then change direction based on what he heard.

They reached a junction, and Fred stopped, his eyes narrowing as he considered their options. The sound of footsteps echoed down one of the hallways, growing closer with each passing second.

"Which way, Fred?" Crash whispered, his voice tight with tension.

Fred's gaze flicked between the two paths before him, then settled on the one to the right. He let out a soft bark, indicating they should go that way, and the group quickly followed his lead.

They moved swiftly but carefully, Fred's instincts guiding them through the labyrinth of hallways. As they turned another corner, @Encryptor stopped abruptly, his eyes widening as he caught sight of a security camera ahead.

"Hold up," he hissed, quickly pulling out his device and typing furiously. The camera blinked, then turned off, its feed disrupted by the hackers working tirelessly from afar.

"Clear," @Encryptor said, and they continued on.

The tension was palpable, the air thick with the weight of their mission. Every sound, every shadow felt like a potential threat, but

Fred remained focused, his mind working at a speed that seemed impossible given his condition.

Finally, they reached the stairwell that led to the surface. Fred hesitated, his breathing labored, but there was no time to rest. The footsteps were getting closer, the sound of voices echoing down the hall.

"We're almost there," Crash urged, his voice filled with both hope and fear. "Just a little further, Fred."

Fred looked up at him, his eyes filled with a mix of exhaustion and resolve. He let out a final, determined bark, then led the way up the stairs, his movements slow but deliberate.

As they emerged into the cool night air, the sense of relief was overwhelming. But there was no time to celebrate. The facility was still on high alert, and Leonard's men were undoubtedly closing in.

Fred paused at the top of the stairs, his eyes scanning the area for any signs of danger. The street was quiet, but they knew it wouldn't stay that way for long.

"Which way?" Crash asked, his voice urgent.

Fred's gaze locked onto a side alley, barely visible in the darkness. He barked softly, then started moving toward it, his steps more confident now that they were outside.

The group followed, their hearts pounding as they slipped into the shadows. Fred led them through a series of narrow alleys and side streets, his hyper-intelligence guiding them away from the main roads and any potential threats.

As they moved further from the facility, the sounds of pursuit began to fade, replaced by the distant hum of the city. Fred's pace slowed, his exhaustion catching up with him, but he continued to push forward, determined to get them to safety.

Finally, they reached a small, abandoned warehouse on the outskirts of the city—a temporary safe house that @ShadowNet had secured for them. As they entered, Fred collapsed onto the floor, his body trembling with the effort it had taken to get them this far.

Crash knelt beside him, his heart aching at the sight of his friend so worn out. "You did it, Fred," he whispered, his voice thick with emotion. "You got us out."

Fred let out a weak bark, his eyes closing as he finally allowed himself to rest. Crash gently placed a hand on his side, feeling the rise and fall of his breath as Fred drifted into a much-needed sleep.

The room was silent, the tension of the escape slowly ebbing away. Crash looked around at the faces of those who had helped him—@Encryptor, the barista, and the others—each one showing the strain of the night's events, but also a deep sense of relief.

"We made it," Crash said softly, his voice filled with both gratitude and exhaustion. "We got him out."

But even as they allowed themselves a moment of rest, they knew their work wasn't done. Leonard was still out there, and they still needed to expose his plans to the world. But for now, they had Fred, and that was enough.

The sun had barely risen when Crash found himself seated in Leonard's opulent office, the room bathed in the soft glow of early morning light. The office was a stark contrast to the chaos of the previous night—a place of calm, order, and power. But for Crash, it felt more like a lair, the den of a predator who had been manipulating the world from behind the scenes.

Crash's heart raced, but he forced himself to stay calm, his expression unreadable as he waited for Leonard to arrive. He knew this was the moment that would determine everything—the future of his community, the fate of Fred, and his own path forward. There was no turning back now.

The door to the office opened with a quiet click, and Leonard strode in, exuding his usual aura of confidence and control. He paused for a moment when he saw Crash sitting there, alone and seemingly unarmed, but his surprise quickly faded, replaced by a cool, calculated smile.

"Crash," Leonard said smoothly, as if greeting an old friend. "I must admit, I wasn't expecting you. But I'm glad you're here. We have a lot to discuss."

Crash remained seated, his gaze steady as he watched Leonard move to his desk and sit down across from him. The room was silent, the tension between them palpable, as Leonard leaned back in his chair, his fingers steepled thoughtfully.

"I have to say, I'm impressed," Leonard continued, his tone almost admiring. "You've proven yourself to be resourceful, determined—qualities I respect. It's clear that you have potential, Crash. A great deal of potential."

Crash didn't respond immediately, his mind racing as he considered his next move. He knew Leonard was trying to gauge him, to find a way to manipulate him once more. But this time, Crash wasn't going to fall for it.

"I know what you're doing, Leonard," Crash said finally, his voice low but firm. "You think you can offer me something that will make me forget about everything you've done. But I'm not that person anymore."

Leonard's smile widened, as if he found Crash's words amusing. "Come now, Crash. Let's not be hasty. I'm offering you an opportunity—something you've wanted your entire life. Fame, success, a way out of that dead-end existence. Isn't that why you came here? To finally get what you deserve?"

Crash's jaw tightened, but he forced himself to remain calm. "I came here to make sure you're stopped," he replied. "You've been using people, manipulating them for your own gain, and I'm not going to let you do that anymore."

Leonard sighed, as if disappointed by Crash's response. "Crash, you're thinking too small. I'm offering you a chance to be part of something much bigger. This community—it's nothing compared to what you could achieve with my help. We could change the world, you and I."

Crash felt a surge of anger, but he kept it in check, knowing that this was exactly what Leonard wanted—to provoke him, to make him doubt himself. Instead, Crash leaned forward slightly, feigning interest as he spoke.

"And what exactly do you have in mind, Leonard?" he asked, his voice carefully neutral.

Leonard's eyes gleamed, sensing that he was gaining the upper hand. "Think about it, Crash. With your influence, your connection to the community, we could shape the future of this city. No more poverty, no more crime—just progress, innovation, and prosperity. You'd be at the forefront of it all. Imagine the power, the recognition. You'd never have to worry about anything again."

Crash let Leonard's words hang in the air for a moment, pretending to mull them over. He could see the anticipation in Leonard's eyes, the subtle shift in his demeanor as he believed he was winning Crash over. But deep down, Crash felt nothing but disgust.

"I have to admit," Crash said slowly, carefully choosing his words, "it's a tempting offer. After everything I've been through… everything Fred's been through… it would be nice to finally be on top, to have control."

Leonard's smile grew, his eyes narrowing slightly as he leaned in, sensing victory. "That's right, Crash. You deserve this. All you have to do is say yes."

Crash reached into his pocket, his hand closing around his phone. His heart pounded in his chest, but he kept his expression calm, almost contemplative. He could feel the weight of the decision bearing down on him, but he knew what he had to do.

"You know," Crash began, his voice steady as he met Leonard's gaze, "you're right. I do deserve better. But not like this."

Leonard's smile faltered, a flicker of confusion crossing his face. "What do you mean?"

Crash's eyes hardened, and without breaking eye contact, he pulled out his phone and tapped the screen. The command he sent was simple, but it set in motion the final part of their plan.

"I mean," Crash said, his voice filled with quiet resolve, "that you're finished, Leonard."

For a moment, Leonard didn't react, as if he couldn't quite process what was happening. Then, slowly, realization dawned on him—Crash had been playing him all along.

"What have you done?" Leonard demanded, his voice sharp as he stood up, his calm facade crumbling.

Crash remained seated, his phone still in hand. "I just gave the signal. In a few moments, everything you've built—your surveillance, your manipulation, your lies, the decades of back door government contracts and sweetheart tax deals—will be exposed to the world."

The moment Crash sent the command, it was as if a switch had been flipped. Across the globe, a carefully coordinated digital assault began to unfold, orchestrated by Fred and his network of hackers. This was the moment they had all been working toward—the moment Leonard's empire of lies would come crashing down.

In a dimly lit room, @ShadowNet's fingers danced across a keyboard, executing the first phase of the plan. A wave of digital signals spread out like wildfire, infiltrating forums, social media platforms, and news sites. It was subtle at first—a trickle of posts and articles, carefully worded to pique curiosity and spread like a virus through the internet's vast, interconnected veins.

Within minutes, the trickle became a torrent. Posts began to appear on every major platform, each one linking to a treasure trove of documents, videos, and audio recordings that exposed the full extent of Leonard's operations. There were contracts detailing illegal surveillance agreements with the government, evidence of tax evasion on a massive scale, and videos showing Leonard's manipulation of key community figures to further his own agenda.

Fred, though still recovering, was at the heart of this operation. He had designed the algorithms that would ensure the information reached the right eyes—targeting influential figures, journalists, and even ordinary citizens who would be outraged by what they saw. The sheer volume of data was overwhelming, and it was everywhere.

On the streets of cities around the world, people's phones buzzed with notifications as the evidence spread like wildfire. In offices and homes, screens lit up with breaking news alerts as major outlets picked up the story. It was impossible to ignore—Leonard's name, once synonymous with innovation and progress, was now being dragged through the mud as his darkest secrets were laid bare for the world to see.

In a high-rise apartment in New York, a woman stepped out of her shower, only to see her smart display flashing with urgent messages. "Exposed: The Dark Truth Behind Leonard Armitage." She wiped the steam from the mirror and watched, stunned, as the display began to scroll through the damning evidence, her disbelief turning to horror.

In a bustling café in Paris, patrons gathered around a television, their conversations falling silent as the screen showed images of Leonard's face, juxtaposed with the incriminating documents. The newscaster's voice trembled with the gravity of the situation, detailing the shocking revelations that were flooding the internet.

In Tokyo, commuters on the subway stared at their phones, the normally silent car now abuzz with the sound of hundreds of people reading, watching, and sharing the information that had suddenly consumed the digital world. The headlines were inescapable, plastered across every screen, every device.

In San Francisco, where it had all begun, the local news stations were in overdrive, scrambling to cover the breaking story. Crash's neighborhood was at the epicenter, the once-quiet community now thrust into the spotlight as the world watched the fallout from Leonard's downfall.

But it wasn't just the major cities that were feeling the impact. Fred's carefully crafted algorithms ensured that even the most remote corners of the internet were saturated with the evidence. From small-town blogs to niche forums, there was no escape from the tidal wave of information.

In the heart of the storm, Leonard's office—now empty save for Crash—was eerily silent. But outside, the world was exploding with the revelations that had been unleashed. The smart display on Leonard's desk flickered to life, showing headlines from around the globe. The evidence was undeniable, the damage irreversible.

Fred, though still weak, had done his part, guiding the hackers to ensure that every piece of evidence was delivered with precision and impact. Crash could almost hear Fred's satisfied bark in his mind, knowing that they had succeeded.

Across the world, people were waking up to the truth. Leonard's carefully constructed facade had been shattered, his reputation irreparably damaged. The headlines continued to scroll, the reports growing more damning with each passing minute. Leonard Armitage—once untouchable—was now the most hated man in the world.

Leonard's face twisted with rage, his hands clenching into fists. "You little fool! You think you can stop me? I have connections, power beyond your imagination! You'll regret this, Crash!"

But Crash was unmoved, his resolve stronger than ever. "Maybe. But at least I'll know I did the right thing. You can't control people forever, Leonard. And now, everyone's going to see you for what you really are."

The tension in the room was electric, the air crackling with the intensity of the confrontation. Leonard's eyes blazed with fury, but there was also a hint of fear—fear that everything he had worked for, everything he had manipulated, was slipping through his fingers.

The sound of notifications pinging on Leonard's computer filled the room, as reports, videos, and files began to flood the internet, revealing the full extent of Leonard's schemes. Crash's message had gone out, and the world was watching.

Chapter 16
A Symphony of Oddities

Leonard's expression darkened, but he forced a smirk, trying to regain control. "You think this will change anything? People forget, Crash. They move on. I'll rebuild, and you'll be nothing."

Crash stood up slowly, meeting Leonard's gaze with unwavering determination. "Maybe they will. But not this time. Not after what you've done."

Leonard's smirk faltered as he saw the conviction in Crash's eyes. The power dynamic had shifted, and Leonard was no longer the one in control.

"You're done, Leonard," Crash said, his voice quiet but firm. "It's over."

Before Leonard could respond, the door to the office burst open, and a group of law enforcement officers stormed in, their weapons drawn. "Leonard Trice," one of the officers barked, "you're under arrest for conspiracy, illegal surveillance, and multiple counts of fraud."

Leonard's face drained of color as the officers moved to restrain him, his confident demeanor shattered. He looked back at Crash, his eyes filled with a mix of disbelief and fury.

"This isn't over," Leonard hissed as the officers cuffed him. "You'll pay for this."

Crash watched silently as Leonard was led away, the reality of what he had just done slowly sinking in. The battle was over, but the consequences would continue to ripple through the city, through the lives of everyone Leonard had tried to control.

As the office emptied, Crash took a deep breath, feeling a weight lift off his shoulders. He had done it. He had stood up to

Leonard, and in doing so, he had protected his community, his friends, and himself.

He looked down at his phone, the screen still displaying the command he had sent to the hackers. "Arf Arf."

Crash looked around the office. He had dreamed for so long of sitting behind a desk like this one. He left, his muddy Van's leaving permanent stains in the carpet.

The morning after Leonard's downfall, the neighborhood felt different—a palpable sense of relief hung in the air, mingled with the renewed energy of a community that had faced the worst and come out stronger. The streets, once marked by fear and uncertainty, were now filled with a sense of purpose and hope. The news of Leonard's exposure had spread quickly, and with it came the realization that they had weathered the storm and could now begin to rebuild.

Crash walked through the heart of the neighborhood, taking in the sight of shop owners sweeping their doorsteps, neighbors chatting animatedly on street corners, and children playing in the parks that had once been shadowed by Leonard's influence. The transformation was subtle but profound—a shift in the collective spirit of a community that had stood together against a powerful adversary and emerged victorious.

The grocery store, the heart of Crash's world, was already buzzing with activity. His mother and grandmother were inside, busy stocking shelves and chatting with customers. The store had always been a symbol of the neighborhood's resilience, and now, more than ever, it represented the strength and unity that had carried them through.

But the community wasn't content to simply return to the way things were. They were determined to build something better—a future that honored the past while embracing the possibilities of what could be. In the wake of Leonard's defeat, a new idea had taken root, one that would harness the historic charm of their centuries-old neighborhood to bring in new customers and visitors.

Crash had been at the center of these discussions, his experiences over the past few weeks shaping his vision for what the neighborhood could become. He had seen firsthand the power of community, the importance of standing together, and the value of protecting what made their neighborhood unique.

As he approached the town square, he could see a group of community members gathered, discussing plans for the new cooperative they were forming. The cooperative would focus on revitalizing the neighborhood's historic elements, from the old architecture to the local businesses that had stood the test of time. They wanted to attract new visitors who appreciated the authenticity and history of the area, while also ensuring that the neighborhood remained a vibrant, welcoming place for those who called it home.

Crash joined the group, greeted by nods and smiles from the people who had become more than just neighbors—they were now friends, allies, and partners in the journey ahead.

"We've been talking about the old theater down the street," one of the community members, Mrs. Nguyen, said excitedly. "It's been closed for years, but it's such a beautiful building. If we can restore it, maybe we could host events, show classic films—bring people back to experience what this place has to offer."

"That's a great idea," Crash agreed, his mind already racing with possibilities. "We could tie it in with other local businesses—offer special deals, organize walking tours of the historic sites. We have so much to offer, and people are looking for something real, something with history and meaning."

The group nodded in agreement, the conversation flowing easily as they brainstormed ideas for the cooperative. There was a renewed sense of purpose in their words, a recognition that they had the power to shape their future—together.

As the discussion continued, Crash felt a hand on his shoulder and turned to see his grandmother standing beside him, her eyes filled with pride.

"You've done well, Crash," she said softly. "You've shown this community what it means to lead—with heart, with determination, and with a deep respect for what we've built here."

Crash smiled, feeling a warmth spread through him. "I couldn't have done it without all of you. This neighborhood is special because of the people who live here—people who care enough to fight for it."

His grandmother nodded, her gaze sweeping over the bustling square. "And now we're going to make it even better. For us, for the next generation, and for anyone who wants to be part of this."

As the day went on, more and more people joined in, offering their ideas, their skills, and their enthusiasm. The cooperative was beginning to take shape—not just as a business venture, but as a symbol of the neighborhood's resilience, creativity, and commitment to a better future.

Crash felt a deep sense of fulfillment as he watched the community come together. The challenges they had faced had been immense, but they had proven that by standing together, they could overcome anything. And now, they were poised to create something lasting—something that honored their history while embracing the future.

The neighborhood, once on the brink of being consumed by Leonard's ambitions, was now a beacon of hope and possibility. And Crash, having grown from the uncertain boy who once questioned his place in the world, was ready to take on a leadership role in guiding the neighborhood forward.

Crash looked around at the faces of his friends, his family, and his community. They had fought, they had struggled, and now they were ready to rebuild—stronger, wiser, and more united than ever.

As he walked through the door, the familiar chime of the bell greeted him, along with the comforting sight of his mother and grandmother busy behind the counter.

His mother, Somjai, looked up from the register, a smile spreading across her face as she saw Crash enter. "There you are," she said warmly. "How did it go today?"

Crash returned her smile, feeling a deep sense of contentment. "It went great, Mom. The cooperative is really coming together. Everyone's excited to get started."

Jan, his grandmother, emerged from the back of the store, wiping her hands on her apron. "I'm so proud of you, Crash," she said, her voice filled with emotion. "You've done so much for this neighborhood—more than I ever imagined. You're not just part of this community—you're helping to lead it."

Crash felt a lump in his throat as he looked at the two women who had raised him, supported him, and believed in him even when he doubted himself. Their pride in him was evident, and it meant more than he could put into words.

"You've both been there for me every step of the way," Crash said softly. "I couldn't have done any of this without you."

His mother reached out and placed a hand on his shoulder. "We've always known you were capable of great things, Crash. But it's not just about what you've done—it's about the man you've become. You've shown this community what it means to care, to stand up for what's right, and to create something lasting."

Jan nodded in agreement, her eyes shining with pride. "You've built a legacy here, one that will endure long after we're gone. And that's something to be truly proud of."

Crash's heart swelled with gratitude and love for his family. He had been through so much, faced challenges he never expected, but he had come out stronger on the other side. And now, he was ready to continue building that legacy, not just for himself, but for the entire community.

Each day, Crash went to work at the store with a renewed sense of purpose. The once-routine tasks of stocking shelves, ringing up customers, and managing the daily operations now felt like vital contributions to the life of the neighborhood. He welcomed each customer with a genuine smile, greeting them by name, asking about their day, and making sure they felt like they were part of something special.

The store had always been the heart of the community, but now it pulsed with a new energy—an energy that Crash had helped to cultivate. He was no longer just a boy working in his family's shop; he was a vital member of a community that had faced adversity and emerged stronger.

As the weeks passed, Crash noticed a change in himself as well. He was more confident, more at ease with who he was and the role he played in the neighborhood. He found joy in the little things—like helping Mrs. Nguyen find her favorite tea, chatting with Mr. Patel about his garden, or giving the local kids free samples of the latest snacks.

And then there was Mrs. Lee's granddaughter.

She had started coming into the store more frequently, always finding an excuse to strike up a conversation with Crash. Her name was Mei, and she had a quick wit and an infectious laugh that made Crash's heart skip a beat every time he saw her. They had gone out for coffee a few times, and each date left Crash feeling more certain that he had found something truly special.

His mother had noticed, of course, and she couldn't resist teasing him about it. "So, Mei seems like a nice girl," Somjai said one evening as they closed up the store. "She's certainly been spending a lot of time here lately."

Crash felt his cheeks flush, but he couldn't help grinning. "She is," he admitted. "She's amazing. I'm really lucky to have met her."

Jan chuckled, shaking her head with a knowing smile. "I'm happy for you, Crash. You deserve all the happiness in the world."

Crash smiled, feeling a warmth spread through him. His life had taken so many unexpected turns, but here he was, surrounded by the people he loved, contributing to a community that had become stronger through their shared struggles, and finding new happiness with someone who made his heart soar.

As he locked up the store that night, Crash took a moment to stand outside and look out at the neighborhood. The lights in the windows glowed warmly, and the sounds of laughter and conversation drifted through the air. It was a peaceful, contented evening—a reflection of the harmony and unity that had been restored.

With Leonard defeated and his secrets exposed, Fred no longer had to hide. For the first time, he was free to be himself, and the neighborhood quickly grew to love him for it.

Fred had retired from the high-stakes world of hacking. He had spent too many nights hunched over computers, outsmarting surveillance systems, and unraveling complex codes. Now, he was ready for a change—a more carefree, goofy life that allowed him to enjoy the simple pleasures he had missed out on while living in the shadows.

The first thing Fred did was swap his keyboard for a skateboard. It was an unlikely sight—a sea lion gliding through the streets of San Francisco, his green bucket hat flopping with each turn as he expertly navigated the pavement. The neighborhood kids would cheer as Fred rolled by, always ready to show off a new trick or give them a ride on his board. He was a natural, of course, his sleek body perfectly balanced on the board as he zoomed around corners and skated down the steep hills of the city.

Fred had also taken a liking to the local coffee shops, where he had become something of a regular. He would waddle in, plop himself down in a cozy corner, and spend hours lounging with a cappuccino and a stack of newspapers. The baristas loved him, always ready with a fresh cup of coffee and a fish-shaped cookie. Fred had even developed a bit of a reputation as a connoisseur, his discerning taste leading to a few lively debates about the best blends in the city.

Despite his newfound laid-back lifestyle, Fred still enjoyed spending time at the Wharf. But now, instead of hiding in the shadows, he did it in his own style—lounging on the docks in the sun, his hat tilted just so as he watched the boats come and go. Tourists would stop to take pictures, delighted by the sight of the sea lion with the green bucket hat, who always seemed to be in on some private joke.

But Fred wasn't entirely retired from his old life. He still had a soft spot for helping out the people in the neighborhood, especially when it came to their Wi-Fi problems and forgotten passwords. It was a different kind of challenge, one that Fred found amusing in its simplicity. He would roll into a neighbor's home, fiddle with their router or reset their password, and then accept his payment in the form of fish snacks or a warm seat by the fire.

The neighborhood had embraced Fred fully, seeing him as one of their own. He was no longer just the mysterious hacker who had saved them from Leonard's grasp—he was a beloved figure, a symbol of resilience, and a reminder that even the most serious challenges could be faced with a bit of humor and a lot of heart.

Crash often found Fred hanging out at the coffee shop or skating down the street, a grin on his face as he watched his friend enjoying life in a way he never had before. They would chat, laugh, and reminisce about everything they had been through, knowing that they had forged a bond that would last a lifetime.

There were moments when Fred would grow quiet, a faraway look in his eyes as he reflected on the past. He knew that his skills were still sharp, that he could easily dive back into the world of hacking if he wanted to. But for now, he was content to let others take up that mantle. Fred had earned his peace, and he wasn't in any hurry to give it up.

Maybe someday, he would take himself seriously again—return to the world of codes and firewalls, of digital battles fought in the shadows. But not yet. For now, Fred was happy to be exactly where he was, living life on his own terms, surrounded by a community that loved him just as he was.

As the days passed, Fred continued to weave himself into the fabric of the neighborhood, his presence a constant source of joy and laughter. He had become a part of the community's story, just as they had become a part of his. And together, they were creating something beautiful—a life filled with friendship, laughter, and the knowledge that they had faced the worst and come out stronger for it.

Fred's journey had taken him from the depths of secrecy to the heart of a loving community, and he wouldn't have it any other way. He was exactly where he was meant to be, living life to the fullest, one skateboard trick at a time.

Crash stood at the edge of the Wharf, leaning against the railing as he watched the water gently lap against the docks, Fred doing queer tricks in the water. It was a place he had come to many times before, but tonight felt different—quieter, more reflective.

As he gazed out at the horizon, Crash allowed his thoughts to drift back over the past few months. So much had changed since the day he first crossed paths with Fred, the hyper-intelligent sea lion who had turned his life upside down in the best possible way. Together, they had faced challenges Crash never could have imagined—battling against powerful forces, protecting their community, and ultimately, finding their place in a world that often seemed overwhelming.

Crash smiled to himself, thinking of how far they had come. He had started this journey as a young man uncertain of his place in the world, torn between his responsibilities to his family and his desire for something more. He had felt trapped, frustrated by the limits of his circumstances, and unsure of how to break free. But meeting Fred had changed all of that.

Fred had shown him that there was more to life than he had ever imagined—that it was possible to live with purpose, to stand up for what was right, and to make a real difference in the world. Through their adventures, Crash had learned that true strength came not from power or fame, but from the connections we build with others, and the responsibility we take for our actions.

As Crash reflected on all they had been through, he felt a deep sense of gratitude—for Fred, for his family, for the community that had supported them every step of the way. The neighborhood had become more than just a place to live; it was a living, breathing entity, full of people who cared for one another, who were willing to fight for what was right, and who believed in the power of community.

Crash thought about how much he had grown since those early days. He had found his voice, his confidence, and his purpose. He had discovered that he was capable of leading, of making difficult decisions, and of standing up to those who sought to harm what he loved. But most importantly, he had learned the value of ethical responsibility—the importance of considering the impact of his actions on others, of protecting those who couldn't protect themselves, and of always striving to do what was right, even when it was difficult.

The sound of laughter echoed from behind him, and Crash turned to see Fred skating down the Wharf, his bucket hat perched jauntily on his head. Fred executed a perfect spin, much to the delight of a group of kids who had gathered to watch him. Crash chuckled to himself, shaking his head at the sight. Fred had found his own peace in the aftermath of their battles, embracing a carefree life that brought joy to everyone around him.

Crash's smile faded slightly as he thought about the challenges they had faced—the moments of doubt, the fear that they might not succeed. But those memories were now tempered by the knowledge that they had made it through, stronger and wiser for the experience. They had built something lasting, something meaningful, and that was more than enough.

Crash turned his gaze back to the water, to Fred, bucket hat on head lounging on the pier, feeling a profound sense of calm settle over him. He had found his place in the world—a place where he could contribute, where he could make a difference, and where he was surrounded by people who believed in him. The uncertainty that had once plagued him was gone, replaced by a quiet confidence and a deep sense of fulfillment.

Crash took a deep breath, inhaling the salty air and feeling the weight of the journey they had undertaken. He knew that there would always be challenges ahead, but he was no longer afraid. He had learned to trust himself, to trust the people around him, and to trust that they could face whatever came their way—together.

Crash glanced over at Fred, contentedly munching on a fish-shaped snack. Crash knew that their journey was far from over, that there would be more adventures, more battles to fight, and more lessons to learn. But for now, in this moment, he was at peace.

He had found his place in the community, his role as a leader, and his responsibility to protect what they had built. And as he stood there, watching the world settle into the calm of evening, Crash knew that he was exactly where he was meant to be.

The room was dimly lit, the only light coming from the flickering screen of a large, wall-mounted television. The news anchor's voice droned on, recapping the details of Leonard Armitage's spectacular fall from grace. Images of protests, news articles, and headlines flashed across the screen, detailing the extensive reach of Leonard's surveillance and the public outcry that had followed its exposure.

In the shadows, a figure sat watching, his face partially obscured by the darkness. His uniform was crisp, his posture rigid, exuding an air of authority and control. This was a man who was used to getting what he wanted, a man who had orchestrated countless operations with precision and ruthlessness.

The General's eyes were cold, his expression unreadable as he absorbed the news. He had been following the developments closely, though not with the same sense of shock that the rest of the world had shown. To him, Leonard's downfall was not an unforeseen disaster, but rather an inconvenience—a wrinkle in a much larger, more calculated plan.

As the broadcast continued, the anchor shifted to a different segment, showing footage of the community that had played a central role in Leonard's defeat. The camera panned over the familiar sights of the neighborhood—people smiling, children playing, and businesses thriving in the aftermath of their victory.

And then, almost as an afterthought, the camera captured a brief image of Fred. He was lounging by the Wharf, his bucket hat perched on his head, looking every bit the carefree sea lion he had become. It was a fleeting shot, barely more than a few seconds, but it was enough.

The General leaned forward slightly, his gaze narrowing as he focused on the screen. Fred's appearance was unmistakable, even after all these years. The General's lips pressed into a thin line, a cold calculation flickering in his eyes.

He reached for the remote, pausing the broadcast on Fred's image. The room fell into silence, save for the faint hum of the television. The General stared at the screen for a long moment, his mind working through the implications.

"Fred," he muttered under his breath, his tone laced with a mixture of recognition and disdain. "So, you're still alive."

He reached for a phone on the desk beside him, his movements precise and deliberate. With a few taps, he initiated a secure call, his eyes never leaving the paused image of Fred on the screen.

The line clicked open, and a voice on the other end answered, tense and expectant. "Sir?"

"It's me," the General said, his voice cold and measured. "The situation has changed. Leonard is no longer in play."

There was a brief pause on the other end, the tension palpable. "Understood, sir. What are your orders?"

The General's eyes narrowed further, his mind already several steps ahead, calculating the next move. "Fred has been found. The deal with Leonard is off. Prepare for contingency operations. We can't allow this to go unchecked."

"Yes, sir. Should we proceed with the original plan?"

The General considered this for a moment, his expression hardening. "No. We need a new approach. Fred's survival complicates things, but it also presents an opportunity. Monitor the situation closely. I want a full report on Fred's activities and any potential threats. And keep this off the radar. We can't afford any more mistakes."

"Understood, sir. We'll begin immediately."

The General ended the call, placing the phone back on the desk with a quiet click. He leaned back in his chair, his eyes still locked on the frozen image of Fred. A slow, calculating smile crept across his face—one devoid of warmth or humor.

"So, the experiment continues," he murmured to himself. "Let's see how this plays out."

The General reached for the remote again, turning off the television and plunging the room into darkness.

About The Author
Chase Fiore

Chase Fiore is a designer, writer, and lifelong fan of the weird, the wonderful, and the wildly unexpected. With a professional background in themed entertainment, show set design, and immersive storytelling, Chase has spent years helping bring magical worlds to life—usually from behind the scenes, buried in layers of technical drawings and narrative logic.

He holds degrees in technical writing and themed entertainment design, blending precision with imagination in everything he creates. His career has taken him from theme parks and live events to production studios and backstage basements, where he's learned that the most interesting stories often happen just out of sight.

Chase's writing is deeply personal and playfully absurd—rooted in themes of belonging, self-discovery, and the awkward humor of being human. His debut novel reflects a love of quirky characters, surreal situations, and the kind of meaningful nonsense that helps us make sense of the world.

When he's not building attractions or writing late at night, Chase can usually be found overthinking things, doodling ideas on napkins, or searching for the perfect snack.

He lives somewhere between imagination and practicality—ideally with a good view and a better cup of coffee.

www.ingramcontent.com/pod-product-compliance
Lightning Source LLC
Chambersburg PA
CBHW050320110726
47899CB00007B/2306